AZAR on FIRE

ALSO BY OLIVIA ABTAHI

Perfectly Parvin

AZAR ON FIRE

OLIVIA ABTAHI

 Nancy Paulsen Books

NANCY PAULSEN BOOKS
An imprint of Penguin Random House LLC, New York

First published in the United States of America by Nancy Paulsen Books,
an imprint of Penguin Random House LLC, 2022

Visit us online at penguinrandomhouse.com

Library of Congress Cataloging-in-Publication Data
Names: Abtahi, Olivia, author.
Title: Azar on fire / Olivia Abtahi.
Description: New York: Nancy Paulsen Books, [2022] | Audience: Ages 12+. |
Audience: Grades 7–9. | Summary: "Fourteen-year-old Azar Rossi sets out
to find her voice and win her local Battle of the Bands contest"—Provided by publisher.
Identifiers: LCCN 2022019483 (print) | LCCN 2022019484 (ebook) |
ISBN 9780593109458 (hardcover) |
ISBN 9780593109465 (ebook)
Subjects: CYAC: Bands (Music)–Fiction. | Contests–Fiction. | High schools–Fiction. |
Schools–Fiction | Iranian Americans–Fiction.
Classification: LCC PZ7.1.A186 Az 2022 (print) | LCC PZ7.1.A186 (ebook) |
DDC [Fic]–dc23
LC record available at https://lccn.loc.gov/2022019483
LC ebook record available at https://lccn.loc.gov/2022019484

Printed in the United States of America

ISBN 9780593109458
1st Printing
LSCH

Edited by Stacey Barney
Design by Suki Boynton
Text set in Rotis Serif Pro Greek

Your defects are the ways that glory
gets manifested.

—RUMI

For Four

AZAR on FIRE

APOLOGIES IN ADVANCE

YOU'RE PROBABLY WONDERING why the book you're holding in your hands is full of such underwhelming garbage. I know. I feel the same way. When Dad gave me this fancy notebook for Christmas and said it was to share my lyrics with the world, I thought he was joking. Why would I share my lyrics? There's already enough pain and suffering on this planet.

"Azar, I see you writing down songs on all these little scraps of paper. It's time your words had a home. Even if you can't sing them out loud, you should still keep them." And then he pretended to strum his air guitar, and Nonna smacked him upside the head with a wooden spoon and told him to serve dessert, even though we were all stuffed and could barely eat a sesame seed. But you don't mess with Italian grandmothers from Jersey, especially during the Feast of the Seven Fishes.

I'm back with Mom in Virginia now, but I still have this stupid book. It's bound in leather, and it has a ribbon to keep track of where you are in your miserable ramblings. It's even in my favorite color: lime green. Aha! Did you see that? This book is trying to seduce me. Shut up, stupid book. Even your lime-green ways can't bewitch me now.

Little Green Book
Wants to open me up
Swallow me whole
Make me feel like a chump
Little Green Book
Trying to lull me to sleep
Take a peek at my dreams
Steal them out from under me
Little Green Book
Trying to crack my spine
Share my songs with the world
But these songs are mine.

Nice try, Moleskine.
You lose.

BACK 2 SKEWL

ANOTHER SEMESTER. ANOTHER five months of talking to nobody, hiding in the band room for lunch, and never raising my hand in class. I am in a prison of my body's own making.

Worse: I am out of Pop-Tarts.

Just then, Mom sticks her head into my room, her brown curls a ball of positive energy and argan oil. "Azar, I made kale chips for your lunch today!" She pronounces it Aw-zár, the traditional Iranian way of saying it.

Did I mention I'm in hell?

As if spending Xmas talking to no one but my family wasn't humbling enough, I now have to be reintroduced to the public, where people can tell I have no friends, much less a life.

"Azar? I made some tahini dipping sauce, too!"

I am going to die alone.

The kitchen reeks of the yerba mate Mom always preps for her drive to DC. It tastes like oregano gone bad. Mom says it is an indigenous plant grown in the north of Argentina, where her dad, my abuelo, is from. I think she secretly just likes it because it requires being sipped from a traditional gourd.

"Good morning, Azar," she says formally. I give her a look like, *Do I have to?* and she nods gravely. I clear my throat.

"Good morning, *Mother.*" The words come out scratchy and warbly, like I tried to step on each note with a roller skate and they just slid out from under me. They're the first words I've spoken today, and Mom does not look impressed.

"Did you stay up late again? Your voice sounds worse than yesterday!" She says this accusingly, as if I have committed homicide—or worse, stayed up past my bedtime. Which is nine p.m. Which of course I blew right past, throwing a towel under my door so she couldn't see the light from my laptop as I uploaded more stuff to SoundCloud.

"Mom," I begin to lie, my voice even, just the way Ms. Davolio, my speech pathologist, taught me. "I went to bed at nine p.m., after we watched *Up in the Air.*"

Because we have no lives, I almost add. But don't.

She shakes her head, gold hoops swinging. "Maybe

we need to start quiet time earlier, like eight p.m., just to be safe."

I sigh. Sure. Add it to my tab of misery.

"You're right," Mom says, even though I didn't say anything. We've got our nonverbal cues down to a science at this point. "One thing at a time. Get dressed and shower—I'll give you a ride to school."

I wordlessly trudge back to my lair.

"And don't forget to gargle!" she calls out.

The second I close my door, I grab my acoustic guitar, the one Dad got me a couple years ago when my throat infections started ramping up. Instruments are about the only thing Mom lets Dad buy for me, besides making deposits to my college fund. She's too proud to ask for anything else. I've also got an electric drum kit with pads that connect to my computer, a keyboard, a ukulele, plus I can borrow instruments from school during lunch break. The guitar needs to be tuned, but I strum the chords anyway, singing lyrics in my head.

Azar, gargle with salt water
And wear something that has color.
I'll give you a ride to school
If you become a better daughter.
Don't burn the toast.
You had one job!
To not burn the toast!
And now I'm late for wooOoorrrrrk.

"Azar, are you getting dressed?" Mom demands through my thin bedroom wall. I can hear her blasting reggaeton through her tinny phone speakers in the kitchen, singing along to every word. I switch to a minor chord, the song going from light and fun to dark and dreary.

"AZAR!" Mom shouts. "Did you hear me?"

I get out my phone.

> **AZAR ROSSI** *6:28 A.M.*: yes, mother.
> i heard you.
>
> **MOM** *6:28 A.M.*: Then why aren't you in the shower!
>
> **AZAR ROSSI** *6:29 A.M.*: yes sir captain sir.
>
> **MOM** *6:29 A.M.*: And don't call me Mother!

The saltwater gargle tastes disgusting, but the steam from the shower feels good on my throat. It's way more soothing than the humidifier I run on my nightstand. I feel like one of those beached whales that people keep dumping water over to keep them moist.

The hot water runs out in three minutes, which is normal for our crummy apartment building. A sullen girl stares back at me in the bathroom mirror, her mouth a flat line with freckles spilled randomly across her face. She really, really does not want to return to school after winter break.

I don my jeans, T-shirt, and a bright orange sweater Mom got me for Xmas that she says "makes me more approachable." It feels weird not wearing black.

"You're killing me, Z. We're gonna be late," Mom says, popping her head into my room. There is no such thing as privacy in this apartment.

I reach for a black sweater, threatening to put it on instead. "I'll do it. I'll even put on black lipstick."

Mom groans in frustration (which is really bad for your throat) and heads back to the kitchen, where she is no doubt making me hummus from scratch and grilling tofu for my lunch sandwich.

We don't have a real dining room or kitchen table. I plop into a chair under the counter that serves as our eating space. But when I reach for the orange juice, Mom slides it away from me.

"You know what Dr. Talbot said. Orange juice and acidic foods make your vocal nodules worse."

"Dr. Talbot buys sushi from the gas station. Should we really be trusting his judgment?" I growl. My voice sounds like the lowest gear on a bicycle, unable to switch up to something faster and more fluid.

Mom just stares me down.

"Fine." I grit my teeth.

She slides a cup of tea over instead, and I shiver like someone has cracked an egg on my head, already dreading my breakfast. The tea is called Throat Soothe, and it tastes like marshmallows made from dirt. I take a sip, the hot drink comforting my esophagus despite filling my nose with notes of licorice, mud, and something called slippery elm.

"Can I have some pancakes? With extra whipped cream?" I whine, wishing my voice didn't sound so husky. Without my secret stash of Pop-Tarts, I'm at my mom's organic, free-range mercy. I'm a growing teen. Teens need gluten and preservatives, and that fake maple syrup stuff. It's our birthright.

She just gives me another look and slams a bowl of yogurt with strawberries and honey in front of me instead. Every week, she makes yogurt from scratch in a big metal pot and covers it with a towel, like my maman bozorg taught her. I stare at the yogurt miserably. Yogurt's supposed to be really good for your throat health. But it tastes the opposite of pancakes.

"I bet Adele eats the same thing for breakfast," she says, scrambling to get ready. "She had to cancel a couple concerts last year because she was losing her voice, so you two are in the same boat."

Yes, because Adele being on "vocal rest" from selling out arenas and me having vocal nodules on my throat since I was a baby are the same thing. Mom is the type of person to call a paper cut "a deep exfoliation!" and a debilitating vocal condition "an opportunity for different communication!"

"Her strawberries are served to her individually as models fan her with palm fronds," I point out, my throat slowly warming up. "On a private jet."

Mom sniffs, straightening her button-down business-casual shirt. Even in a plain outfit, she looks beautiful, with bright brown eyes and glowing skin. Her left hand threatens me with a spoonful of raw clover honey. "This is *homemade* yogurt, thank you very much."

"What a thrilling life you lead."

"Less talking. More eating," she barks, now looking in our small kitchen mirror and lining her eyes with the thick kohl she uses on her gargantuan Persian eyelids. I try not to gag as she circles her entire eyeball, even the part of the eye that's on the bottom, right by the waterline.

After taking two bites, I moan, "Can we go now?" Not that I'm super eager to get to school. But being around Mom in this cramped kitchen reminds me that my throat's messed up, while my classmates just think I'm quiet.

There's a difference.

MORNING COMMUTE

I GRAB MY backpack, my Washington Nationals hat, and a fresh pack of gum while Mom puts on her parka. Something crinkles against my foot as I slide it into one of my black faux-leather combat boots.

"Día de los Reyes Magos!" I yelp. It's Epiphany, or what some people call Three Kings' Day, and per my mom's Persian-Argentinian traditions, that means I get candy in my shoes. It's usually raw cacao bonbons, or fair-trade dark-chocolate bars. Whatever it is, at least it'll supplement my abysmal breakfast. I reach into my shoe.

"Cough drops?" I cry. "You got me cough drops for Día de Reyes?"

"Excuse me," Mom says defensively. "I got those small-batch cough drops at the farmers market. They're sweetened with agave and they cost twelve dollars a dozen!"

Fuming, I unwrap a cough drop and shove it into my

mouth, staring at Mom the entire time to really get the point of her child torture across. Notes of orange peel and cinnamon dance across my tongue.

"Ugh," I concede. "These taste incredible."

"I will take that as a thank-you," she says primly.

She opens the door and leads the way to the parking lot. Washington Gardens is the kind of place where there aren't hallways connecting any of the apartments together. The second you step out of your unit, you're outside in the unforgiving wetness that is the DC metro area. We walk past the other units and down the rickety wooden stairs to our car, the January cold slapping me in the face. Winter in Northern Virginia is a cruel mistress.

"Brrr," Mom says. "You buckled in?"

I give her a thumbs-up.

"You ready to make the world a better place?"

I flash a less enthusiastic thumbs-up. More of a sideways hitchhike.

"I'll take it." She reverses out of the parking lot and I fiddle with the window button, since it doesn't work anymore. *Click. Click-click. Click-click-click.*

"Azar, come on."

It's like there's always some random beat in my head and I play it out on my tapping fingers, toes, or decaying Honda Civic (hybrid). I tap the back of my teeth with my tongue instead.

Mom fiddles with a knob and our asthmatic heater coughs on. We pass our neighbor, Nadim Hadad, who's walking to school while rolling a gigantic instrument case. According to our school's morning announcements back in the fall, Nadim is one of a handful of foreign exchange students Polk's hosting this year.

"He goes to your school, right?" Mom says, turning onto the street. "Maybe we should give him a ride?"

I shake my head. If we give Nadim Hadad a ride, then I'll have to make conversation. And if I make prolonged conversation, then he'll hear how messed up I sound this early in the morning. I need to drink at least half my thermos of witch's brew to get out a full sentence in mixed company.

"Azar—" Mom starts.

"Mom." I already know where this conversation is going. *Click-click-click.*

"I'm just saying—what about making some friends this year? We could invite him over, or sign you up for some after-school clubs. It'll look good on your college applications to have a social life."

I shake my head. Being extroverted and talking to people is not in my DNA. Besides, I can't just invite Nadim over to our place. What will he think of Mom's over-growing crystal collection, or how our kitchen counter is completely dedicated to the various fermented foods she makes from scratch? Don't even get me started on the inevitable star chart Mom will force on him. I doubt he'd have a good time, much less want to be my friend.

Anyway, I have my cousin Roya, who *has* to like me, since we're family. She never cares that I'm quiet or that the only decent snacks we have at our house are pita chips and vegan tzatziki. Then again, anything tastes better than the food at my old middle school, where Roya is still serving out her sentence as an eighth grader.

"I just want you to have people you can hang out with, you know? A friend. Preferably one you're not related to, and one who's your own age," Mom continues. "Even if we have to pay them."

She takes a pull of her yerba mate, then nudges me to take a sip of my tea, too. I literally have permission from the school to sip this special tea all day, while my classmates fervently wish they could chug their mochaccino sugar bombs and ridiculous pumpkin-flavored lattes, which are strictly banned from class.

Click-click-click.

I'd kill for a pumpkin latte.

It takes forever for Mom's ancient car to heat up. She hasn't had the money to get a new one, but it's on the list. Her breath steams as she peers through the icy windshield, and a news anchor on the radio talks about more issues with DC traffic. No matter how much she tries to scrape it, the windshield still looks cloudy with ice.

The news anchor shifts gears. "This program has been sponsored by the Northern Virginia Battle of the Bands! Are you a high schooler in the NOVA school district? Enter, and your band could win a record deal, musical equipment, and a ten-thousand-dollar cash prize! Visit us online to enter!"

When I was in elementary school, Mom would take me and Roya to the battle and we'd strum our air guitars like crazy during each act, pretending we were onstage. That was before Mom got busy with work, and before I realized that vocal nodules do not mix well with dreams of being a singer-songwriter. What a sweet summer child I was.

When the radio ad finishes, Mom says, "Now that you're in high school, you could enter and do an instrumental thing. Or have Roya sing for you." *Because you can't sing, she doesn't add. Because when you try to sing, you experience vocal fatigue, and your vocal nodules grow too much from the vibration in your vocal folds, and even though you've dreamed of sharing your lyrics with the world, it is just easier to write them in a notebook and not deal with your esophagus than face the bitter stench of defeat, antibiotics, and vocal rest.*

But all I say is: "Roya can't sing for me. She isn't a high schooler."

I've dreamed of performing at the battle since seeing it live. But being a songwriter who can't sing is too tragic a backstory for even me to swallow.

"Come on," Mom insists. "You don't have to sing out loud to share your music with people. You could still play melodies and stuff."

"Mom," I croak. She frowns at the sound of my voice. Great. "It's a battle of *bands.* One person strumming a guitar onstage does not a band make."

Honestly, do you see the kind of nonstop encouragement I have to deal with?

She just shakes her head and grumbles something

about enjoying instrumental music, but I've already snuck an AirPod into my right ear. Nonna got me them for Christmas, and so far, they've come in handy. The sound quality isn't as good as the huge purple headphones in my backpack, but these pods are ten times stealthier.

I cue up a song and rest my head against the freezing window while our neighborhood slides past. Mom's still mumbling something about "putting yourself out there" and "missing one hundred percent of the swings you don't take," but I've already tuned out.

And then, without permission, a vision of me performing at the Battle of the Bands seeps into my brain. I'm under the hot spotlight, a guitar slung around my neck and a microphone so close I can taste the crosshatches of steel. And when I open my mouth, instead of sounding like a rusty hinge, my voice is clear as a bell.

The lyrics in this stupid notebook suddenly take flight, sounding better than anything I've heard on the radio. My voice is smooth and even and it doesn't crack or warble, the way it does now. Out of nowhere, a drummer and a bassist join in, their faces blurred in my fantasy. I reach for the busted window button, using the clicks as a backbeat.

This is the moment,
Click-click,
When my dreams take flight.
This is the signal,

Click-click,
For my fire to light.
I've been waiting,
Click-click,
For the chance to show you
Everything I can be—
Everything inside me.

The audience cheers, and someone throws roses onto the stage (Is that what they do at concerts? Or just figure skating?), and suddenly I'm being held aloft on someone's shoulders as they announce that I've won and that I'm getting a record deal and—

"Azar? Did you remember your lunch?"

Suddenly I'm slammed back into the passenger seat of Mom's car, where we're already in the drop-off line at James K. Polk High. Instead of the heat of a spotlight, I feel the chilly cough of the radiator, and the cheers of my adoring fans are just the sound of school bus air brakes. The car feels smaller than it did before, the peeling upholstery looking even shabbier.

With an ache I realize that the song I just came up with will never be performed out loud. I'll never sing it onstage or have the guts to upload it publicly to Sound-Cloud or enter the Battle of the Bands. This right here, in my mom's busted sedan, is as good as it gets.

"Azar?" Mom asks again.

"Huh?"

"Did you remember to bring the lunch I packed?"

My hands fumble around near my feet and pull up my reusable lunch tote, filled with gluten-free sandwich bread, organic crackers, and god knows what other wholesome thing she's shoved in there.

"Yeah."

She pulls up to the curb, and I suddenly wish I'd asked her to teach me how to use eyeliner the way she does. Classmates enter the building with new clothes and gear they got for Hanukkah and Christmas, and my orange sweater feels shabby and small by comparison. Black eyeliner could have helped me feel cool. Especially since the coolest thing we did over the holidays was break Mom's no-meat rule and eat an entire Costco rotisserie chicken together on New Year's Eve.

Mr. Clarke, the easily excitable film teacher who's doing drop-off today, practically faints at the sight of Mom when I open the door.

"Everything all right, Mrs. Rossi?" he asks.

"It's *Ms.* Arampour Gomez, Mr. Clarke," says Mom, and she winks at him. Has she no shame?

He turns beet red and I practically hear his heart stop beating through his navy peacoat. Mom is a good ten years younger than every other parent at James K. Polk High, and Mr. Clarke has definitely noticed.

"Of course, of course. Glad to see you today!" he says, hyperventilating, turning away to probably clutch his chest and/or wave the next car on.

I shake my head. "You're cruel."

"I'm the thirty-two-year-old mother of a high schooler.

Give me this one brief pleasure." She squeezes me into a hug, her spicy perfume wrapping around me. "Have a great day at school, Azar. And remember, don't get—"

"I won't get pregnant, Mom." I wish I could shout how *NOBODY* is trying to impregnate me at this school, because to do that, they'd have to know I exist. Invisibility is honestly the best kind of birth control.

Besides, what kind of Mom uses that as a sign-off to a fourteen-year-old? *Mine.*

"But only if you let me have orange juice tomorrow. Otherwise? I'm getting super pregnant. We're talking triplets," I threaten, holding out my pinkie for her to make a promise.

She cuffs her pinkie around mine, shaking her head. "Luckily for you, I *do* negotiate with terrorists."

A laugh slips out of me, the sound sharp and painful. You can't let parents know they're funny, though; otherwise, it goes to their heads.

"Have a good day at school. I'll be home a little late, okay?"

"Okay."

I start to exit the car, the warmth of my fantasy already disappearing like my breath in the cold air. My fingers find the button for the window again.

Click-click.

VOCAL TORTURE

"HOW WAS WINTER break?" asks Ms. Davolio, my speech pathologist. You'd think this was a normal, polite question, but it's actually a trap. She wants to hear me speak, and if she doesn't like what she hears, she'll call my mom. Then Mom will call Dr. Talbot. And then I will be forced into some other form of torture in my already-uncomfortable life.

I pop in a fresh stick of gum to keep my mouth moist (ew). "It was good," I reply, not offering anything else.

Ms. Davolio frowns.

"You?" I ask, trying to change the subject.

"*MY* winter break? INCREDIBLE," Sydney Hotchkiss, the only other student in speech therapy, says next to me. "The Mediterranean? Breathtaking. The water? Actually blue. The food? To die for!"

Sydney's blunt-cut purple hair looks extra vibrant today. She talks with such vigor, it swings around her forehead like a Muppet's. But I have to hand it to Sydney; she knows how to play Ms. Davolio, just like I do. It's Ms. Davolio's first year of being a speech pathologist, after all. We can smell weakness in adults like sharks smell blood in the water.

I give Sydney the faintest smile. She smirks back at me, my partner in speech pathology crime. I don't have any friends here at James K. Polk High, but during our fifty minutes of special elective every day, Sydney and I are thick as thieves. We're the only two kids in the entire first-year class who require speech therapy. It's nice having someone else at school who knows the real reason I'm so quiet. I'm pretty sure she tells her friends she works in the front office this period, the truth too embarrassing to share. Most kids work their speech-therapy issues out by the time they're in middle school. Most kids, but not us.

Suddenly Ms. Davolio slams a textbook onto the table. "Sydney, don't think I didn't notice that you didn't use a single *s* in your sentences. And, Azar? I need a sample size of more than three words if you want me to help you keep your voice."

Sydney and I look at each other. This is definitely not the same teacher we left before winter break.

"Well?" Ms. Davolio gestures to Sydney. "I'm waiting."

She sinks down in her seat. "This is so pointless!" she wails, the *s* in *pointless* revealing her speech impediment.

"So what if I have a lisp? Did you know that in Spain it's normal? They call it Bar*the*lona!" She looks to me for backup, knowing I speak Spanish, but not knowing that Argentinian Spanish and Spain Spanish are practically different languages.

I sigh. "She's right. Se pronuncia Bar*the*lona."

Ms. Davolio just scowls, her pastel pink outfit at odds with the murderous look on her face. She grabs the delicate gold chain around her neck that has the Greek symbol for her sorority on it, clutching it like a talisman. She takes a deep breath, winding up for another lecture, and I assume the brace position.

"When I was in high school, they would have given up on you, Azar." She points at me, pinning me to my chair. "They would have made you learn American Sign Language so fast, your head would spin. And you, Sydney. They would have made you get braces, the ugly kind, *with* the rubber bands, to close the gap in your front teeth. Not to mention a frenectomy!"

Sydney gasps. "Not the rubber bands!" I don't dare google what a frenectomy is.

"Oh, yes," Ms. Davolio says, pacing the room furiously in her sensible beige pumps. "So, I know we've all had fun doing the bare minimum the first semester, but that ends now. I don't want to see y'all next year, and I don't think y'all want to see me, either. So we're going to try harder this time around, okay?" You can tell she's really angry by how her Southern accent keeps slipping in.

Sydney and I share one last look, one that is no longer smug and snarky, but panicked and terrified. In that moment, I know our minds have melded and we're thinking the same exact thing: Neither of us wants to be here again. Especially not for a whole other year.

"Okay. I mean . . . Yes," Sydney says, trying hard to close her teeth on the word. It sounds strange without her lisp.

"Azar? How about you?"

"Deal," I croak. My throat's hurting more than normal today, probably because of the frigid temperature outside.

"Aaaaaaand?"

"And . . . I watched a bunch of George Clooney movies, ate cold pizza, got music lessons for Xmas, and I agree to work very hard this semester, Ms. Davolio, can I stop talking now?"

She smiles. "There we go. Was that so hard?"

Surely Dante wrote about a circle of hell that is 24/7 speech therapy, because this is absolute torture.

"Now, Azar, I noticed your voice raise at the beginning of your sentence before getting back to a good volume. Let's work on modulating the decibels here, okay? If you speak at that volume too much, you could experience vocal fatigue. Better to keep an even, consistent tone, projecting from your diaphragm . . ."

My eyes glaze over as she pulls up a familiar image of an esophagus on the smart board and begins to discuss vocal vibrations. Sydney's already on her phone, no doubt texting her millions of friends with equally vibrant hair as they make plans to converse in person and maybe even laugh or say something at loud decibels.

I wish my throat could be fixed by braces.

Even if it meant getting rubber bands.

MY ESOPHAGUS: AN ORAL HISTORY

WHEN I WAS a baby, I had something called colic, not to be confused with consumption or diphtheria or any of those other old-timey illnesses. Colic, apparently, is just when a baby is really unhappy and cries a lot.

Only, I never stopped crying.

I just cried and cried.

Until one day, I couldn't cry anymore. My vocal cords were shot. I had sobbed myself into silence, and the vocal folds where everything rubs together to make noise had called it quits. They were infected and covered in bumps from all the friction, forming something called vocal nodules. And those nodules never really went away.

A lot of babies get over their colic.

A lot of babies, but not me.

I went from crying a lot to making almost no noise. Doctors who inspected my throat told my mom what a bad mother she was for letting me cry so long. But it's hard to tell a baby to go on vocal rest and drink Throat Soothe.

Mom still blames herself. Just the merest whiff of a throat infection sends her into a WebMD-fueled panic.

It got better as I got older, *sort of.* Mom taught me some basic sign language as a toddler so I could sign for "more" and "milk" and "help." My throat healed up enough to learn to talk, but I always sounded like a Disney villain. Even now with all the speech therapy, I'm still crackly and gravelly, with the kind of voice people use in folksy pickup truck commercials.

The Rules of My Throat

- *I sound the worst in the mornings, when my throat hasn't had a chance to warm up yet. Ditto for late at night when I'm tired.*
- *I keep a humidifier next to my bed to help with the above issue.*
- *Sometimes my voice feels smooth and fine, and it doesn't hurt to talk. Ms. Davolio says this can be because of a number of things, like a good night's rest or a high humidity index or a low stress level.*
- *But other times it hurts like crazy, sometimes for no reason at all. It's definitely worse in the winter.*
- *The more evenly I talk, the better it is for the vibration of my vocal folds and the less I aggravate my nodules.*
- *A few sentences are fine. Reading out loud in class is hard. Singing? Out of the question.*

- *When I shout or laugh or talk unevenly, the bumps on my folds grow.*
- *When the nodules grow, it can lead to an infection.*
- *Infections hurt and I have to take medicine and go on vocal rest.*
- *I get about five to six infections a year.*
- *The more infections I get, the harder it is to recover each time.*
- *God, I am getting bored with this list.*
- *Who cares.*
- *Nobody ever asks.*
- *This is why I can't sing.*
- *Or have a life.*
- *Or have a normal first-period class.*

I wish there was a plaque I could staple to my forehead that read MAKE WAY FOR THE BROKEN-THROAT WOMAN! But other times I'm glad nobody has to know about the inner workings of my esophagus.

Am I quiet because my throat sucks? Or does my throat suck because I'm quiet and don't make an effort? Maybe if I had more people to talk to, I'd try harder to speak evenly, like Ms. Davolio wants.

Sometimes it's hard to know where my condition stops and my personality begins.

But I do know one thing: The bell has rung, so I don't have to think about this again for another blessed twenty-four hours.

THE HALLWAY OF CHAOS

SYDNEY DRIFTS AWAY from me the second we step out of the tiny speech therapy classroom, like I'm her dirty little secret. We're not really friends outside of class, more like coworkers who have to clock in to our daily fifty-minute shift. *See you in the break room at lunch!* I almost shout, but don't.

> *Secret studies*
> *With my therapy buddy,*
> *Who pretends I don't exist.*
> *Secret studies*
> *With a croaking voice*
> *And a throat I need to mist.*

I enter the first-year hallway alone, watching class-mates meet up with their friends, ask how their winter break was, and make squealing and palm-slapping sounds. Even if I did have a friend at school, I would never be able to pull off a "Yay!" squeal like that, much less know how to fist bump without looking like I'm having a mental breakdown.

So many friendships seem to be based on people loudly exclaiming how "psyched" or "excited" they are, their voices rising to unhealthy volumes. I haven't been "psyched" since my sixth birthday, when Mom surprised me with a cake made with real buttercream icing. Even back then, I'd throw classmates' birthday party invites in the trash, knowing my silence would kill the mood.

This is my first year away from Roya. The first time I don't have my younger cousin to shield me from the harsh realities of being friendless. I feel way too visible in my neon-orange sweater.

On go my purple headphones, my anxiety fading out as my *I Hate Crowded Hallways* playlist fades in. The second the beat drops, it's like I have the power to turn my peers into a music video and not classmates who give me FOMO. First-years morph into faceless blobs, and the bridge and the chorus keep me afloat. This is the only way I can survive this massive, more-than-two-thousand-person school: by casting them into the soundtrack of my life. The Neon Borealis track kicks in, regulating my heartbeat better than Mom's homemade chamomile tea.

Tell me, honey, what's the news today?
Is it time to float away?
Say the word, and we can levitate,
Rise into the clouds and play.

This is why I love music so much. It takes regular, mundane things and makes them feel special and in my control. When I break down the world into beats, it's not as overwhelming. Even something as gnarly as vocal nodules can feel easy to swallow when it's got lyrics behind it.

Instruments have always helped me express myself in ways that I can't on my own. Whenever I talk, it's this flat, one-note chord. But when I play my guitar, I can sound happy or sad or playful, or, yes, even psyched. Just deciding whether to strum or pick can change the vibe from serious to fun.

My voice lacks range. But music gives it back to me.

My phone buzzes with a text.

ROYA NAZEMIAN *9:24 A.M.*: Sooo?
How's your first day back?
       AZAR ROSSI *9:25 A.M.*: first day
       is stupid are we still hanging out
ROYA NAZEMIAN *9:26 A.M.*: Do you
still refuse to use punctuation??????
       AZAR ROSSI *9:26 A.M.*: c u at 4

Back at Stonewall Middle, I was the only eighth grader who deigned to eat lunch with a seventh grader. Except, Roya is the one with a billion other friends she could choose to sit with, and *I'm* her social kryptonite. Was I using my younger cousin as a crutch? Yes, yes, I was.

I'm lucky Roya doesn't care about spending time with someone who doesn't talk too much. She does most of the talking, anyway.

Tell me, baby, is there something strange
About the way I seem today?
Tell me, darling, is there something new
About the bars on my own cage?

"Heads up!" I hear someone shout through the pads of my headphones. Too late. A Frisbee hits the side of my head, and I gasp. My headphones fall onto my neck and I stare numbly into the fog of more than five hundred kids in our corridor, my head throbbing.

People have stopped in the hallway, and they stare at me like I'm in one of those nightmares where I forgot to wear pants. Only this time it's real, and pants can't help me now. I spy Sydney in the crowd, and her eyes bug out of her head, horrified. Coming to my aid would mean explaining how we know each other. And explaining how we know each other would risk all her hard-earned high school clout.

I hold the Frisbee out to the crowd, not sure who to

give it back to. Emerson Cheng from World History class steps forward, grimacing.

"Hey, I'm really sorry—I didn't see you when we were throwing it, and—" He reaches toward the Frisbee, clearly feeling bad. I hold it out for him, and when his hand comes closer to mine . . .

I let it drop to the floor.

"Oooooh, dang!" someone yells.

"She's not playing!" another guy calls out.

Emerson looks up at me, confused and a little hurt. I give him a hard stare back, my heavy eyebrows almost daring him to say something to me, while inside I scream at this stupid day for being the absolute worst. I've heard whispers in the hallways from girls swooning over how hot Emerson Cheng is. But all I see is a dude with nervous brown eyes and spiky hair, his face clearly saying *Please don't tell a teacher.*

Tears struggle to break through my glare, and my head aches from where I got hit. Thankfully, Emerson stays quiet, and I bite back the pain and humiliation that a single disk of plastic can unleash.

Mom says she named me Azar because it means fire and warmth and all the good things that help give us life. But when it comes to high school, I'm a stone-cold ice queen. I'm untouchable, and I won't let anyone see me crumble, no matter how many things they literally throw my way.

All my life I've been in a bubble with Roya, but now she's not here to protect me anymore. What would she do in this situation? Because all I want to do is curl into a ball in that dark room in the nurse's office, where they let sick kids rest.

I put my headphones back on, cue up my song, and walk away.

Wearing orange today was a mistake.

A QUIET, DIGNIFIED MELTDOWN

I STILL HAVE five minutes before history, and I use them to retreat into the empty speech therapy hall-way and open the janitor's closet, the one they luckily forget to lock in case someone needs to have a private panic attack.

I've only been at school for an hour, yet it's already causing me emotional and physical distress. I almost call Mom, knowing she'd pick me up if I asked her. But then I think about all the vacation days she's been sav-ing up for a trip we probably can't afford, and I put my phone away.

Usually when I get this flustered, I play something. Everything I want to say can get channeled into a gui-tar or my drum pads or a borrowed instrument. But all I have in my backpack right now is a pair of chipped drumsticks, and I left my ukulele in my locker.

Let's be honest, though: this is no time for a ukulele.

I wrap my hands around my drumsticks and feel a bit better. I try not to think about that Frisbee connecting with my head, and instead focus on my breath. *Inhala. Exhala.*

I've seen the real drummers at this school, how they walk around with their sticks and bang them on lunch tables or the bleachers during marching band. Some of them even keep a pair in their car and drum on the dash while waiting to exit the clogged parking lot.

I started carrying my sticks around, too, not that anyone's ever seen me play. Speech therapy's always taken up one of my precious elective spots, and I need to use the other one for a language, per the Polk guidelines. But if I can impress Ms. Davolio enough, she'll let me graduate from her class and it'll free up a slot for me to take band.

That would be amazing.

I experimentally tap a stick against a metal shelf filled with cleaning supplies, making the extra rolls of toilet paper and paper towels shake. Amy Waters' song "Bad Math" has one of the best drum solos on her debut album, and I love playing along to it on my pads back home. Today I'll have to improvise.

Forgive me
Make it everything you dreamed it would be.

Fight me
Leave nothing but broken teeth.

I do a roll, the hits fast and tight. I feel my chest loosen, and the ache in my skull drifts further away.

I've been doing the math, and it just don't add up
When you try to subtract the "you" from the "us."
But I never took calculus. . . .

Before I know it, I'm whaling away on a cardboard box, my hits playing out all the frustration I can't put into words. My knuckles are white from gripping my sticks too hard, but the *thunk thunk thunk* of the box takes all my rage.

Why does high school reward extroverted people so much? *THUNK THUNK THUNK THUNK.* Why can't I just walk through the halls without getting Frisbees thrown at my head? *THUNK THUNK THUNK THUNK.*

The years they've been waiting
With each grain of sand
To take stock of delusions
You called your grand plan.

AHHHHHHHH! I want to scream. The beats do it for me, and I'm reminded again of why music is the absolute best: because it helps me feel like this, like I'm actually a player in the video game of my life and not some puppet beholden to the cruel winds of adolescence.

Time keeps on turning.
Your family grows.
I'm left out of the portrait,
And nobody knows. . . .

I go all out, doing a massive combination on a bucket of road salt, using the metal shelving unit as a hi-hat. The world is my instrument, screw everyone at this dumb high school, I'm not invisible, I'm invincible, AND—

SLAP. I watch as a bottle of bleach falls off the wobbly shelf, then hits a giant cube of stacked toilet paper rolls like a wonky game of dominoes. They fall forward, taking the whole shelf with it, and—

CRASH.

I jump out of the way just in time, feeling the *whoosh* of the shelf as it falls forward, scattering soap bottles and loose paper towels. The road salt has spilled all over the floor, and I stand in a growing pool of suspicious-looking liquid. It seems like a tornado came through here. A tornado of rage and excellent drum technique.

Footsteps pound outside, racing toward the noise. For a split second, I consider hiding, but then I realize it's pointless trying to hide in a ten-by-ten room of industrial-sized cleaning products.

The door blasts open, and my heart goes from andante to staccato.

Principal Saulk stares at me, stunned. In that moment, I bleakly realize that I'm still clutching my drumsticks. I can see his small brown eyes dart between the collapsed shelf and the way I'm stupidly holding them out mid-shrug, like, *Whoops!*

"You," he says, pointing, as if there's anyone else in this cursed place. "Follow me."

OH NO

THE BELL RINGS, but instead of sitting in history class, I'm in Principal Saulk's office. I can only describe the decor as "depressing." Mustard-yellow walls. Faded green chairs in a weird corduroy fabric. A big brown desk with no pictures on it, because who would marry Principal Saulk? I've been sitting here alone for ten minutes as Principal Saulk "assesses the damage."

The door finally opens.

"Remind of your name, Miss . . . ?" Principal Saulk asks, sitting behind his desk.

"Rossi. Azar Rossi."

My mouth is so dry, my name tickles my throat, and I start coughing like crazy. He leans away from my germs, and I chug tea from my thermos and pop in another stick of gum.

"Rossi, Rossi . . ." He enters the name on his computer, the screen facing away from me, and I wonder what my file says. Evidently nothing interesting, because he quietly asks, "Do you want to tell me what you were doing in the supply closet with a pair of drumsticks?"

My face flushes. I wish I could be like Mom and laugh it off and turn it into a funny story, or be like fast-talking Roya and come up with a completely credible lie.

But I have no idea what to say, so I say nothing.

He reads from his computer screen. "No history of disobedience or troublemaking . . . Also, you have a speech condition? But it doesn't say you're in band. . . ." I almost feel bad for him, trying to make sense of this sullen, wavy-haired girl who smells of bleach and Throat Soothe.

"In fact, it doesn't say much about you here at all." He takes off his rectangular black glasses and rubs his eyes. "Are you all right, at least?"

I blink. For a second, I think he's referring to the Frisbee incident, and that he's checking if I'm okay. But then he gestures to my soaked pant leg and suds-covered combat boots, and I remember why I'm really here.

"Yeah. I'm okay." It comes out husky, my throat tight from nerves, but at least I don't go into another coughing fit.

He leans back in his chair and purses his lips. "Unfortunately, Miss Rossi, you've destroyed about a thousand dollars' worth of equipment and school property.

A custodian is cleaning it up right now, but I doubt that's the best use of their time."

"A thousand dollars? For some toilet paper and bleach?" There's no way I can pay that back. Mom can barely afford the copays for my ear, nose, and throat doctor visits. She'd have to sell her car for parts to be able to get that much cash, or worse, ask my grandparents. Mom *loathes* asking people for money.

"The road salt alone was five hundred. The bleach soaked into a month's worth of toilet paper and paper towels, too."

I descend into another coughing fit. "Five hundred . . . for road salt . . ."

"Did you mean to destroy school property, Miss Rossi?" he demands, staring me down.

"No!" I say quickly, voice shaking. "It was an accident, I swear. Please don't tell my mom. There's no way she can pay that back. I'm really, really sorry." I gasp for breath. I haven't talked this much in months.

Principal Saulk holds up a hand, stopping my rambling. "There may be a way you can repay the school without paying out of pocket." He clicks around on his computer some more. "We have a bake sale coming up. And the cheerleaders are doing a car-wash event. Or maybe you could run on behalf of the school at the Hot Chocolate 10K race? We still have a couple spots left. I don't expect you to raise a thousand dollars at any of these, but it'll show me that you're sorry for your actions and are willing to work toward fixing them.

Any amount you raise will go back to the school."

I squint back at him, wondering if this is a joke. Does he actually think I'd be useful in any of these situations? That I can just bake cookies and wash cars and run for fun and pleasure? If anything, I'd probably deter people from giving money to the cause. Who would want to eat my mother's gluten-free, vegan, sugar-free, dairy-free brownies at the bake sale? Who would want their car washed by a gloomy girl who gives dirty looks to gas-guzzling SUVs?

"Maybe I could work here in the office instead?" I plead. "Help you make copies and stuff."

Principal Saulk shakes his head. "We already have student helpers for that."

His eyes stray to the drumsticks I'm still holding. I watch as they widen and a smile blooms on his face. Alarm bells ring in my head like a submarine that's about to be hit.

INCOMING MISSILE! BEGIN EVASIVE MANEUVERS! DIVE! DIVE! DIVE!

"Miss Rossi, have you heard of the NOVA Battle of the Bands?"

I've only been thinking of it constantly since that radio ad this morning.

"No."

"Well, we could definitely use a team entry. No one from Polk has entered so far."

"Okay . . . ?"

"And since you have no extracurriculars that I can see, and the cash prize is ten thousand dollars, well . . . I'd call this a win-win situation, wouldn't you?"

"Um." Doesn't his giant computer screen say that I am medically unable to sing in front of a live studio audience?

"You play the drums, right?" Principal Polk prods me.

"I mean . . . yeah," I admit, not liking where this is going.

"Are you any good?" he asks bluntly.

I bristle. What kind of question is that? I don't ask if *he's* any good at his job, do I? "Yeah, I'm good," I spit. "But I'm a solo act, *Damian*," I say, reading off the plaque on his desk. He doesn't even clock my insolence, though. He just smiles even bigger.

"I propose this: If you win, Polk claims one thousand dollars of your earnings to reimburse the damage. You can use the rest however you see fit. But if you don't place, you're off the hook, and you'll still have an extracurricular to put on your college résumé, which it looks like you desperately need. Plus, our school will have a band represent us. Nice, right?"

He holds his hand up for a high five, but I leave him hanging. This can't be happening.

"But . . . I can't sing." It's like every ounce of saliva in my mouth has evaporated, turning my tongue into sandpaper. "Even just talking is hard."

Principal Saulk chuckles. "You'll figure something

out," he says, eyes twinkling behind his glasses, like he's doing me some big favor.

"And if I say no?" I wheeze.

"Well, then we have a problem. If you don't want to participate in any of the fundraising options I just gave you, then you will owe James K. Polk High one thousand dollars. And I'll have to put you down for destruction of school property, which will go on your permanent record."

"Eraghgnnn" is all I say.

Principal Saulk lowers his glasses, as if he is "leveling with me." I can tell he wants to flip his chair around and sit on it backward so, so badly. "Use this as an opportunity to work with others. Colleges look closely for team activities."

"Is there a fee to enter?" I sigh.

He moves his mouse around, tapping away at his keyboard. Why he needs to type so much to look up basic information is beyond me.

"Nope. No entry fee. And I just entered you for the school's team. You perform the week after spring break. Check your student inbox for more information. I left the band name blank, though."

"What?" I yelp. If Ms. Davolio were here, she'd crucify me for all the uneven modulation of my voice.

"Break a leg, Miss Rossi."

But I can't hear him because I've already started coughing again.

WORLD HISTORY

SOMEHOW I HAVE been recruited to play in a nonexistent band with my nonexistent voice. And if I don't play, I will be permanently labeled as a delinquent and owe this school one grand. The truth is, I would love to perform at the Battle of the Bands.

But *can* I?

That's the bigger question.

I rest my cheek on my cool desk. All I need is for a cartoonlike rain cloud to burst open above me, and then I will have truly hit rock bottom.

"Does *anyone* know the name of the famous Mongol military commander?" Ms. Ahmed asks, her eyes scanning the room. It's Genghis Khan. Everyone knows it's Genghis Khan. People who know nothing about the Mongol Empire still know this, but of course, no one in class seems to care enough to answer.

Ms. Ahmed's eyes fall on me, and I can see her wrestle with the realization that I am probably the only person who's listening, but that I'm also the only student she's ever taught who has a note from her doctor that says "Try not to call on her in class, *for vocal reasons.*"

She swivels away. "How about you, Brayden?" she says, calling on Brayden Abdullah, who is, unfortunately, asleep. I, too, would like to be unconscious.

"Huh?" he asks, yawning. Brayden has the mustache of a twenty-year-old man. It's honestly impressive.

I turn back to Ms. Ahmed, then quickly look away from her frantic *Who can I call on?* face. Normally, I wouldn't really care. But seeing her be ignored reminds me of how I could be in the same situation soon, standing in front of an audience, praying that someone listens to me and cares, unless I find a way out of this mess.

What if I get onstage and I'm somehow still invisible? If I completely bomb, it'll show once and for all that I'm just not cut out for performing, that practicing on my own at home is the best it'll ever get.

The thought makes my gut ache. What are all these lyrics for if I never share them with anyone?

In my mind, I raise my hand to answer Ms. Ahmed's question, then I speak out loud in a perfect voice. Suddenly my fantasy morphs into Ms. Davolio telling me my throat's all better and I don't have to go to speech therapy anymore, and Sydney's rushing to my side, asking me if I want to go to the nurse after the Frisbee hit my head.

"Okay, well, if you open your book to page one ninety-two, we can learn more about this famous ruler . . ." Ms. Ahmed says, defeated.

I shoot my arm up, startling her. It's like someone made a record-scratch noise. Even Ebenezer Lloyd Hollins, Fifth of His Name, looks up from the corner of the room where he's been playing paper football with Emerson Cheng, perpetrator of the Frisbee assault.

"Ms. Rossi?" Ms. Ahmed asks, looking genuinely confused. She probably thinks I need to go to the bathroom.

Everyone's eyes feel like hot coals on my back. But if I can't answer a simple question in history class, how am I ever going to perform my music in front of a live audience?

I clear my throat. There's more detritus in there than I'd like. "It's Genghis Khan," I say, my voice warbling like a seventh-grade boy's. "Of the Mongol Empire," I add, hoping those extra words will smooth out the running start I gave my throat in the first half of my sentence, but alas, it has joined the ranks of gravel and sandpaper.

"Very good!" Ms. Ahmed squeals. Squeals! I give an uncomfortable grimace and turn back to my book.

"Nice," Colton Tran, my desk partner, whispers to me.

I can't even say "Thanks," since whispering is just as bad for your vocal folds as shouting, if not worse, as Ms. Davolio likes to inform me. I give him a tight-lipped smile instead.

"I didn't know you could speak," he continues quietly as Ms. Ahmed turns back to the board.

I give him a look, like, *Excuse me?*

Okay, maybe this is why I can't make friends. I have too much "sass," as Nonna calls it.

"No, no, it's just . . . everyone at school says you can't talk. Like, medically."

I didn't know anyone else at school knew. How would they have even found out? Clearly *I* didn't tell them. Hmm.

"I can talk," I say quietly. "Just not too much. It's bad for my esophagus."

Colton nods. "What's wrong with it?"

"I got really sick when I was a baby and it affected my voice." Okay, so I'm really simplifying things here, but no one's ever bothered to ask before.

Colton winces. "That sucks."

I nod. It sucks, big-time. Especially in moments like this.

"Mr. Tran?" Ms. Ahmed asks, suddenly turning to us. "Do you know the answer?"

Colton reels off some facts about the Great Wall and I go back to our reading, wondering what the heck just happened. That was my first unprompted conversation with a classmate in the entire history of my high school career.

It wasn't terrible.

SANCTUARY

YOU KNOW THOSE movies where the girl has nobody to sit next to at lunch, so she just eats her sandwich in a bathroom stall? Who actually does that? Are her jeans sitting *on* the actual toilet seat? Or is there some lid on the school toilet seat that I don't know about?

I'd honestly rather eat my lunch alone in the parking lot, no matter how cold it is, than on a germ-infested toilet seat. But I guess a parking lot isn't as cinematic as a bathroom.

Not that I'm in a bathroom stall right now. I mean, where I am is equally tiny, but there isn't a toilet. One of the cool things about going to Polk is that the music program lets you borrow instruments during lunch if you use the sign-out sheet posted outside Ms. Kaiser's door. Today I'm in one of the small, five-by-five practice rooms with a mandolin, which is kind of like if a guitar and a violin had a baby, and you play it on its side with a pick. Next door I can hear another student practicing on a weird-sounding instrument, like a cross between a clarinet and an oboe.

"Why is this so haaaard?" she whines after flubbing a complicated run. Good question, random person next door. Good question.

I chew my hummus and tofu sandwich as I quietly freak out, wondering what I'm going to do about this Battle of the Bands thing. This feels like the first time all day that I've gotten to take a deep breath and process this complete catastrophe.

I can't ask Mom to pay for the damage. There's just no way. The other day I saw her dribbling saline solution into a drying tube of mascara to "make it last longer," and that seemed like a pretty good metaphor for our finances. Worse, if I told her why I needed the cash, she might even sell her beloved George Clooney autograph collection, and she's already sacrificed a lot for me. Namely, her twenties.

I look around the practice room and note the peeling paint, the mangled blinds, and that one overhead light with the flickering bulb. My toe taps against the gross, threadbare carpet. I used to look forward to lunch, but today my practice-room sanctuary just feels pathetic and depressing.

Here I am, in what is essentially a cubicle, eating a bean sandwich. Today has been a new low.

My phone buzzes with a new email from the Battle

of the Bands registration. I ignore the letter and click the homepage link.

> *NOVA BATTLE OF THE BANDS!!!! SHOW THE WORLD WHAT YOU'VE GOT AND YOU MAY JUST GET A RECORD DEAL!!!!*

The website is black, with Comic Sans type and neon coloring to make it look like a vintage website from the '90s.

> *Join us April 14th at the Dogwood for a night of music and teen excellence!!! All NOVA students are welcome to enter for the chance to win 10K and an EXCLUSIVE record deal and mentorship from Anthony Staples, founder and CEO of Staple Sounds!!!!!*

My breath catches. Anthony Staples? As in, the guy who single-handedly discovered Amy Waters and Neon Borealis?

The thought of working with him makes me light-headed and a bit clammy. But for the first time since Principal Saulk's chat, I feel my anxiety morph into something else: excitement.

Okay, so I've never performed on a stage before. And I've never played with others. But what if I find bandmates and we sound good? What if we win this freaking thing?

I'd have to really put myself out there. No hiding behind purple headphones and emitting two words per day. Talking to people like Colton Tran would be just the start; I'd have to talk to *multiple people, multiple times a day.*

Suddenly the dingy practice room feels bigger. I can almost imagine sitting here with another band member, working on a particularly hard riff. Now the space feels cozy and full of possibility. This wouldn't be a cubicle of solitude—it would be a womb of creation!

What is this tingly feeling running through my body, making everything feel light and wonderful?

Oh, yeah. Optimism. I click back to my email.

Thank you for registering for NOVA's Battle of the Bands! All band members must be enrolled in a NOVA district high school. Please plan to arrive at 2pm on April 14th for sound check prior to the performance. Get ready to ROCK!!!

Yeah!

I finish my food and prop my phone on the music stand so I can pull up a YouTube video that shows me where to put my hands on the mandolin. Time to get serious and use this time wisely.

Dear kombucha,
I've got a bone to pick with you.
How do you taste like vinegar
But stick in my mouth like glue?
What's with the gross strands at the bottom?

I know they're called the Mother,
But I think you have a problem. . . .

I strum, mouthing my made-up lyrics in time to some basic chords.

What if the voice in my head isn't as bad as I think it is? Maybe I could even sing at the battle. Mom says I tend to be overly pessimistic about my condition. I haven't tried it in a while.

The singer in my head sounds crystal clear, without any abrasions or rough edges holding her back. I can almost *feel* the sound pushing out of my mouth and into existence. I take a deep breath, ready to sing, and—

Nothing.

I can hear the air pushing past my throat, but it's like a trumpet that's between octaves. This happens sometimes when I try to talk and the folds in my throat just don't line up. Instead, all I hear is the scratchy sound of static.

I throw my kombucha into the recycling bin.

Time to find a lead singer.

STILL HELL

THIS FIRST DAY back from break has dragged on forever, and I've already talked outside of speech therapy thrice—a new record. According to my strict winter break schedule, I should be eating a bowl of cereal in my pajamas right now, but instead I'm in English class, listening to Mr. Nuñez go over the second-semester syllabus.

"I'm going to pair you with a partner for the rest of the semester, and each team will do a report on one of the books on our list. You'll be expected to meet outside of class to complete the assignment."

My heart sinks like a stone. I've done group work in science class where we each have to do a certain task in a set of instructions, but I've never had to meet up with someone outside of class to finish a project. How does that even work? We aren't juniors with cars who can just drive to each other's houses. I'll have to ask my mom for a ride, or worse, bring them to our apartment.

This already sounds incredibly awkward and full of talking.

Across the room, I see Colton thunk his head on his desk. I guess he's not a big fan of group work, either. But he glances up and gives me a hopeful smile. I look away, trying hard not to smile back, because yeah, I wouldn't mind being paired with Colton Tran. Everyone knows he gets straight As.

"Colton Tran and Sydney Hotchkiss, you two will work on Pearl S. Buck's *The Good Earth*." Damn it. I peek at Sydney in the back row, and she looks like she just won the lottery, she's grinning so hard. English class is not Sydney's strong suit, and now she's guaranteed a good grade for sure.

Mr. Nuñez reels off a bunch more names, and I zone out again, hoping there might be an odd number of students and I'll be off the hook and able to do my book report alone. It's happened before.

"Eben Hollins and Azar Rossi, you'll be working on *The Heart Is a Lonely Hunter* by Carson McCullers."

I turn around and look into the faceless sea of classmates behind me, trying to find Ebenezer Lloyd Hollins. He gives me a head nod, like, *Sup?* He has the kind of features you'd see in an L.L.Bean catalog: auburn hair, square jaw, and a wholesome, open face that looks like "Gee!" and "Golly!" could come out of it. Though I practically live under a rock, even *I've* seen girls in the hallway faint at the sight of his dimples. He twirls a lanyard, unbothered. This has to be a joke, right? Can Eben even read???

"Why are we only reading from white authors? I don't see any authors of color on this list," says Fabián Castor, influencer celeb of Polk High. Other students mutter agreeing noises.

Mr. Nuñez starts handing out books. "I know it's tough to read novels in which you don't identify with the main characters as much, but I encourage you to do your best."

"Seriously?" Fabián huffs. "I have to read about a bunch of kids who go Hunger Games on each other?" he says, smacking *Lord of the Flies* onto his desk. "This is messed up."

Mr. Nuñez grimaces. "It's out of my control, Fabián. I'm really sorry."

"It's not a big deal," Eben says, accepting his copy of our book assignment from Mr. Nuñez, and I can't help noticing how he looks a lot like the authors we've been assigned. "They'll all be boring anyway."

I wince. I hear Colton Tran thunk his forehead on his desk again.

"What?" Eben says, combing his hair back with his fingers in a way I know is considered objectively attractive. "What'd I say?"

I shake my head. I can already see Fabián rolling his eyes.

This is not going to be a fun project.

Eben waits for me outside class. I don't think we've ever spoken face-to-face before. It's unnerving having his amber eyes stare directly into mine. Sometimes it feels like everyone in this school is a faceless, amorphous shape until I interact with them.

"So . . . when do you want to meet?" he asks.

"Whenever." I try extra hard to make my voice sound normal, lowering the pitch a little, focusing on keeping it even and smooth, like in Ms. Davolio's lessons.

"Yo, Five! See you at tryouts?" A sophomore I don't know claps Eben on the back.

"See you soon!" he shouts, his face lighting up.

"Five?" I ask him.

"My suffix," he explains, staring down at me, since he's a good foot taller. "Ebenezer Lloyd Hollins the Fifth."

"Oh." If Mom were here right now, she'd say something like *And does that name come with a butler?* But who am I to judge? My full name is Azar Gomez Arampour Rossi. Not that I'd ever say it out loud in public. Plus, I've already spoken three words this entire conversation, and I'm not about to go wild now.

"I have lacrosse tryouts after school today, but could we meet in the library after?" he asks.

"Sure," I mumble, relieved to have someone else figure out this whole meet-outside-of-class thing. Whoever invented group work should be publicly humiliated and then given an F.

Eben holds a hand out for my phone, and I give it to him, watching as he punches his contact info way too hard into my touch screen. He gives it back to me, and I see that he sent himself a text from my phone that reads "Hi!" from the contact named COOLEST PERSON EVER!!! So humble. So modest.

He grins. "All right. See ya later." He walks away, slapping palms with athletic upperclassmen like a teen movie star. All he needs is a letterman's jacket to solidify the gap in our social standing.

"Bye."

Five words. I said five words to him total. I wonder if I'll be able to get away with as few words this afternoon, during our meetup.

"You're so lucky." Sydney Hotchkiss swoons, her lisp oddly reassuring. "He's, like, so hot."

"I don't see it," I reply, my vocal fry coming out. Around Sydney, I don't have to pretend. She's seen my voice naked, after all.

Her purple bangs flap against her forehead, her blue eyes wide. "How can you NOT?" she practically screams. Her notebook is covered in photos of K-pop bands and heart stickers. It seems like fangirling is one of her favorite pastimes.

Behind her I can see Nadim Hadad, that kid who lives in my apartment building, glance over at us. He quickly looks away.

"Umm . . . I guess he's just not my type," I mumble.

God, this is so unspeakably awkward. It reminds me of

the times Roya would try to wheedle who I had a crush on out of me and get frustrated when I'd tell her "Nobody." Or when Mom's tried to get me to "spill the gossip."

Sydney just shakes her head, the gap in her teeth visible. "Let me know if you need help talking to him. I can be your interpreter or whatever."

"Um, thanks, Sydney. I'll let you know."

"No prob!" She skips down the hallway, linking up elbows with one of her BFFs as they squeal about something on their phones.

I wait before my meeting with Eben in the practice room after school, fiddling around with a drum pad until I perfect my traditional drumroll. A lot of drummers do a matchstick drumroll, where you hold the two sticks in front of you with your palms down, but traditional is when you play with your left hand palm up and hold the stick between your middle and ring fingers.

It's an old-school technique from when drummers in the army would sling a snare drum over their shoulder, making one side higher than the other. Even though it's tricky, I like knowing I can switch it up. It beats sitting in the library waiting for Eben to finish his tryouts.

COOLEST PERSON EVER!!! *4:45 P.M.*:
Finishing up, see ya soon!
[smiley face emoji] [shooting star emoji]
[rocket ship emoji]

I put the practice pad and sticks away and head down the empty hall to the library, not looking forward to this already-awkward class assignment. Maybe we can finish quickly and I can head home in time to watch something over FaceTime with Roya.

Then I hear a voice, and I freeze in my tracks.

Throwing all my hopes and feelings
Into laughing, living, screaming.
Life always made sense
When you were by my side. . . .

The popular Neon Borealis song reverberates through my body like it's a cymbal and someone just smacked it. Who's singing that? Between his perfect pitch and warm, rich voice, it's like I'm watching an episode of *The Masked Singer.*

Despite the cinder-block walls, the voice sounds clear and strong, the way I wish *my* voice sounded.

I push open the gym's double doors and scan the empty space, wondering where it could be coming from.

When you left me, I was reeling,
Trying to give my life meaning.
But I'm stronger now,
Enjoying the ride. . . .

I press an ear against the boys' locker-room door, and yep, it's definitely coming from in there, where I can also hear someone showering. Whoever is singing can project their pipes a good 150 feet, and through multiple rooms.

God, I hope nobody walks into the gym and sees me doing—What exactly am I doing? Trying to be a pervert through the door with my ears?

The voice suddenly cuts off, along with the water from the shower, and I feel like a deer in headlights. Should I just wait here like a stalker until whoever is in there exits, and accost them, demanding to know where they got their voice from?

Or maybe I should just walk away from the doors because this is stupid. There are better ways to ask people if they want to be in your band than a locker-room ambush. I speed-walk out of the gym, already late for my meetup with Eben.

I HATE GROUP WORK

I RUSH TO the library, out of breath from jogging all the way from the gym. Miss Villanueva, the librarian, gives me a concerned look as I gasp for air, so I give her a reassuring wave. She just frowns. Everyone's a critic.

Eben's not here yet, so I grab us a table by the window and get out my copy of *The Heart Is a Lonely Hunter,* wondering who at James K. Polk is the owner of the mysterious voice in the locker room. I throw on my Nats hat and slump into my seat, popping in a fresh stick of gum.

What if that voice wouldn't mind being the lead singer for the band? For once, I'd have a decent shot at performing outside our school's practice rooms, all while fulfilling Principal Saulk's requirement. It's the perfect plan. I make a mental note to hang out by the locker rooms again tomorrow and at least see which face matches the voice.

"Hey, sorry I'm late." Eben walks up, clutching a lacrosse stick and a duffel bag. He's wearing mesh pants and one of those sporty thermals that has what Mom suspiciously calls "drying technology."

"No worries." I freeze, a funny feeling prickling all over my body. Eben's hair is wet, his auburn hair dark from the moisture. He notices me staring dumbly at his red freckles.

"What?" he asks. "Do I still smell?" He sniffs his shirt and I struggle to connect my mouth with my brain.

"You shower at school?" I ask, my thoughts spinning into overdrive.

There's no way that voice could belong to Ebenezer Lloyd Hollins the Fifth, lacrosse enthusiast and boy who I know for a fact pronounces the *J* in jalapeño.

He gives me a weird look. "I mean, everyone else went home to shower, but I had to meet you, so . . . ?"

There's just no way.

"What?" he asks, reading my face. "What's wrong?"

I stare into his eyes and practically feel my own pupils dilate. I still need more proof than a coincidental shower, though.

"Do you like Neon Borealis?" I ask casually. "Any favorite songs?" I take a sip of water, noticing how dry my throat's already getting from just four sentences.

Eben relaxes, reaching for his copy of the book. "I love Neon Borealis! Their song 'Reeling' is my favorite."

Suddenly my water's gone down the wrong pipe and I'm coughing like crazy. *HOW????*

"Are you okay?" He gets up, motioning like he's about to slap my back with his huge lacrosse hands. My eyes water as I try to clear my throat and wave him off.

Ms. Villanueva looks over and shakes her head. I distinctly hear her sigh and say, "Not again." A single trickle of water is all it takes to set off a coughing fit. My reputation as a choking hazard is legendary.

"All right?" Eben asks, still looming over me like he's about to perform the Heimlich. Sydney would probably pay good money to have Eben Lloyd Hollins the Fifth give her CPR.

I clear my throat, finally inhaling again. "I'm good."

He sits back down, his broad shoulders making him look more like a linebacker than a lead singer. "Sorry tryouts ran over. I'm going for varsity, and it's kind of intense."

I nod politely, but in my head all I'm thinking is *GOOD GOD, MAN! This is no time for lacrosse, not when you have the voice of a rock star!*

"Okay, so we have to outline each chapter, right? You wanna take evens and I'll do odds?"

I watch as he skims through his worn copy of the book, diligently writing some stuff down in his planner. For a dude who loves sports, he sure has nice penmanship.

I suddenly can't take it anymore. I grab his book and snap it shut. He snaps his head up, surprised.

"What was that for?"

"Eben," I say, trying to sound sweet. But instead of honey smooth, I just sound the way a snow cone crunches. "Have you heard of the NOVA Battle of the Bands?"

He raises his eyebrows. And before I know what's happening, I do the last thing I ever thought I would do at this high school: I try to make a friend.

PLOTTING

"THE BATTLE OF the Bands? Yeah, I've heard of it." Eben looks super confused, and I don't blame him.

"Listen," I begin, the words tumbling out of me. "I'm a songwriter, but I suck at singing. Maybe you could sing my songs for me? I heard you belt 'Reeling' from the locker room earlier and I think you'd be perfect . . ."

I stop talking, my throat too sore to go on. Water doesn't seem to be working.

Eben's normally smiling face looks completely bewildered, and a little panicked. Even his eyebrows are that same reddish-brown color, and they seem to splay frantically at me. "Okay, number one: What? Number two: I'm flattered. But number three: What?"

"For reasons I will not get into right now, I am entering the Battle of the Bands contest. And while I have a bunch of songs ready to go, I can't sing them."

"Because of your throat thing, right." Eben nods.

It's my turn to look bewildered. "Does *everyone* know about my throat?" The only person I've ever told at this school is Ms. Davolio, who brings it up in class with Sydney. And Colton Tran, I guess. And Principal Saulk.

Principal Saulk. That gossip.

Eben looks at me like I'm a complete idiot. "Azar, we've been in the same class since kindergarten. Everyone knows."

"Oh." I guess this wasn't as tortured a secret as I thought.

"So, you like my voice?" Eben says, his expression going from confused to intrigued. "Like, you think it's pretty good."

"It's a classically strong voice, yes."

"The choir director at my church says I have a good voice, too," Eben continues. "She's always trying to get me to sing for them more, but it's tough with lacrosse. I've never sung for anyone at Polk, though."

"I promise it won't take up too much of your time," I say quickly, my throat really aching now. "We can work around your lacrosse schedule, and I'll handle all the beats and lyrics. All you'd have to do is sing."

Eben's face falls. "Oh, so I'd just be your front man. Or whatever."

I nod, relieved. "Exactly. I'll take care of all the music—you just have to perform it."

"Ah." His hair's practically dry now, turning back into the floppy do that Sydney swoons over.

"Yep," I say.

"So you're saying I just have to show up to a couple rehearsals and the concert on . . ."

"April fourteenth," I finish.

I'm getting excited now. He seems to be really considering it. I may just be able to pull this thing off after all.

"Won't we need a real band, though? Like, a drummer and a guitar and stuff like that?"

I wave a hand. "That's for me to worry about. You just gotta show up."

He runs his fingers through his hair, making it stick up even more. "I don't know, Azar. This sounds crazy, right? I'm flattered, but who'd want to see me in a band?"

I roll my eyes, ignoring the fact that he mispronounced my name. "Trust me, Eben—lots of people would like to see you in a band. Plus, you could put it on your college application. You know, show you're into stuff outside of school and sports." I feel bad, manipulating him the same way Principal Saulk tried to manipulate me. But it's a good point.

He nods, chewing his lip. "Can I think about it?"

The bpm of my heart slows down a few clicks. I was hoping Eben would be just as excited as I am, but from the way his eyebrows are knitted together, I can feel my soaring adrenaline start to plunge.

Why would Eben want to help me? This was such a stupid idea. What was I even thinking?

I nod, trying to hide my disappointment. "Sure, of course. Take your time." I know that he probably won't ever bring this up again. Mom calls it American Manners, where people nod and smile and tell you they'll *totally* read the link you sent them, or they *can't wait* to meet you for lunch, but then they'll go radio silent instead of just saying no up front. It drives her nuts at work, even though she is, technically, 100 percent American.

He exhales. "Cool, thanks. My schedule is just really busy these days. Anyway, we still haven't talked about the book. Want to take evens?"

I shrug. "Yeah, that sounds fine."

He looks at the texts blowing up his phone. I can't see what they say, but he's clearly popular.

"Here's the book report outline I started." He hands me a binder with different tabs for things like PLOT, THEMES, CHARACTERS, NARRATIVE ARC, and CHAPTER SUMMARY. It's super detailed, with each chapter already labeled in that neat blocky handwriting. Roya would drool over how well organized Eben's binder is. It makes her spreadsheets look like child's play.

"Whoa." I flip through the summary pages, each one with different boxes for us to fill in. "You did this?" I ask.

Eben looks hurt. "Yeah?"

"This is really good," I say, quick to not sound judgmental. "I just thought . . ."

"You just thought that since I like sports, I can't be good at school, too?"

"No . . ." What happened to smiley, happy-go-lucky, golden-retriever Eben Hollins?

"Or that I can't be more than a mouthpiece instead

of a real member of your band?" Eben finishes, crossing his arms.

"I didn't say that . . ." I mumble, my face bright red. Clearly, I have underestimated him.

"I just thought you wanted me to be a part of your team, you know? Then I could show everyone that I can be creative, too. I'm not some dumb jock."

"I didn't mean . . ." I croak. For someone who's so afraid of being judged and putting myself out there, I sure just judged the crap out of him.

Eben looks away, flushing. I get the feeling he doesn't get angry often. "I gotta go pick up my sister. Let's plan on finishing a chapter a week, okay?"

"Okay," I say, sufficiently scolded. He leans over to grab his binder, and he smells like clean laundry, the kind that is definitely bad for the environment but smells really good.

"Bye," I mumble.

He strides out of the library, and then I plonk my forehead onto my copy of *The Heart Is a Lonely Hunter*. Right on cue, I begin to cough all over again.

Miss Villanueva groans.

SECONDARY PARENTAL UNIT

I GINGERLY PLACE my headphones over my Frisbee bruise and prepare for the trudge home with my *MOOD* playlist, the one with songs that help me decompress after weird situations, like seeing Dr. Talbot, or being blackmailed into a Battle of the Bands competition, or learning that you've been paired with one of the most popular guys at school and he has the best voice you have ever heard in person. The Pink Medal song "Fury" comes on.

Why did no one tell me
That high school would feel so scary?

I nod along to the beat and walk fast to keep warm. Virginia cold is so wet that my pants feel like they've been dipped in ice water. My fingerless gloves are useless.

I pass the major road that divides the "nice" houses

from the "undesirable" apartment buildings in my tiny pocket of Northern Virginia. These houses have big front yards, brass door knockers, and professional gardeners who put up and take down the holiday decorations. Mom says those houses are flimsy, but I think she's secretly jealous.

I'm just about to cross the road when Dad calls, his grinning picture taking up my whole screen. I hit "accept."

"Azar," he says. It sounds like he's outside his fancy Wall Street building—I can hear cars honk and the sound of jackhammers down the block, which means he's finally taking his lunch break.

"Hey, Dad," I reply, crossing the street.

"So? How was your first day back?"

"It was good," I lie. *It was absolutely awful and I don't want to talk about it.*

My throat's seriously hurting from all the speaking I did today, even though normal people wouldn't think that was much talking. A small part of me registers that that's a really bad sign, but the larger, bigger part just hopes I'll be able to fix it by being silent and going on vocal rest.

"Hmm," Dad says after hearing me speak.

"Can we switch to text?" I ask.

He doesn't ask why.

"Sure, one sec," he says, hanging up.

DAD *5:35 P.M.:* So, it was good?

I press "play" on my soundtrack and start walking and texting.

> **AZAR ROSSI** *5:35 P.M.*: i have a new assignment in English. i have to team up with a partner

DAD *5:36 P.M.*: That's fun, right?

> **AZAR ROSSI** *5:36 P.M.*: sure dad

DAD *5:37 P.M.*: Guess what? The bank I work at is expanding their branch down in Tysons Corner, Virginia. Maybe they'll approve my transfer request.

> **AZAR ROSSI** *5:37 P.M.*: ~~kewl~~

DAD *5:37 P.M.*: Yeah, I could be closer to you guys.

> **AZAR ROSSI** *5:37 P.M.*: that would be nice

Dad's always talked about moving here, but his company's always kept him in New York. It *would* be nice having Dad ten minutes away. Maybe we could see more shows together. Mom is always down to try the latest vegan café, but with Dad, I can see concerts and go to record stores in Manhattan. He fuels my musical side.

> **DAD** *5:38 P.M.*: We'll see what happens. What do you want to do this month? I'll take the train down in a couple weeks.

AZAR ROSSI *5:38 P.M.:* hmmm there's an Amy Waters concert we can go to.

DAD *5:38 P.M.:* You sure? Her stuff is so bleak.

AZAR ROSSI *5:38 P.M.:* it resonates with me emotionally

DAD *5:38 P.M.:* She's no Nirvana but I guess we can go.

AZAR ROSSI *5:38 P.M.:* [old man emoji]

DAD *5:39 P.M.:* Hey!

AZAR ROSSI *5:39 P.M.:* see you soon, dad

DAD *5:39 P.M.:* I love you bug.

AZAR ROSSI *5:39 P.M.:* you too

"Azar, right?" a cautious voice calls out behind me. I pause my music and see Nadim Hadad, rolling that big instrument case on the sidewalk. He even pronounced my name right, with the emphasis on the first syllable. *AW-zár*. Has that ever happened with a schoolmate before? But then again, have I ever explained how it's actually pronounced in the first place?

"Hey," I say, looking up at his tall frame. He must be six feet at least, with long, gangly arms and hands that look too big for his body. We've never spoken to each other before.

"I'm Nadim. I think I live in your building." He has a thick accent, one that kind of sounds like my maman bozorg, but different.

"Ah, that's right," I say, pretending I haven't seen him walk to school by himself every day. His hair is dark and thick like mine, his cheeks covered in stubble.

And then . . . nothing. Nadim looks at me expectantly, and I have no idea what he wants me to say.

"I'm an exchange student." He starts walking, and I keep stride. "From Libnan."

Lebanon. "Nice," I say.

He nods. "Yes. Very nice."

More silence.

"So . . ." He fills the silence uncertainly. "What kind of activities do you like?"

What is this, a *How to Make Small Talk* primer?

"Um . . . I like listening to music," I say, gesturing to my headphones. "What about you?"

Nadim bites his full lips, like he's trying to remember his own hobbies. "I like talking to friends, watching TV, and hanging out."

This conversation sounds way too canned to be real. I round on him. "Did my mom pay you to talk to me?" I should have known she'd pull something like this. She's been scheming since breakfast.

"No!" Nadim replies, horrified. "She gives money to your new friends?"

I shrug. If she can bake her own gluten-free sourdough, she's capable of anything.

"My teacher says I need to try to talk to more people. To improve my English," Nadim explains. *En-ge-lish.*

"Sorry," I say. "I didn't realize." Between this and Eben's outburst, I'm feeling like a very judgmental jerk. It's okay when I'm sarcastic and suspicious in my head, but clearly it does not translate well out loud. Thankfully we're a block away from home and I can turn left out of this conversation.

"Maybe we can walk and talk tomorrow?" Nadim asks. "That would be cool. If you want. I don't know." He looks anxious, like he's worried he made a mistake.

I smile back, trying to make up for accusing him of being a paid actor. "Very cool," I agree, even though I would rather listen to music by myself.

We're at our building now. Nadim waves bye, and I watch as he makes his way to a ground-floor apartment.

I trudge up the stairs to our unit. Then I close the door behind me, collapse onto our sofa, and curl up into the fetal position.

That's enough talking for forever.

MY CAVE OF SOLITUDE

I THROW ON a pair of pj's and drag the comforter off my bed and onto the couch. This is no time for a dinky quilt.

Then I unearth my laptop from a pile on my desk and video chat Roya instead of answering the zillions of text messages she's left me. My pile of homework will just have to wait. The thought of Eben's binder full of neat handwriting makes me want to die.

"Azar, finally!" she says. She's in her parents' big house a couple neighborhoods over, in a bright pink bedroom that was uncool two years ago but is now hip again.

I wave at the computer screen. Under my duvet with music notes on it, I look kind of like a babushka.

"So? How was your first day back? Thanks for answering none of my texts, by the way. I'll go first: Mrs. Adams from next door asked me to babysit Atticus every Monday until spring break, which means I'll hit my second-semester target!" Roya's practically vibrating through the screen, she's so ecstatic. "So with that, plus the money from watching Ashkan, I'm off to a good start this year."

"Roya, what is the point of you making all this money if you never use it?" She's like one of those dragons hoarding her gold in a cave somewhere, a dragon who begs to babysit her little brother so she can add more to her bank account.

"Excuse me, I am building generational wealth."

"But your parents have plenty of money."

Roya pinches the bridge of her nose like I'm a complete idiot and she can't believe she has to explain such basic concepts to me. "It's for *my* generation, Z. That's the difference."

I roll my eyes. "You wouldn't happen to offer loans, would you? To the tune of one grand?"

Roya looks confused. To be fair, I've never asked her for money before. "Do you need a new instrument or something?" she asks.

I slowly shake my head. Roya clicks around on her own computer, and I know she's opening her master spreadsheet, the blue glow bouncing off her brown eyes. She looks at this thing at least once every hour. The fact that she's even referencing it is just for show—she has all those numbers memorized.

"Hmm, I could loan it out at fifteen percent interest over a year if that works for you," she says, her eyes still scanning the document. "Obviously you'll have to pay a penalty if you pay it off too quickly."

"Fifteen percent?" I yelp. "So I'd owe you another hundred and fifty dollars? Don't I get a family discount?"

Roya tosses her sleek black hair; she's one of the few Persians I know whose hair is stick-straight. "That is how loans work, and yes, that includes the family discount. It's the same rate I give my brothers, you weirdo. What do you need this for, anyway?"

I take a deep breath. This is going to require a lot of talking. "Emerson clocked me in the hallway. So I went to work off some steam with my drumsticks and I accidentally knocked over a shelf. Then Principal Saulk blackmailed me into entering the Battle of the Bands."

I chug water. That monologue was not pleasant.

"Yeah, I'm gonna need a bit more than that." Roya crosses her arms, an eyebrow raised. For an eighth grader, she sure is intimidating.

I hold up a "give me a second" finger and type what happened over text message instead. My fingers fly, explaining how Emerson Cheng humiliated me, how I found solace in the janitor closet, and how it cost me a thousand dollars that I now owe in the form of a musical performance. I watch Roya's eyebrows hitch higher and higher up her forehead with each message, and by the time I send the last one, they're practically in her hairline.

"What?" she cries. "Like, a real show? With an audience and everything?"

I nod grimly.

"THAT IS SO COOL!" she shouts. "Now you *have* to perform your lyrics out loud! Can I handle your merch table? For a fee, of course."

I laugh. "Yeah," I say. "Sure." It's decided. I'm going to put together an actual band and perform at the Battle of the Bands instead of paying for road salt that must be laced with diamonds. It feels good to give in to Principal Saulk's ultimatum and not be panicked about it. I try not to think about how I still have to recruit musicians despite having zero friends. For this one moment, I'm going to bask in the feeling of being the hip, exciting older cousin.

"This is the kick in the pants your butt needs," Roya says sagely, steepling her fingers together like she's a genius mastermind.

"Um, thanks?"

We sit there a bit longer, Roya clicking around as she looks up the Battle of the Bands website, me wondering if I can just hire a vocalist on fiverrr.com to sing my lyrics, then blast a prerecorded song from a laptop at the show.

"You don't happen to have a fake high school ID so I can recruit you into being in this band, right?" I ask.

"Nah, none of the ones on the black market here have the right barcode, so the scanner never works. Whoa, the prize is ten thousand dollars? I thought you just got one thousand for the school or whatever."

"Yep. I give them one thousand if we win, and then the band keeps the rest."

"Wanna play something?" Roya suddenly asks. "I

have some time before my new friends Aspen and Kinsley come over. And this way if you win, you can reimburse me for all the times I helped you practice."

"Wow, what an offer," I say flatly. But I don't let Roya see my smile as I move the laptop to my bedroom and plug the mini piano Dad got me into my laptop.

Roya switches her audio to headphones so she can hear the beat I'm about to feed her. Her voice isn't perfect, but it's a hundred times better than mine. I can usually count on her to audition whatever lyrics I've got.

"Here." I text her a song I've been tooling around with. Maybe it can be for the battle.

"Hum it for me?" she asks.

I start to hum in my crackly voice, accompanying it with the piano. Roya reads along in time to my head bobbing.

"Okay, I think I've got it."

I lead her in, conducting at the screen when it's time to start singing. Her voice is plain but even, and she starts right on cue.

With a girl like me
And a town like mine,
The odds have been against us, baby,
Since the dawn of time.
With a story like yours
And a knife so fine,
We'll cut this world open wide,
Singing songs the whole time.

Roya stops before I transition into the chorus. "Oooh, I like this one!" she says. "It feels bigger than your other stuff, you know? It's less specific, more universal. Good work!"

"Dang," I wheeze. "Thanks, Roya."

She ties her long hair back into a ponytail, her sparkling brown eyes turning serious. "All right, let's take it from the top. We gotta get you that ten K."

I bite my lip to hide the dangerously happy look spreading across my face. "One, two, three, four."

KOMBUCHA O'CLOCK

MOM BURSTS THROUGH the door holding grocery bags. Roya and I just finished recording the song with her vocals, and I can't wait to add instrumentation on my computer tonight.

"Hi, Roya jan!" Mom calls out from the kitchen. "How's school?"

"Hi, Holleh! It's good!" Roya replies through the phone, referring to my mom as "Aunt" even though she's technically her second cousin once removed. I position the laptop on the kitchen counter so Roya can see the two of us.

"You're already in your pj's?" Mom asks me, her curly hair wrapped into a big scarf and piled high on top of her head. She slips off her shoes and puts on her house moccasins.

"You know me," I say hoarsely. "Taking a disco nap

before I rage tonight." I can feel a tickle begin in my throat, the kind where the top of my nasal cavity stings whenever I swallow.

"Oh my god," Roya says. I can't see the screen from this angle, but I can hear the eye roll from here.

Mom's eyes narrow. Oh no. Wordlessly, she puts a hand on my forehead.

"Hmm. You're pretty warm." Mom's always on the lookout for a throat infection, and one of the first signs is a high temperature. If she catches one whiff of a sore throat, she'll force-feed me antibiotics and insist I eat yogurt at every meal.

I wriggle out of her grasp and move to the fridge.

"Roya, you wanna come over for dinner? I just went grocery shopping!" Mom says into my laptop.

Roya takes one look at all the dark leafy greens sticking out of Mom's reusable shopping tote and visibly shudders.

"Um, no thanks, Holleh! I should probably get going. Bye!"

I snort. Roya's favorite food is energy drinks, and the only time she eats vegetables is if they're in khoresht, aka Persian stew.

Instead of giving Mom any time to comment on my throat, I start putting kale, collard greens, brown eggs, and soy milk into the fridge while she takes her huge gold hoops out of her ears.

"How was school?" she asks innocently, reaching into the fridge for a bottle of kombucha. She opens it carefully in the sink, making sure not to let it bubble over. I gag at the sight of those weird strands of gloop at the bottom of the glass bottle.

"It was fine," I reply, trying to speak from my diaphragm, like Ms. Davolio insists. "I got partnered up with some lacrosse dude for English, though."

Mom sips her drink. "Is he a good guy?"

I remember how Eben had already outlined our entire project for us, and how he has one of the most beautiful voices I've ever heard. "I don't know him that well," I say. Thankfully, Mom doesn't seem to be listening too hard.

"What do you want for dinner, Z? Seitan? Kale Caesar? Quinoa?"

I give her a pitiful look. "I talked to that Nadim kid on my walk home today. I think I deserve a little more than a kale Caesar, wouldn't you say?"

"Seriously, Azar? I *just* went grocery shopping."

"Can we get delivery?" I beg, my face twisting in agony. "Pretty please?" I make my voice crack on purpose on that *please* for dramatic effect. It's my one superpower.

Mom gives me a hard stare, one that lasts so long, I can count the freckles on her nose. I have the same kind of freckles, but they're lighter.

"Fine." She throws her hands up into the air. *Yesss!* I watch as she gets out her cell.

"Salaam," she says in Farsi, then continues. "What are the specials of the day? . . . Uh-huh . . . baghali polow?"

I do a silent fist pump. Baghali polow is my favorite kind of rice. Mom places our dinner order for delivery, and I give her an angelic smile.

"You're evil, you know that?" she says, flopping down onto the couch. I curl up next to her.

"I'm not evil. Just persuasive."

"Delivery actually sounds like just what I need after the day I had." She strokes my hair. "Thanks, Z."

"Is everything okay?"

"Just work stuff. Too many projects to manage and not enough time. Same old, same old."

I snuggle in closer, and Mom wraps a blanket around the two of us. She cues up *Ocean's Eleven,* one of her favorite George Clooney movies. Maman Bozorg and Mom have an unhealthy George Clooney obsession, ever since his role on *ER*. It spiraled out of control when George was caught doing a beshkan, or a two-handed snap, in a viral video. Watching *Ocean's Eleven* means that Mom is trying to cheer herself up, and that her day at work must have been especially rough.

Half an hour later, just when Danny Ocean's got almost all his team assembled for the big heist, the doorbell rings.

"Salaam, Azar jan. Niloofar." Kian, our delivery guy, licks his lips in Mom's direction. He always rushes over any orders we place—probably because he keeps hoping Mom will marry him and make homemade yogurt for all the sons she'll doubtlessly birth. Having a kid at a young age must make her look especially fertile. Barf.

"Salaam, Kian," I reply, signing the delivery receipt. "Khubi?"

"I'm good." His cologne is so strong, my eyes water. "The construction here is getting worse, though. Pah! Tysons Corner is going to become the next LA, at this rate."

I make some sympathetic noises, ready to end this conversation so I can breathe clean air.

"How about you, Niloofar?" Kian calls out, flexing his huge biceps for Mom. Who wears muscle tees in January?

"Hi, Kian." Mom smiles politely from the couch, not moving.

"I have tickets to the Iranian Arts Showcase at the Kennedy Center this weekend. Want to come?"

"Maybe some other time," she says, her smile not reaching her eyes.

"Cool, cool, yeah, no worries." He nods, shaking off the rejection like it's no big deal.

"She'll come around," I whisper. Mom better not endanger our delivery hookup or I'll be devastated.

"No doubt. No doubt. Shab bekheir, Azar jan." Kian puffs up his chest, already convincing himself that my mom just "needs more time" or something. He finally hands me the plastic bag of unrecyclable Styrofoam boxes and I close the door, taking a gulp of air.

"Kian's starting to think you don't like him," I scold her, bringing the food over to the counter. "Then he'll stop giving us extra lavash." I unpack the thin folds of flatbread and fix us both plates.

Mom just waves her hand. "He's an Aries. You know I don't date fire signs. They're too chaotic."

I sigh. "If you did, we'd get free kabob every night. Can't you just take one for the team?"

Mom frowns. "Azar, are you sure you feel okay? Your voice sounds like it hurts." I bite my lip. It *always* hurts. But having a normal night of watching George Clooney with my mom is worth some vocal discomfort. I stay silent and put the veggie kabob, rice with dill and fava beans, and bits of yogurt and feta cheese onto each plate and carry them back to the living room.

Mom takes a sip of kombucha, still appraising me. "Maybe we should just call it a night. The later you stay up, the worse it gets."

We eat our dinner in silence. There's so much I wanted to tell her. How I got hit with a Frisbee that landed me in the principal's office with an entry for the Battle of the Bands (omitting the thousand-dollar-damage part, of course). How I'm nervous and scared and in over my head. How I could really use some advice here.

But Mom's clearly already had a rough day. How much more can I dump on her? So instead of saying anything, I scrape my plate, load the dishwasher, and go to my room. I'll have to figure this out on my own.

FEVER DREAMS

I WAKE UP the next morning with crusty eyes and a sweaty forehead. Everything feels wrong. My throat feels scratchier than ever. My head's pounding. Just swallowing my own saliva hurts. The air in the room feels stale, and I've got a mossy feeling in my mouth that I only get when I'm sick.

"Azar?" Mom gently knocks on the door, a far cry from her blasting reggaeton and yelling at me to finish getting dressed like she did yesterday.

"Mom?" I sound like a bullfrog. Sunlight pours into my room at a weird angle for 6:30 a.m. "What time is it?"

"It's ten a.m. You slept through your alarm."

"What?" I jolt up in bed. How can it be 10:00 a.m.? Immediately, I feel dizzy and the ache in my head pulses even harder. Hair's plastered to my face, and the sheets are all tangled and ropy from whatever thrashing I'd been doing.

"Take it easy, Z. You have a fever."

I fall back onto my pillows. "Oh."

I don't say anything. We both know what this fever is from: my throat. The tickle I had last night must have grown.

On my nightstand is an arsenal of over-the-counter medication I don't remember taking. Fever reducer, cherry-flavored throat-numbing spray, and, of course, Vicks VapoRub, the only thing Abuelo swears by. Mom must be desperate. Vicks is usually for chest coughs and I don't have one (yet). She hovers over me in a sweater and jeans, an outfit she'd never wear to work.

"You don't have to stay home for me." What I don't say out loud is how excruciating getting that one sentence out feels, how my entire esophagus feels like it's on fire. *Please don't go to work.*

"Baby, I think we need to visit the doctor."

Doctors will swab the back of my throat and prescribe me antibiotics. Then Mom will make me eat a bunch of yogurt and fermented foods so I can "rebuild my intestinal flora." Then we'll wait a few months and the cycle will start all over again.

I'm surprised she's talking about an in-person visit. Last time, Mom just did a phone consultation and picked up the prescription, since our family doctor knows how often this happens. That's probably what she meant.

"Wake me when you get the drugs." Clindamycin. Metronizadole. A Z-Pak, if I'm lucky, which has only six pills instead of ten days' worth of antibiotics. I snuggle back into bed. Just having this conversation feels like walking underwater, each word a gargantuan effort.

"No, baby. Your physician wants you to go to Dr. Talbot. This is your fourth infection in six months."

I freeze. "Dr. Talbot?" He's my ear, nose, and throat doctor. We only go to him when things get *really* bad.

Mom nods gravely. "Dr. Talbot."

The ENT clinic is deep in Fairfax, in one of those developments full of town houses that look like regular homes but are secretly businesses, doctors' offices, and bagel cafés. Mom pulls into an office park with dark green awnings outside every front door, along with brass plaques and welcome mats. JAMES TALBOT, MD. | OTOLARYNGOLOGY | EAR NOSE AND THROAT SPECIALIST | HEAD AND NECK SURGERY.

Just unbuckling my own seat belt makes me woozy, and my whole body feels like it's buzzing. I shakily open the car door, and Mom helps me walk up the office's neat front steps. I breathe slowly through the mask she insisted I wear in case I could infect anyone else.

Tracy, the receptionist, gives me a friendly wave when we enter. On the lip of her desk are some forms for Dr. Talbot to sign along with his lunch, which looks like it's a sub from the local Chinese restaurant. Why does he insist on subjecting himself to the worst food ever?

We've been here many, many times, and Tracy's been here ever since I started seeing Dr. Talbot. If I had visited him when my throat issues first started, they would have operated on me immediately and put in a pig's aorta to line my throat. But I'm too old for that now, because it would have to be a huge pig to pull that off. They say it's a miracle I can talk as much as I do. Because I'm just *sooo* chatty.

We sit down in the waiting room, and I don't even get my phone out or flip through a magazine, because I know what's about to come and I just want to get it over with.

Visiting the ENT isn't like visiting a regular family physician, where they take your temperature and the worst thing that happens is they swab your throat. Nope, visiting the ENT usually means they get a good look at what's going on in your esophagus, which means threading a tiny camera up through your nostril and down the back of your throat, forcing you to watch it on a big screen. *Please let this be a camera-free day.*

I wonder what Eben's doing right now. Probably slapping someone's back, or saying something like "Yeah, no, for sure!"

I still can't believe I asked him about being a lead singer yesterday. Why did I do that? The hurt look on Eben's face oozes into my brain, followed by how he stormed out of the library, all because of me. Is that why I'm sick right now? All the "stress"?

He's probably laughing it off with his cool lax bro

friends. Or texting Emerson Cheng about the whole conversation, the two of them cackling about me over Slurpees, the blue raspberry kind that looks subatomic and tastes like heaven. Why did I have to open my mouth? Maybe Roya knows someone else who can be the lead singer. She knows more people at my high school than I do.

"Azar, chill," Mom says, pointing at my bouncing knee.

"Azar?" Dr. Talbot asks through the doorway. He pronounces it wrong, like *quasar*. We've never bothered correcting him. He motions for me to join.

"Want me to come with?" Mom asks.

I try to stand and instantly fall back in my chair from the head rush. She gently holds my arm.

Dr. Talbot leads us to the room with the camera equipment inside, and my nostrils quiver in fear. Camera scopes hurt way worse when you have an infection.

"Sit, Azar," he says, gesturing to the examination table. "I'm just going to feel for bumps."

He runs his hands up and down my throat to feel for swollen lymph nodes. He's so close, I can see the different shades of blue in his irises and the small veins that run under his white, papery skin. I close my eyes, everything feeling way too close and awkward. He stops on a lump right below my right jawbone. I wish I could bat it down like a game of Whac-A-Mole.

"Tell me what you ate for breakfast," he says, his hand still on the lump.

"Tylenol. And Throat Soothe." The room reeks of

bleach and Dr. Talbot's talcum-powder aroma. It's taking everything in me just to sit up straight and not keel over on the examination table.

He sticks a thermometer into my ear. "One hundred and one point three. That's pretty high. Can you remove your mask?" he asks. I tug my mask down as Dr. Talbot puts his on. "You should wear one too, Niloofar." He hands one to Mom.

I watch as Dr. Talbot grabs a very long cotton bud and brace myself.

"Do you need a tongue depressor?"

I shake my head. I've had this done to me so many times, my body doesn't fight it anymore. He quickly touches the cotton bud end to the back of my throat, then sticks it into a plastic baggie filled with solution.

"We'll have the lab rush this one. From what I can see, it looks like strep. You've got the telltale white patches and your throat inflammation is substantial. How do you feel?"

I give him a dead-eyed stare. "Fantastic."

"Niloofar, do you feel all right? Streptococcus is very infectious."

Mom shrugs. "I feel fine. I'm just worried about her."

Dr. Talbot turns back to me. "It seems your throat is much more susceptible to infection than others'. Let's take a look."

Take a look. He makes it sound so chill and low-key, when the truth is he's going to STICK A CAMERA UP MY NOSE. I wish I could pass out like women in those

Victorian movies and just wake up with everything over and done with.

"We're not going to need the straps, right?" Dr. Talbot's tone is both light and menacing, as if he's saying, *This isn't going to be a problem, is it?*

When I was younger, I'd fight this procedure so much, they'd have to strap me down to the table before they could insert the scope. I shake my head at Dr. Talbot. The straps just make it worse, and lying back makes it harder to swallow.

He gets out the camera, which is really just a wire that's thinner than my phone charger cord. At the end is a little light where the camera lens is.

Mom holds my hand as I sit on the edge of the examination table, her palm soft from all the coconut oil she uses. The camera looms, and I try to take deep breaths.

"Wait!" I yelp.

It's the loudest I've spoken in weeks, not close to a shout but definitely louder than the normal "room temperature" volume Ms. Davolio likes. "Can I listen to music? It'll help me relax." I say it quickly, my throat aching.

Dr. Talbot looks surprised. "Sure, if it helps." I don't think he likes doing these procedures, either. I wonder why I didn't think of listening to music sooner.

I grab my bright purple headphones and press "play" on that *MOOD* playlist, the music making it seem like I'm in control, even though I feel completely helpless in this moment. Maybe if I'm lucky, I'll dissociate from my body.

I see you glow.
What will your crystal ball show?
In a future no one knows. . . .

He puts the scope in my right nostril. I take deep breaths in time to the beat of the dark, haunting Amy Waters song. This part doesn't hurt that bad; it's just like if you get a nosebleed and you stick a tampon up your nose to stop the blood. He pauses when he gets to the top of my nose, right where the bridge meets my eyes, and looks at me as if waiting for permission.

"Okay," I confirm. Here it comes.

I flinch as the worst part happens, the part where the cord pushes past my nasal cavity and into my sinuses before it dips into my throat. My sinuses feel like they're made of magma, they burn so much. Mom squeezes my hand and I clutch it, my eyes closed so tight, I see spots. The cord feels huge, even though I know it's only a couple millimeters wide.

It slowly wends its way down the back of my throat, and it feels like postnasal drip, like when my allergies are bad. I want to cry. I want to yank this thing out of my face and hog-tie Dr. Talbot and his stupid lunches. I want to go back in time and grab my mom by the shoulders and tell her to schedule surgery the second I become colicky. But instead I just raise the volume on my headphones as Amy screams and thrashes and sings all the things I can't say out loud.

Take your clothes, take the keys,
Take the best parts of me.
When you look back at this day,
See our names in that tree,
Carved permanently.

Dr. Talbot says something through the music, and I feel the tube stop moving. I open my eyes. There's a big monitor in the middle of the room and my throat flickers on-screen in real time, in black and white, like night vision. There's a big black circle in the middle with white-and-gray tissue surrounding it.

Hello, throat, you piece of garbage.

I can't hear what they're saying, but Dr. Talbot points to tiny white circles on the screen. Those are the stupid vocal nodules that keep my vocal folds from vibrating properly.

I try to swallow, but it's hard with the cord still inside, like the back of my throat can't form a full seal. I shiver as saliva drips down my esophagus, tasting like copper. Mom says something, and then Dr. Talbot turns to me and starts removing the camera. It feels like he's sucking my soul out, it's so weird and strange. Luckily, they record each session, so he doesn't need to stay in there too long.

Finally, the scope exits my nostril. I tilt my head back and Dr. Talbot gives me a tissue for the nosebleed that always comes. Amy's agonized chorus fades out, and I finally swallow. It feels like a Dementor has just given me a kiss.

"Well, Azar, I think it might be time to discuss laser surgery."

"Really?" I croak.

It feels like we've done everything to avoid it. Speech pathology. Steaming my throat. Avoiding acidic foods. Getting eight hours of sleep and trying to keep my stress levels down.

"Obviously, you're too old for an esophageal graft." I shiver, thinking of the poor pig they'd have used on me. "The reason we use surgery as a last resort for children is because poor throat hygiene means the nodules can come back even after the procedure. But you've clearly been responsible, and it isn't making a difference. The risk is that the surgery can sometimes lead to more infection, something you're already prone to. You'll need a few days of complete vocal rest."

"But how would I go to classes and stuff?"

He perches his short, elfin body on one of those rolling stools.

"We could wait until the end of the semester for summer break, but I'm worried you'll get more infections. If we do it now, you could risk undoing all our hard work by having to speak at school. Even just a few words or clearing your throat could lead to a post-op infection. Could you learn some basic ASL? It's a shame we didn't catch this over winter break."

"What about after?" I ask, my throat still feeling raw from the camera. I cough a little, clearing the slime trail the scope left. "Will I sound . . . more normal?"

Dr. Talbot gives me a smile, his teeth so white, they look blue. "Normal as in your voice won't sound so strained? Yes, it will eventually be a little smoother. You should be able to hold a conversation without pain."

"What do you suggest we do?" Mom asks. Here we go. Whatever he suggests, I know it's going to suck.

"I recommend we do the procedure right before spring break. That way she'll have a whole week off to heal without accidentally undoing our hard work, and we can tackle extra quiet time with Ms. Davolio."

Mom nods. "How long is the procedure? What kind of anesthesia will you use?"

Suddenly the room feels too small, like the cord's still in my nose and I can't swallow properly. I hear Dr. Talbot say words like "ambulatory" and "general anesthesia," but my blood's buzzing, and I can feel myself floating out of my body. Whatever fever reducer Mom gave me is wearing off.

"Can I go to the bathroom?" I ask. I need to get out of here.

Dr. Talbot blinks. "Yes, of course."

"You go ahead, Z. I'll meet you in the waiting room," Mom says, already taking notes on the legal pad in her giant purse. Her job as a project manager means she's *always* taking notes.

I throw on my mask and stumble out of the examination room. "Azar, which flavor lollipop do you want?" Tracy calls out. "I've got green apple! Your favorite!"

I wave her off and burst through the exit. I need to breathe. I reach Mom's car and gulp for air, its coolness soothing my singed throat. Dr. Talbot had always mentioned surgery before, but never this urgently. Now it's really happening.

With shaky hands, I pull up my phone, ignoring all of Roya's texts. For some reason, I load up the website for the Battle of the Bands, probably out of a perverse need to feel even more terrible. I scroll through and see that spring break is the week before the battle—right when I'll be in the middle of healing.

Of course it is. When has anything ever been easy for me?

Maybe Sydney could be the lead singer. We'd call our band the Sibilants, and all our lyrics would have s's in them. Between Eben's reluctance to join and the fact that I won't be able to talk the entire week leading up to the performance, it's clear I'm going to have to go onstage alone with a guitar and just take the public humiliation solo. My band name can be Girl with a Laptop, and my opener will be called "Crippling Embarrassment."

I collapse into Mom's car in the frigid parking lot, wishing I could scream at the sky like a normal teenage girl.

I raise the volume on my headphones instead.

SICKBED

BURN AFTER READING. *O Brother, Where Art Thou?* *Syriana.* At one point we got so desperate, we watched *Michael Clayton*—one of Clooney's most boring movies, in my humble opinion. Mom took the whole day off work and sat with me on the couch, force-feeding me Throat Soothe and sauerkraut to "rebuild my intestinal flora." Have you ever burped into a face mask after eating sauerkraut? It is not ideal. It beats staying home alone, though.

By the time 6:00 p.m. rolls around, I am ready to crash. Mom puts a cool hand on my forehead. "Your fever's still there. Let's see how you feel tomorrow."

I nod and take my second antibiotic for the day. Then I brush my teeth, scrape my tongue, cleanse with the bottle of bulk argan oil Mom keeps on our bathroom counter, and pass out.

When I sleep, there's no song stuck in my head. No dreams, just black.

∩

The next morning, I wake up in cool sheets with normal-smelling breath. When I swallow it doesn't hurt, though I still feel a little off.

Mom knocks and opens the door, carrying The Tea. "You look way better," she says. "How do you feel?"

"I feel . . ." I test the words out in my mouth. They're still rough, but it's definitely not as painful as yesterday. "Okay."

"Here," she says, handing me my pill. I swallow it and then she hands over a thermometer. "Let's see what we're working with."

"Ninety-eight point nine." I give it back to her.

"Do you feel up to going to school? Dr. Talbot said strep isn't contagious after about a full day of antibiotics."

I shrug. Going to school sounds awful, but cutting into Mom's vacation days sounds even worse. "I guess so."

"Great!" she exclaims, the relief clearly displayed on her face. She's probably way behind at work from taking yesterday off. This may just be one of the last times she stays at home while I'm sick if this surgery works as well as Dr. Talbot claims.

Surgery. Dr. Talbot says it's a simple in-and-out procedure. The lasers will eliminate my nodules like a video game, leaving nothing but a smoking circle. They'll give me vein champagne, then I'll wake up and go right back home. *Zap zap zap.*

Maybe my voice will finally sound okay afterward. Maybe I won't sound so rough and patchy. Maybe . . . just maybe, I could sound as good as Roya, or even Eben, one day.

Eben. I can practically see his name spelled out in that perfect handwriting. Hopefully we can just ignore each other at school today and pretend our conversation never happened.

"Get dressed, Z. I'll drop you off on my way to work."

🎧

I barely listen to Ms. Davolio in speech pathology, my thoughts floating in a post-fever haze. Dr. Talbot's apparently consulted with her on the surgery and all the post-op therapy I'll need, along with how my throat will be too raw for class today. Thankfully she's too busy trying to get Sydney to pronounce the word *sixth* to even notice that I am mentally checked out. I pop in a stick of gum, chewing it like a depressed cow and her cud.

I have a little over three months to find a lead singer, or a serviceable instrumental arrangement that won't get me laughed offstage at the Battle of the Bands. That's plenty of time, right? I package the anxiety up, gift-wrap it, and place it on a high shelf in my head. There. Nice and out of sight.

The bell rings, and Sydney and I head to English, the two of us drifting away from each other like we always do. I head to my locker, but then she taps me on the shoulder.

"Hey," she says through her curtain of purple bangs. "Are you okay? Do you want me to take you to the nurse?"

I flinch. It feels like Sydney and I are breaking some sort of unspoken rule by having a real conversation outside of speech therapy that isn't about how hot my English partner is. Still, I'm kind of touched.

"I'm okay," I finally croak. "Just a lot on my mind."

Sydney nods. "I hear you. I have a quiz in . . . *sixth* period."

I bark a harsh "Ha!" sound. She pronounced the word without a lisp. "Nice!"

"See ya in English."

She goes off to her locker, and I stand there, calculating. That was my first joke with someone in high school. Do we have an inside joke now?

I grab my textbooks, but just seeing the cover of *The Heart Is a Lonely Hunter* makes me flush. My shame knows no depths. I rest my face against the cool metal of the locker, hoping it'll help with the redness that I can feel creeping into my cheeks. If only Mom had given me enough melanin for moments like this.

Someone clears their throat behind me.

I turn around, only to come face-to-face with Eben.

"Hey," he says. "Were you sick? Your face looks really red."

My thudding heart goes from pianissimo to fortissimo. Oh boy, here it comes: He's going to tell me off for being a jerk on Monday. Or, even worse, he's just going to pretend the whole band thing never happened, silently hinting that we should just put this whole strange incident behind us.

A strangled *"Yeeeeeuuuugh"* noise crawls out of my throat.

He continues as if I'd actually said hello. "So, I've been thinking about our conversation . . ."

I brace myself for the crushing blow of rejection. My throat makes another unattractive gurgle.

". . . and I think it would be cool. But only if I get to be a real band member, you know? Help with lyrics and beats and stuff. Not just some attackman who cherry-picks goals."

"Eurgh."

"Because I have ideas. Good ones," he says, his face lighting up enough to reveal two earnest-looking dimples.

"Mhmmm."

"Yeah, and it's time to show everyone that I'm more than just a lacrosse player. I'm creative. And stuff."

"Yes," I say, and nod, completely thrown. "That." My head spins.

He holds out a hand to shake. "Let's do this, Azar."

I flinch at the way he mispronounces my name. I reach for his hand, then stop. Eben was real with me just now. He spoke about what he really wants, and that takes guts. Maybe it's time I start doing the same thing.

"Deal. But on one condition," I add.

"What's that?"

"You have to say my name properly," I say, looking him in the eye. "It's pronounced *AW-zár*."

"Isn't that what I said?" Eben asks.

"No, it's *AW-zár,* not *A-tsar.*"

Eben tries again. I shake my head. This is gonna be like Sydney and the word *sixth* all over again.

"Say *awww,* like you just saw a cute kitten."

"Awww!" Eben repeats. "I love kittens."

"Good, now say *pat.*"

"Pat," Eben repeats gamely.

"Now say the *a* from *pat.*"

"*A,*" Eben repeats, the *a* sounding harsh and flat, the perfect pronunciation for it in Farsi.

"Now say *zar,*" I say, using that same harsh *a.*

"Zar." Eben nails it.

"Put it all together. *AW-zár.*"

"Azar!"

"Yes!" Warmth blooms in my chest. There's something so powerful about hearing your name pronounced properly, like that person is in your inner circle now. You both invested time in teaching it and learning it. Maybe Eben really will be a good team player in this band of ours.

"Just let me know when the first rehearsal is, okay?" Eben says.

The bell rings. I'm still smiling like an idiot. "Sure."

He slings his backpack over his shoulder. "Okay, well, see you in class."

"Uh-huh," I say, trying to keep my cool, but inside I feel gooey and happy. Nobody in my class has ever said my name right before, except Nadim. Eben and I are bonded now, whether he realizes it or not.

He ambles away, the easy gait of someone who unknowingly dropped a bombshell onto my life.

This is it. This is my chance. I let my Battle of the Bands fantasy wash over me, the details already in place from the daydreams I've had since I was a kid. It's like picking up a good book I can't wait to continue reading, but I have to keep returning it to the library because it isn't mine. Well, guess what? Now I can imagine the concert as often as I want. I *own* this book, suckers.

But as soon as my brain catches up with my joy, a splash of cold water soaks the whole thing. It's one thing to fantasize about something, but a totally different feeling to have a dream come true.

I groan out loud. "Crap. Now I really have to do this."

THE BLESSÉD WEEKEND

Shoot for the stars,
Go for the gold—
What's the point when you're 14 years old?
I see my dreams; they're just within reach,
But that gold star taunts me when I speak.

By the time Saturday rolls around, I am too emotionally spent to be a contributing member of society. Mom lets me sleep in, and when I finally wake up, I take an extra-long shower where I just stand under the running water, letting my throat warm up in the steam. Weekends are the only time when the hot water doesn't run out after a few minutes, and it feels good to just stand with my forehead against our chipped tile, thinking.

I stayed up half the night listening to SoundCloud and writing lyrics, trying to figure out what the heck I was going to do with Eben's "yes" to make an actual game plan. Maybe we could be a rock band, with Eben as a strutting lead singer who somehow wears lots of denim. Or maybe more of an indie-pop sensation, where he and I perform and it would be okay to have a laptop onstage providing the rest of the instruments. That would solve the recruitment issue of a drummer and a bassist.

Despite staying up until 1:00 a.m., I still haven't narrowed down the kind of sound I want us to have. Looking back, I'm amazed I even asked Eben in the first place. The Azar who asked him that day in the library was a gutsy, confident fool. What would we even perform in? Lacrosse jerseys?

"Azar!" Mom knocks on my door. "Don't forget we're going to Abuelo and Maman Bozorg's soon!"

Through a slit in the shower curtain, I see an arm snake into the bathroom. Something clinks on the vanity and the door shuts; I peek and see a cup of Throat Soothe sitting next to the sink.

"We leave in an hour," Mom says from the other side of the door.

I cannot catch a break.

♩

My grandparents live about fifteen minutes away, in a nicer part of town. Their neighborhood is so old, you drive on converted cow paths that loop and wind into the woods, ending in driveways a quarter of a mile long. When we pull up, I see Roya's family car already there, and barbecue smoke spilling over from the backyard, even though it's the middle of January.

"You excited for your sleepover?" Mom turns off the ignition.

I flash a thumbs-up. Once a month, Roya and I spend the night here, and Mom uses that time to go on a date or go out with her friends. I usually take the bus up to New York and see Dad once a month, too, though we haven't seen each other since winter break.

"What are you going to do while I'm gone?"

Mom sighs. "Honestly? Probably just relax and watch a movie. I'm too tired to plan anything."

"You should spend the night then, too!"

It's okay if *I'm* a total loser with no friends, but somehow knowing my mom also has no social life makes me feel even worse.

Mom shivers. "Thanks, but I've spent enough weekends in that house to last me a lifetime."

When Mom got pregnant with me in her first year of college, she had to drop out and move back home while Dad finished his degree, since he was a senior and about to graduate. My grandparents helped, but I know they weren't happy housing a single mom/college dropout.

"Come on," she says. "I bet they've got all the processed junk food you want."

I run to the house.

We head to the back patio, where everyone's sitting under heat lamps. Abuelo envelops me in a big hug, his bushy white mustache tickling my face.

"Azar!" he cries. "¿Tienes hambre? I made you chorizo and lomo saltado!"

"And we have chimichurri and kabob," my maman bozorg adds, her elegant black outfit at odds with Abuelo's apron, which is really just an Argentinian soccer jersey.

"Pah!" Abuelo sneers. "That chimichurri is from the jar! It doesn't count."

"Hey, Maman," Mom says to Maman Bozorg. "Hi, Papá."

My abuelo is from Argentina, while my maman bozorg came from Iran. Their cultures are pretty different, but if there's one thing they both know how to do, it's grill meat.

"Toma, toma," Abuelo instructs, holding out a piece of chorizo for me to try. I look at Mom for permission, and she gives me a tight nod. I take a bite of the salty, spicy sausage.

"Yummm," I moan. I miss eating pork, which Mom doesn't allow. Technically, Maman Bozorg doesn't allow it, either. I see Maman Bozorg sniff, but she doesn't say anything.

"Azar!" Roya calls out from where she's huddled under

a heat lamp. In the corner of the yard, I can see Ashkan hitting a soccer ball. Roya's older brother, Darius, is too busy at George Mason University to come by for Saturday barbecues anymore.

"Hey, cuz." She gives me a hug, running her hands up and down my arms to warm me up. My hair's under my Nats hat today, while Roya's wearing a cute beret and a parka. I look like an unfriendly beanpole with no chest next to Roya's curves. I miss going to the same school as her. Just walking next to her made me seem friendlier, even if I'm not.

"Salaam, Azar!" Roya's mom, Neda, calls out.

Mom sits down next to Holleh Neda, catching her up on everything going on. Neda is basically my mom's sister. Kind of like how Roya and I are.

Roya's dad, Jamshid, chugs black tea under an outdoor heater while he looks at his phone. Roya's entire family is Iranian, while I'm only a quarter. You wouldn't know it from looking at us, though. My dad's Italian side seems to have teamed up with my Iranian genes, making me just as hairy. Even though Abuelo's from Argentina, he's got some Italian blood in him, too.

"Are you hungry, joonam?" Maman Bozorg asks, handing me a cup of tea. "You look so thin! Why you are not eating?"

Maman Bozorg looks accusingly at Mom, who just rolls her eyes. "I do feed her, you know. We had baghali polow this week! Tell her, Azar."

"Yeah, and *Kian* delivered it."

My maman bozorg lights up. "Kian saw you? And what were you wearing?"

Mom snorts, pouring herself a glass of tea. "Sweatpants? I don't know!"

Maman Bozorg tsks so loudly, I'm sure Kian can hear it all the way from here. "How you are going to get married if you don't even try?"

Mom just takes a sip and ignores her. Roya and I giggle. It's one thing to have Mom rag on me all week, but it's another thing to see my maman bozorg rag on her instead.

Before they can keep bickering, Abuelo hands out plates heaped with food: chorizo nestled between split pieces of baguette for choripan, thin cuts of beef, aka lomo saltado, and cubes of chicken kabob all rest on top of white rice and a grilled tomato. My mouth waters as the scents of saffron and char waft over me. There's no way Mom would let me eat this much meat in one day at home. She slyly adds some fresh herbs onto my plate for roughage.

"Yum," I say out loud, not caring that my voice sounds crackly.

"Mom says Holleh Mariam is the best cook in the family, but I think you might give her a run for her money," Roya says to Abuelo.

He beams. He loves putting on his "apron" and grilling. In the summer, they grill just about every meal except breakfast out here. Even Roya's dad, who's stayed pretty quiet until now, attacks his plate like he hasn't eaten in weeks. Ashkan toddles over and eats kabob with his hands, too impatient for forks or spoons. That's how good the food is.

"Azizam, bokhor!" Maman Bozorg prods me. *Eat!*

I take a bite of choripan and groan happily. The spicy chimichurri sauce on top of the chorizo tastes amazing. Mom has already abandoned her "pescatarian" lifestyle and seems to be inhaling chicken kabob. I take a sip of the soda Maman Bozorg snuck me and revel in the flavors of a perfect meal.

You know the food is good when everyone's quiet for the first ten minutes. I don't think anyone even minds the cold at this point, we're so hunched over our steaming plates. Finally, when we come up for air, Abuelo points at Mom.

"Querida, when are you going to save up and buy a house? Then you could have people over for your own barbecues!"

Mom sighs. She never catches a break from them. "I'm trying, but work's been intense lately. And the only houses in our budget in Azar's school district are serious fixer-uppers. Being a project manager doesn't mean I make loads of money."

Abuelo shrugs. "Just let us help you with the down payment."

My holleh Neda nods, stroking Roya's hair absentmindedly. "I can help you find a good deal, too. I've got some clients looking for houses in the same area, and I've seen some decent properties."

Roya's mom is always insisting on helping us get an "investment property" or a "starter home." I think she's where Roya gets her entrepreneurial spirit from.

"Those are generous offers, but I want to do this on my own. You both have already helped so much."

It's my turn to feel awkward now. When I was born, Neda and my grandparents practically raised me, since Mom was a nineteen-year-old who needed all the help she could get.

"Want to go inside?" Roya whispers. I nod vigorously.

"We're gonna finish eating in the basement," Roya announces, loading her plate up with more food. The adults wave us away, their conversation on homebuying starting to heat up. We hear words like "mortgage" and "equity" and "appraisal" ricochet off the pergola above the deck. We barely make it out alive.

ROCK BAND

MY GRANDPARENTS' BASEMENT has its own bedroom, living room, bathroom, and soda fridge. Every time Roya and I spend the night, we basically take over the whole floor and hog the huge flat-screen TV. I once asked Mom if she missed living here, but she looked at me like I'd asked her if she enjoyed eating red meat.

Roya turns on the TV and I plug in Mom's old Xbox, and we begin playing our favorite game: *Guitar Hero*.

Except we don't play it the way you're supposed to, which is where you mash a bunch of buttons on a tiny plastic guitar in time with the music. No, our version includes points for choreography, hair tossing, and general performance. You can't just stand there and squint at the screen while you hit the keys—you have to *feel* it. We've been playing this game for years, and it never gets old.

"Me first!" Roya shouts.

I hand her the dinky guitar and she cues up one of her favorite songs. She shouts the lyrics at the top of her lungs, headbanging between verses for good measure. Roya plays it perfectly, the notes blaring back at us through the basement's fancy sound system. Then she finishes with a twirl and pretends to smash the guitar onto the ground.

I clap loudly and whistle like a real audience member. She takes a bow and hands me the guitar as I shake out my shoulders, preparing for the concert like I just sold out the entire arena.

The song begins, and I start slow, building my performance in a crescendo of energy. I hit the buttons with precision—we memorized the songs a long time ago—and as soon as it gets to the chorus, I kick my foot up onto the sofa and really get into it. I can almost imagine it's a real concert, with Roya cheering me on and clapping in time to my guitar solo. I fall onto my knees, swishing my hair back and forth before spinning the tiny plastic guitar around my neck.

By the time I'm done, Roya is chanting my name and I'm out of breath, the two of us smiling like complete dorks. We collapse onto the huge sectional sofa, and Roya rummages around the mini fridge for more soda. We might not be able to smash a champagne bottle over our heads, or whatever rock stars do, but at least we'll always have our sugar.

"Here," she says, and tosses me one. Mom would kill me if she knew I drank more than one soda in a day. But what Mom doesn't know won't drain her energy crystals.

I pop it open and gulp it down, tired from my Madison Square Garden–level guitar solo.

"So," Roya begins, catching her breath. "Have you figured out the band yet?"

I waver. Should I tell her about Eben? It feels like the second I tell Roya, it'll truly become real. Right now, it's just between me and him.

I hedge. "I've got to do a book project with this guy on the lacrosse team. That's what I've been focusing on."

Roya's eyes narrow. "Do I know him?"

I shrug. "Maybe? His name is Eben Lloyd Hollins. The Fifth."

Roya gasps. "The lacrosse star? He won state championships for us at Stonewall, remember? I think he has a Lax Bro sponsorship! He must pull in at least ten thousand dollars a year in merch."

"Really?" I had no clue that Eben was semi-famous.

She pulls out her phone and searches for Eben's socials. "See?"

I scroll through photos of him at lacrosse practice and a couple where he holds a huge trophy with his family. Judging from the massive house they're standing in front of, they're definitely wealthy.

I hand the phone back to Roya, my stomach sinking. Eben is clearly way more popular than me, what with the sports stardom and rich parents. If I had known how different our social standing was, there's no way I would have approached him to sing.

So why did he say yes to being in my band?

"What's wrong?" Roya asks, pocketing her phone. I can already see all the texts and DMs she's ignoring just to be here with me. It makes me feel more pathetic than ever.

"Well . . ." I say in a tiny voice. "I may have asked Eben to be lead singer. For the band."

"No. Way." Roya looks ecstatic. "He can sing?"

"Dude," I say, shaking my head. "His voice is incredible."

"Singer, lacrosse star, homecoming court, sponsorship deals . . . this guy has everything." She and Sydney should start a fan club. "What did he say?"

I gulp. "He . . . he said yes."

Roya squeals, and for a second, I feel like I'm back in the first-year hallway watching my classmates. "OH MY GOSH, AZAR, THAT IS SO COOL!" She jumps up from the couch and pretends to strum a huge chord on the toy guitar. "That's such an awesome idea! You'll finally get to share your lyrics with everyone! *And* perform in public! And most important, win NINE GRAND MINUS MY MERCH FEES!"

I smile. Maybe we'll win, and get a record deal, and—

"So what's your band called?" Roya asks, turning back to her phone. She types something into a website with suspiciously familiar '90s typography.

"Why are you on the Battle of the Bands website? Please tell me you are not scoping out the competition."

"Listen, if you have Eben in your band, of course I'm

going to take the over on you winning. He's always a sure bet. Name, please? I know someone in the Polk subreddit is already taking bets."

I falter. "Name?"

"Yeah, like, what's your band's name?"

Sweet gluten, I haven't even thought of a band name. Or when we're going to have our first rehearsal. Or which songs we should do, or the best arrangement for Eben's voice. What was I thinking?

"Roya," I say, suddenly panicked. "What if our band sucks? What if I can't find a bassist or a drummer? Or what if Eben doesn't want to sing any of my songs? Or he can't read sheet music and I have to sing the lyrics out loud to him so he gets it? Or . . . Or . . ."

Roya places her hands on my shoulders. "Deep breaths."

I gulp in air.

"Maybe all of those things *will* happen," she says. "But the most important thing is that you tried. You can't keep writing lyrics in your notebook forever, where nobody can hear them."

I think of that claustrophobic feeling I had in the school's practice room. The one where I felt too big for that tiny closet of a space, hoping to break free. "Okay."

"But, seriously, you need to win. Because I just put all of my babysitter money on UNNAMED JAMES K. POLK FIRST-YEAR BAND."

I throw the plastic guitar at her head.

FARSI SCHOOL

AT 11:00 A.M., Mom grabs me from my grandparents' and shuttles me off to Farsi school in DC. Farsi's harder for me than Spanish, since the alphabet is different. But at least Farsi's a smoother language for my throat, the words all connecting so I never lose momentum. English is all hard consonants starting and stopping, the engine of my voice stalling all the time. Farsi is a gentle cruise.

I turn to a section of "All the Hemispheres," a poem by Hafez that we're translating in class.

All the hemispheres in existence
Lie beside an equator
In your heart.

Aghaye Khosroshahi continues reading out loud while I want to weep with admiration. I will never write lyrics that good. What are songs if not poetry in motion?

These classes give me a bar to reach. Another way of looking at songwriting, even if it is sadistic to compare my own writing to these legends. My lyrics are always specific, but Hafez's poetry somehow switches between huge ideas and small ones.

It's a reminder that I should leave my words open to interpretation, that I don't need to make the subject of every song crystal clear. I'm always so worried about not being understood that I try hard to make all my lyrics narrow and clear. Must be nice to trust that people will just "get" you.

I shift in my chair in the last row of the classroom. There's an odd number of students, so I don't have a partner, but I don't mind. I wish Roya came to Farsi school, though. Then we could do translations together and carpool. But she gets enough Farsi at home, and her parents are way too cheap.

There are a few people from Polk in my class, including a girl named Parvin and her boyfriend, Amir. They always sit next to each other and share their textbooks while making heart eyes at each other. I can practically smell the oxytocin from here. Nobody seems to care that I don't talk much, and Aghaye Khosroshahi knows not to call on me.

As soon as class ends, I shuffle out to the parking lot while everyone else heads to the café. By "café" I mean a little broom closet where you can buy Iranian treats, like black tea, saffron-infused rock candy, gaz (a kind of nougat), and soup. Mom waves from her car.

"Hey, Z, how was it?" she asks.

I shrug. "Fine. We learned some new poetry."

"Good, good," Mom says, distracted, looking around the busy parking lot while other kids meet up with their parents.

My eyes follow hers and land on a dad who's helping his daughter get into her car seat. The girl must be in one of the younger Iranian classes, where all the kids do is learn numbers and sing songs.

"Who's that?" I ask casually, trying not to spook Mom. It's clear she's interested in this guy.

"Hmm? Oh, no one. Just another parent."

I take another look at the man's tan skin, big nose, and distinctly Iranian features. He waves goodbye to us, and her face flushes as she gives a small wave back.

She never used to stay the whole lesson in the parking lot. Usually, she drops me off and runs errands or something. But lately she's been staying the whole time with the other Iranian parents outside. Now I know why.

"I'm telling Kian you're cheating on him." I smirk, holding my phone with House of Kabob on speed dial.

"What's that? You want tempeh for dinner? Excellent choice, Azar."

Damn it.

MORNING COMMUTE

MOM HAS TO go to the office early today, which means I have to walk to school in the icy cold. I burrow my hands deep into the pockets of my puffy jacket and wish my baseball hat had those weird little earflaps. The tip of my nose feels like it's going to turn into an icicle and crack off.

"Azar!" a familiar voice calls out.

There's Nadim Hadad, towing that massive instrument case again. I give a frozen nod and wait for him to catch up. He's wearing a parka, snow pants, earmuff hat, and ski gloves. He looks ready for a bomb cyclone.

"Oh my god, it's so cold!"

"Yeah," I agree, unsure of what else there is to say. Maybe if we were somewhere warmer, I'd feel more talkative. Just kidding. I am never talkative.

Nadim's teeth chatter, and I press on, leaning into

the harsh wind working its way into the exposed strip of wrist between my sleeves and gloves. Puffs of air steam out of Nadim as he tries to walk quickly with his instrument case, his tall frame hunched over. I doubt Lebanon ever gets this cold.

I unwrap my scarf a tiny bit so my mouth can peek out from my jacket collar. "What instrument is that?"

"Bass," he says. "I played it back in Beirut."

There's no way that could be a bass. It's almost as tall as he is, and twice as wide. I've never gotten my hands on one, but I know they're only a little bigger than a guitar.

"*That's* a *bass*? It's huge." Up ahead I can already see the school, and I walk even more quickly.

He laughs, his breath coming out in quick puffs. "No, it's like this." He tilts the instrument case so it's upright, then does a plucking motion with his hands.

"Oh," I reply. "An acoustic bass."

"Yes, exactly!"

How different can an acoustic bass be from an electric one, though? I've switched between my acoustic guitar and electric guitar and it's been pretty easy. Maybe Nadim is the answer to my band recruitment problems.

"How would you like to learn electric bass for my band? We're going to perform at the NOVA Battle of the Bands after spring break."

Nadim's face cracks into a smile. "Really? An American rock band?"

"Yeah?" I reply. "I mean, I guess it's kind of like rock and roll." The frigid air enters my throat like a dozen shards of glass. We hurry through the school's front doors, and I gasp in the warmth.

"Cool beans. When do we start?" Nadim asks, propping the huge bass against a wall so he can remove his scarf. I don't have the heart to tell him that nobody says "cool beans" anymore.

I falter. When *do* we start? We still need a drummer before our first rehearsal, and I've never talked to the other drummers at this school. There are a bunch of percussion students in band, but do they know how to play on a full drum kit? I'll be playing lead guitar, obviously.

"Do you happen to know anyone who plays the drums?"

Nadim starts unwrapping his layers like a mummy. "No, but I can ask my friend if he knows anyone. He might have some ideas."

"Who is this friend?" I ask sharply. I'm not sure I'm ready to start advertising to the world that I'm forming a band.

"Fabián Castor. He knows everything. Even how to dabke."

I give Nadim a blank look.

"It's a dance. It's an Arab thing."

"Fine. Ask him."

We walk through the first-year hallway together, and for a second I savor the feeling of entering the school with someone, like all those classmates coming back from winter break that first day.

It's a nice change from walking in alone.

THE FOURTH BAND MEMBER

WHEN THE END-OF-SCHOOL bell finally rings, I hustle to the front entrance, where I'm pretty sure the exchange students hang. I found an electric bass I can rent from the band room during lunch, and if Nadim's serious, he needs to start playing it ASAP.

I spy him sitting by the buses with his friends, but before I can take another step, my path is blocked by someone with enough product in their hair to be water-repellant.

"Azar Rossi." Fabián Castor holds out a hand.

I shake it slowly. "Hi?"

He pivots around to walk with me. "I hear you're putting a band together."

"I take it Nadim talked to you?"

"He did." Fabián smiles in a scary, all-seeing way.

Suddenly, I feel like a fly caught in Fabián's very well-connected web. "I have a new band member for you."

"You found a drummer!" Relief floods through me. I may just pull this thing off.

Fabián keeps stride with me. "He's a sophomore who's really talented, and he's been looking for a way to express his musical side." Nadim catches my eye and waves from across the parking lot.

Wow, is this really that easy? What's in it for Fabián? Then again, I'm not about to look a gift horse in the veneers. "Great," I tell him. "Have him come to the band room at five p.m. this Friday to try out. And tell him to bring his own sticks."

Fabián blinks. "Five p.m.? On a Friday? You're really cramping my boyfriend's style here."

Aha! I must have a weird look on my face because Fabián raises his eyebrows defensively.

"What? He needs an edge. And being in a band means his portfolio to music school won't be a bunch of whiny lovesick ballads. Sidenote: You use the practice rooms during lunch, right?"

I frown. Ballads? What kind of drummer spends all their time writing soulful ballads? And how did he know I'm in the band room at lunchtime? Before I can say anything, Fabián's already typing something into his phone.

"Fine, five p.m. on Friday it is. He'll be there." In lieu of saying goodbye, he just pirouettes dramatically away.

Nadim walks up just then.

"Wow . . . you talked to him!" he says.

"I think he just found us a drummer," I say, still surprised.

"He's so cool," Nadim sighs as Fabián walks away. "And so American."

My phone buzzes. I've been tagged in someone's Insta story.

"Can't wait to see my boyfriend play in Polk High's HOTTEST new band! Stay tuned for their debut show at the NOVA Battle of the Bands! ¡Chau, familia!" Fabián blows a kiss to the camera, and I shove the phone back in my pocket.

I said I'd *try out* his boyfriend. I never agreed to make him our permanent drummer! This whole thing was supposed to be a quiet, secret side project that would hopefully pay off in a big way. Thanks to Fabián's equivalent of skywriting my hopes and dreams above our high school, everyone will know.

And how did he have time to make a video for Instagram so quickly?

Nadim stares wistfully at Fabián's retreating back. "So American."

IN SEARCH OF MUSE

AFTER COMBING THROUGH all my songwriting journals for material for the band, I have concluded that absolutely nothing I've written is good enough.

> **AZAR ROSSI** *4:13 P.M.*: hey Eben,
> first rehearsal is tomorrow at 5 p.m.
> in the band room
> **COOLEST PERSON EVER!!!** *4:13 P.M.*:
> Awesome can't wait! [strong muscle emoji]
> **AZAR ROSSI** *4:14 P.M.*: don't forget
> to warm up your voice. Or whatever.

Eben responds with a happy puppy emoji, because of course he does. I tap my notebook impatiently. The pressure of a full band waiting for me is not helping my creative process. According to my Battle of the Bands email, each band will have the chance to perform two songs. That means you only get about ten minutes to impress the judges and show them you're worthy of winning.

Ten minutes for them to decide if your dreams are worth turning into a reality.

I pick up my pen, the inkling of a fast song coming on.

Everyone's shouting, texting, messaging,
So much that I can barely think.
Whatever happened to the silence?
I miss the still and the quiet.

What is there left to say
That hasn't been said today?
White noise can be deafening.
Just let me go so I can think.

Sometimes the quiet is worth hearing,
The loudest ones can be misleading.
The noise drowns me and I can't see,
So please help me find the feeling, and—

(Chorus)
Shut up, nobody actually cares.
Shut up, with the picture of your hair.
Shut up, you're out of data anyway.
Nothing left to say.

I quickly close my notebook before more lyrics can spill onto the page. That one hits way too close to home, and I don't like the feeling of my most bitter thoughts laid bare.

I need something epic. Something amazing. Something that will show that my lyrics are worth listening to.

I open up a fresh page, ready to start over.

THE HEART IS A LONELY HUNTER

SOMETHING WEIRD HAPPENED this Friday morning at school. I walked in with Nadim, the two of us desperately trying to thaw out in the first-year hallway, when Sydney said hi to me. And not just because we were heading to speech pathology in ten minutes. She said hi like we were normal friends and then turned back to her locker.

Then *Fabián* said hi to me, too. He was talking to the Iranian couple in my Farsi class, and he just casually said, "Hey, Azar," and turned back around. Amir even gave me a head nod. I probably gave some kind of weird grimace and kept walking.

And then, right before I ducked into speech therapy, Eben Lloyd Hollins gave me a fist bump. A *fist bump*.

"Nice!" he said, lightly pounding my back as he headed to his own class. I can still feel where Eben touched me, and it feels like the combination of an itch and a heating pad.

Last semester, I would go weeks without making eye contact with anyone. But today I've said hi to multiple people, like I'm a normal high schooler with friends and not a fourteen-year-old with the esophagus of a screamo band's lead singer.

Hours later in English class, I'm still stunned. I honestly don't think I've recovered.

"Okay, everyone!" Mr. Nuñez says, snapping me out of my shock. "I hope you've met with your book report partner, because presentations will be right after spring break. Even though it's only January, that's still not much time. I'm expecting a presentation that will really wow the entire class, all right?"

I open my planner, and my stunned feeling turns to dread. That means our presentation will be the week after my surgery, and days before our performance. I may not be able to present if Dr. Talbot thinks my throat still hasn't healed.

Mr. Nuñez passes out the rubric he'll be using for our presentation, which is a full 20 percent of our grade. We spend the rest of class going over what he's expecting us to present, and I feel worse and worse with every new requirement. When the bell rings, I wait until everyone's gone before I approach his desk.

"Mr. Nuñez?"

He looks up from his computer, where I can see he's inputting attendance. "Yes, Azar?"

"I'm supposed to have surgery over spring break. Throat surgery. So I might not be able to speak out loud for the presentation. I can give you a doctor's note."

Mr. Nuñez frowns. But instead of getting upset, he looks concerned. "I didn't realize your condition was so severe, Azar. Does it hurt to talk to me now?"

I shrug. "A little."

He tilts his head, thinking. "Have you talked to your presentation partner about it?"

I remember that afternoon in the library, when Eben said he already knew about my throat. "Sort of?" I reply.

Mr. Nuñez clasps his hands together. "Okay, how about this: You're going to help Eben with the presentation, and then you'll email me all the chapters you worked on yourself, all right? I'm sure Eben won't mind presenting on his own, but I still need to make sure that you did the work."

"Thanks, Mr. Nuñez."

When I leave the classroom, Eben's waiting for me. This day just keeps getting weirder and weirder.

"Hey," he says. "I overhead what you said to Mr. Nuñez."

My face flushes. "Yeah, you'll need to present our report, since the procedure is over spring break."

Just the thought of surgery makes me light-headed. Is it going to hurt? Will my throat feel sorer than it feels now? All the worries I've been pushing to the back of my mind surge forward, eclipsed by my greatest fear of all: What if the surgery doesn't work? What if it'll hurt to talk forever? Dr. Talbot said this is a last resort, but what if even this last resort doesn't hold? I think back to that claustrophobic feeling in the examination room, and it makes me queasy all over again.

"Spring break?" Eben asks. "Isn't that right before the concert?"

We get to my locker, and I finally look up into his eyes. The blur of his silhouette solidifies, and I stare into Eben's smile-free face—a rare sight. "Yep."

He says nothing, leaning against the wall next to me like that's totally normal and we're the best pals in the world.

"Man, I'm sorry. I didn't know you'd need an operation for it."

I slam my locker shut, making us both jump. This pity party is getting old. "That's why I've got you, remember?"

His face lights up, the dimples popping back out. "Yeah! We're gonna kill it!" He pumps his fist in the air like I just gave the team a rousing halftime speech, or whatever they do in lacrosse.

His excitement rubs off on me. "It's gonna be great," I confirm.

"You're heading to assembly, right?" he asks, motioning to the auditorium. Is he asking because he wants to sit next to me? Won't sitting next to me be social suicide?

I nod. He steers us toward the auditorium, and I hold my breath, waiting for him to peel away.

WINTER ASSEMBLY

OUR ASSEMBLIES ARE a joke. Principal Saulk always rambles on, peering into the audience for any laughs or smiles, and then he stumbles when he realizes that *nobody cares*. I still can't believe this clown managed to strong-arm me into a thousand-dollar repayment plan.

"The spring band concert will be held end of April, but hopefully those April showers will hold back, eh?" he says, his brown tie flapping pathetically against his mustard-yellow shirt.

Nadim turns to me. "Is this color popular?" he asks. "He looks like a . . . a tied-up blob of dough. With salt."

"A pretzel?" I ask. I'm glad Nadim waved us down inside the auditorium, or I would have been sitting alone with Eben, someone who I can now tell is smiling without having to look at him. Even though our arms are inches away on the shared armrest, it's like I can still feel his body heat through the space. He leans forward in his chair, and suddenly I want to lean forward, too.

Eben laughs under his breath at Nadim's comment. Never did I imagine myself sitting between Nadim Hadad and Ebenezer Lloyd Hollins the Fifth at assembly. Sydney turns around from a couple rows in front of us and throws me a huge wink. Ugh.

Still, it beats having to sit alone in the cluster of empty seats in the back wings, like I normally do. Principal Saulk's embarrassing lectures are easier to deal with when you realize it's not just you who feels awkward—it's the entire first-year class.

"Polk is thrilled to host Model UN this weekend in the gymnasium, so feel free to stop by and see our team's captain, Colton Tran, make us proud! U-S-A! U-S-A!" Principal Saulk starts to chant, motioning for students to join him.

Nobody does. Somewhere up front, I hear Colton Tran thunk his head against the back of a seat.

A teacher scurries over to Principal Saulk and whispers in his ear.

"I've just been informed that our Model UN team is, in fact, Equatorial Guinea. So . . . go, Guinea! Go, Guinea!"

Crickets.

By the time Principal Saulk wraps up assembly, I feel like I've just seen a terrible film at a movie theater with Eben and Nadim and we don't know what to say. We shuffle out behind the rest of our class.

"Are you supposed to feel bad for teachers here?"

Nadim asks. "In Libnan, they're very respected."

Eben guffaws. I watch as a couple lacrosse players give him nods as we head into the hallway.

"You're *always* supposed to feel bad for teachers in America," I state.

"I'm Eben, by the way," he says to Nadim, extending his hand.

"Sorry," I blurt out. "I forgot to introduce you two. Eben, Nadim's our bassist."

Nadim grasps Eben's hand and grins. "Nice to meet you, Mr. Lead Singer."

"Haha, yeah, for sure," Eben replies tightly. I file that reaction away for later. He gives my back one of those bro taps before going in the opposite direction, and my body seems to spontaneously combust.

"See you tonight!" Nadim calls after him.

"He's perfect for singing," Nadim adds when Eben's out of earshot. "He looks like a famous Chris."

"A famous Chris?"

"You know, like how all the famous people in this country are named Chris. Chris Evans. Chris Pine. Chris-t."

"You mean . . . Christ?"

Nadim smiles. "Exactly."

FIRST REHEARSAL

FRIDAY AFTERNOON. OUR first rehearsal. Writing "UNNAMED POLK HIGH BAND" on the band room request form feels very official.

Nadim helps me clear space near the instrument lockers and I put together a makeshift kit for Fabián's drummer boyfriend. I drag over the snare and toms along with some cymbals from the percussion pit, placing a bass drum in the middle of it all. Rarely do I get to play on a real setup like this.

I reverently open my guitar case and gaze at my baby. This thing has helped me through so many highs and lows, through bad lyrics and good ones. Even though I can't be the "front man," I can still play lead guitar, and that counts for something.

Eben strolls in, his hair wet from practice. He looks like an Under Armour commercial, sporting mesh track pants, a hoodie, and a huge lacrosse bag slung over his shoulder. The surroundings of the sad, carpeted band room look at odds with the shining boy wonder who just walked in.

"Hey, Azar. Nadim." His hands, I notice, are shaking a little bit. There's no denying it: Eben's nervous. So why did he agree to be in the band if it sets him on edge? For some reason, I am still glowing from the way he pronounced my name.

"Hey, Eben."

Just then, Fabián and his boyfriend enter the room, carrying something that takes all the wind out of me. He's carrying *a guitar*.

"Hi, guys." I try not to sound confused, but I can't help it. My voice warbles upward on *guys* and ends in a weird crack. Thirteen-year-old boys and their surging testosterone have nothing on me.

"Hey, y'all, this is Matty," Fabián says, appraising the room. Compared to Fabián's aggressively coiffed hair, Matty's looks much softer, his hair shaggy and brown, as he sports a white T-shirt with holes in it. On his arms are worn leather bracelets, and his fingertips end in chipped blue nail polish.

"Hi, everyone," he says.

"Is this it?" Fabián asks, unimpressed.

I wonder what he sees. A tall skinny kid holding a bass wrong, a jock looking uncomfortable beside a microphone, and a half mute with a guitar. Fabián seems less than thrilled. Matty gives a small wave, his hands suspiciously delicate for a drummer.

"Yep. Just waiting on the drummer . . ." I trail off, still confused about why they brought a guitar.

Matty's pale skin flushes, and his eyes shift uneasily to Fabián. "Babe, you said they needed a *guitarist,* not a drummer."

"You told him what?" I round on Fabián.

Fabián holds up a copper-skinned hand as if to say, *Slow your roll!* He's wearing a cream-colored sweater and big boots that make him look like a hip sailor. I can see Nadim eyeing the outfit, like he's taking notes in his head.

"Azar, I know just about everything that happens at this school, and I can assure you that the best drummer at Polk is already in this room."

I share a look with Nadim, who shrugs. Is he secretly a drummer? I turn to Eben, but he seems unfazed, and, worst of all, he's tapping his foot to a song that he's listening to with one of his AirPods.

"What are you even talking about?" I ask.

Fabián sighs dramatically. "*You,* Azar. I hear you play the drums in those practice rooms all the time. My friend Parvin says she can hear you through the walls when she's practicing her bassoon."

Parvin, the girl in my Farsi class. So much for Persian solidarity, that turncoat. "Yeah, but that isn't, like, *real* drumming. It's just . . . playing around."

Fabián's eyes narrow. "Listen, I propose you play drums and Matty plays guitar. That way Matty can also be backing vocals for Eben, see? And everyone knows having a girl drummer is awesome."

My head spins. I thought the worst part about rehearsal today was going to be sharing my songs with everyone, but Fabián just upended everything. What little control I was going to have slips out of my grasp, and I'm left scrambling for a new hold.

"Why do you want Matty to be the guitarist?" Nadim pipes up, equally confused. *Thank you, Nadim. Excellent question.*

"Because . . . because . . ." Fabián says, struggling to find the right words. It's weird seeing him flail. He always seems so sure of himself that watching him fumble to respond is strange.

"Fabián's trying to make my music viral," Matty says, and rolls his eyes. "Listen, Azar, if you want to play guitar, you should play guitar. We didn't mean to blow up your band." He starts gathering his things, throwing furious looks Fabián's way.

I take a shaky breath as he packs up. The truth is, I don't personally know any drummers at Polk, and I doubt I'll be able to find one and have time to rehearse with them before the Battle of the Bands. After all, it's practically February. We don't have much time.

Could I play drums? I've only played on a full kit a handful of times. But at least I've got my silicone practice pads at home. Before I know what I'm doing, I raise a hand.

"Wait," I say. Matty and Fabián stop, their bodies almost out the door. "Let's do it."

"Really?" Matty asks. "You'll play the drums? You

don't have to, you know." He shoots another look at Fabián, who shrugs innocently.

"I don't know any other drummers who'd be up for it, and Fabián's right—I think I could do it. You could be the guitarist if you're still interested."

Matty grins. "Yeah, for sure."

I smile weakly in return. Drums got me into this mess. I guess they'll have to dig me out of it, too.

FIRST REHEARSAL, CONTINUED

MATTY SITS BACK down in the circle of chairs I've assembled and waves goodbye to his boyfriend.

"Wait, can't I stay and watch?" Fabián asks.

I shoot Fabián the surliest look I've got in my arsenal.

"Yikes. ¡Okay, chau, mi amor!" he says, and then leaves.

"So," I begin shakily. Everyone's eyes are on me, waiting for what I'm going to say next, and it's not a feeling I'm used to. I wish I'd chugged a soda before all this talking. "NOVA Battle of the Bands is April fourteenth, which means we've got a little less than three months to learn two songs."

Eben raises his hand, like we're in an actual classroom and I'm the teacher. I nod in his general direction.

"Do we have a band name already? I was thinking

we could be called the Misfits." He grins from ear to ear, psyched at the thought.

"Er, I think that name's already taken," I say. Eben's smile goes out like a broken bulb, the first time I've seen him look bummed. "Anyway, we've got a bassist, a lead singer, a guitarist, and a drummer . . . sort of." I gesture to each band member in turn.

Eben raises his hand again. I sigh.

"Can I play keyboard?" he says. "People play the keyboard in bands, right?"

I almost yelp in astonishment. "You play keys?"

"Yeah, I play piano at church. I'm pretty good."

"Okay," I say, happy to have a surprise go in my favor today. "That's great to hear. We could definitely use a keyboardist."

Eben beams. I try not to beam back, like a fridge whose door light I have to slam closed.

"I've been working on a couple arrangements for our two songs." I rummage through my backpack and pull out my sheet music. It took me all night to get the sounds right for each instrument. As I pass them out, I finally feel like this first rehearsal is going my way.

Nadim looks impressed. "You wrote all of the parts? By yourself?"

I shrug. Shrugging, Ms. Davolio says, is not communicating. Tell that to my shoulders.

The band takes a minute to read through their parts, and I'm relieved that everyone can read sheet music.

It would have sucked trying to hum everything out loud so they'd get it.

Matty frowns, looking at the pages. "I don't see any guitar solos."

Nadim also looks confused. "Do American bands usually have sheet music of their songs? I thought they all kinda . . . you know . . . jam-sessioned."

Only Eben seems interested in the paper with his lyrics on it. Now Matty raises his hand.

"Can we stop raising hands, please?" I whine.

"When Fabián said you were putting together a band, I thought we were *all* going to have input, you know? I thought bands wrote songs together. It's more freeing to collaborate."

"Yes!" Nadim cries. "The jam session!"

"I thought this was the deal," I growl. "I put together the band, so we get to sing the songs I've been working on. Right?" I make eye contact with Eben, and he gives me a reluctant nod.

Matty shakes his head. "That's not how bands work, though. In jazz band, every instrument gets a chance to shine, and we all have a say over how we perform each song. It's a team sport."

I don't know what to say. I've had such a fierce grip on my vision for this band that I'm not sure how to respond.

Instead, I take a seat and cross my arms. Yeah, I'm sulking, but guess what? I'm allowed to sulk. Even if my lyrics aren't great, I had a really hard time figuring out the arrangements. At least I came prepared. After all this work, I feel the band slip away from me.

"Azar?" Nadim asks quietly. "What do you think?"

I look away. *Don't cry. Don't cry!* "What do I think? I think this was clearly a stupid idea. All I wanted was to get my songs out there. Do you think I can do this alone? Do you think people who sound like me can just go onstage with an unaccompanied guitar and sound all cute and nab a record deal? No. No, they can't."

The band room's silent, and my throat aches from the tightness I'm holding there. Even Eben looks awkward, if that's possible.

Finally, Nadim pipes up. "Maybe . . . maybe we can try the songs first. They may have guitar solos we can add."

"Sorry, Azar. We should give them a chance," Matty says. The kindness in his voice makes me feel like I'm a pity project. "Maybe we should do everyone's star charts now, just to get it out of the way," he adds. "It will help build camaraderie."

"What's a star chart?" Nadim asks.

Matty and my mom would get along really well.

"Um, maybe later." I blink back my tears, praying no one noticed them. Matty just sighs and writes something in his notebook that looks suspiciously like *Scorpio.*

I thought the hardest part of being in a band would be playing the music. I didn't anticipate all this other emotional stuff.

I take a seat on the drum stool, moving the cymbals and hi-hat to my sticks' reach. Matty arranges the sheet music on his stand, and Nadim tries to work his left hand around the neck of the bass. Eben rolls his shoulders like he's a quarterback walking onto the field.

"You guys ready for a run-through?" I call out. *Please work. Please let it sound amazing.*

There are various nods and shrugs, so I grab the drumsticks and tap out the beat. "One, two—one, two, three, four!" I shout, praying Ms. Davolio isn't anywhere near the band room and my loud voice. I'll be paying for that yell come morning.

I hit a simple 4/4 on the bass, snare, and hi-hat while Nadim squints at his sheet music, alternating his gaze between his hand placement and his simple downbeats. So far, so good. Then the guitar comes in.

Matty flubs the first line, but it's okay, we've still got it. Instead of staying calm, though, I rush the beat, speeding up the song the tiniest bit.

Eben's voice comes in right after, and that's when the wheels come off. Nadim loses track of where he is, and Matty misses a chord. I'm rushing the tempo so much that Eben's completely off by the time his voice enters. But we keep going. *We have to.*

My cymbals crash in the wrong place. Nadim's bass drops out altogether, and Matty rushes to catch up. Eben's voice gets shakier, and by the time he gets to the chorus, he's a whole measure behind.

Instead of finishing out the song at once, we all trail off on our own, ending with a whimper and not a bang. And that's when I know there's no way my song will make it through the weird democracy our band has become, much less win us a record deal.

"Well," Eben begins, probably trying to put some positive spin on this.

I hold my hand up for silence.

"That," I croak, "was a disaster."

DRUM LESSONS

AFTER WE ~~PLAYED~~ destroyed my song, we all agreed to practice the arrangement and let everyone come up with their own ideas for the second song, which I guess is a fair compromise.

The embarrassment, though . . . the embarrassment will stay with me forever.

"Azar, are you going to mope around here all weekend?" Mom calls from the kitchen.

Saturdays are when Mom makes batches of all the food we go through during the week, like hummus, yogurt, jam, pickles, and tofu. She's kind of a fanatic about making sure everything is the healthiest version of itself. Sometimes I wonder if she'd be this way about food if my throat was okay.

I peek into a pot of sour cherry jam. We buy the sour

cherries in bulk every year at one of those "pick your own" cherry farms in Maryland. The magenta magma bubbles slowly in the pot, and Mom dips in a candy thermometer to check the temperature.

"Wanna tell me what's wrong?" she asks.

I heave the biggest sigh in the world. "You know that Battle of the Bands thing happening in April? Well, I found a band and a lead singer, but yesterday we had our first rehearsal and it was awful."

Mom spins around. "Wait, you got a band together? You're really entering?"

Oops. Guess I forgot to tell her that part. Maybe it's for the best that I don't mention Principal Saulk's ultimatum. Instead, I just nod.

She gives me a big hug. "Oh, querida. I'm so proud of you! I know how much you've been dying to get your songs out there. That's so exciting!"

"But we suck," I point out.

"So?" Mom replies. "Bands always suck at the beginning. Everyone knows that. You just gotta put in the work, get everything as tight as you can. Here."

She holds up a spoon of jam and blows on it so I don't burn my tongue. I take a tiny lick, and it's the perfect combination of sweet and sour that Mom says all Iranians are obsessed with.

"Yum." I feel the jam coat my throat, waking it up.

"What instrument are you playing?" she asks, turning back to the stove.

I hop up onto the counter. "Drums. But I'm terrible."

"What about those music lessons I got you for Christmas? You could use those. They don't specify an instrument."

"That's right!" I cry. Well, I don't really cry. More like I let the end of my sentence go up with "ascension," like Ms. Davolio taught me, instead of the "descension" that makes my voice sound flat. "Do you think they have drum teachers?"

I could really use help finding my way around a drum kit. It's one thing to know how to play a snare and hit a cymbal, but it's a completely different thing to know how to hit them all at once.

"They've definitely got drum teachers—I remember seeing it on the website. What are you waiting for? Go call the number on the gift card." Mom squeezes my shoulder before turning back to the bubbling jam, and I jump off the counter and unearth the gift card from my desk. Here goes nothing.

🎧

After Farsi school the next day, Mom drops me off at Fox Instruments, an instrument store that also offers private lessons in the back.

"You're gonna be great. Just listen to what the teacher says."

I nervously pop in a fresh stick of gum. At the front are boxes of sheet music and beginner's booklets, and cupboards run all along the sides of the store. On top of those are antique instruments I've never seen before, some looking like ancient brass marching-band pieces along with wooden ones coated in dust. I head to the cash registers in the middle to check in.

"How can I help you?" the man behind the register asks. He looks like a music person, with his long white hair in a ponytail and tiny glasses perched on the end of his nose. Is he my drum teacher?

"I'm checking in for my lesson. Azar Rossi?"

He scans the old, boxy computer in front of him. "Ah, here you are. Come on, I'll take you to your teacher."

"Y-you're not my teacher?" Am I going to get some weird-smelling hippie who went to Woodstock and does drumming lessons to relive the good old days? Or one of those scary ex-military people who played in an army band?

"Nope. I'm a flautist." He leads me to the private rooms in the back, knocks, and swings open the door.

And there, in the middle of the practice room, is the last kind of person I thought would be my drum instructor.

THE COOLEST GIRL
I'VE EVER MET

THE NICE CASHIER gestures for me to step into the room, then closes the door behind me, leaving me face-to-face with a girl in ripped jeans, a leather jacket, black lipstick, and an intimidatingly shaved head.

"Hey," she says in a voice that's even flatter than mine. "I'm Victoria. You must be Azar? Am I saying that right?"

I nod, glad she got it right. I thought my teacher would be some old person. Not a walking incarnation of everything I hope to be when I grow up. Victoria looks like a *badass*.

"First things first: Why do you want to learn the drums?"

I stand awkwardly behind the snare drum she's set up in the middle of the room, as if it can shield me from her imposing vibes. "Umm . . . because I'm starting a band for the Battle of the Bands contest in April . . . and I could really use some help."

Victoria looks surprised. "Oh. Most people say because they want to look cool, or because they saw a Travis Barker video. That's . . . actually a good reason."

She turns to the Bluetooth speaker in the corner of the room. "Before we begin, we're going to play a little game called Real or Fake. You ready?"

Before I can stammer out an answer, Victoria presses "play" on a song I've heard before. It's a Top 40 pop hit that was huge last summer. I listen as the music washes over me, wondering what she wants me to listen for.

"A lot of artists think they can just use machines to replace drummers, but that's absolutely not true. We're going to hear the difference," she shouts over the music. "Tell me if the drums in this song are from a real drummer or if they're a fake drum sound from someone's laptop. This is your first lesson!"

I listen hard to the drumbeat in the back of the song. It sounds clean and even, the drummer hitting the note perfectly each time.

"Real drummer?" I guess.

Victoria slams her drumsticks on the snare. "WRONG!"

Is Mom still in the parking lot? Is it too late to run out?

"Next song!" she barks.

This one's acoustic, with a gentle lead singer and a smoky guitar. I close my eyes and strain to hear the beat.

This drum sound has more echoes. It isn't as clean as the last song, but each hit feels juicy and raw.

I open my eyes. "Real drummer," I say definitively. It has to be.

Victoria grins. "You're getting the hang of the game."

She switches to a rap song, and the drums sound so even and the hits so flat that I blurt out "Fake!" before they even get to the chorus.

Victoria turns the music off and gets in my face. "See? See what a difference a real drummer can make?"

"I–"

"Drummers are the most important part of any band!" Victoria hits the snare again. I try not to jump a mile. "*We* set the tempo," she declares. "*We* are the beat that holds the band together. Without a drummer, bands often rush or drag. We provide the texture that separates a stupid open-mic night from a Grammy winner. Drummers are the unsung heroes of the music world!" She accentuates every sentence with a snap of the snare.

Suddenly, I can see myself performing at the Battle of the Bands again, only this time I'm not leaning into a hot mic. In this fantasy, I'm at the back of the stage, twirling my drumsticks like a pro. I slam cymbals, roll across toms, and pump my bass pedal as the crowd claps in time to my drum solo.

Yeah. That would be cool.

She hands me her sticks. "Show me what you got."

I reverently take them from her. I'd underestimated

drummers before today, but now I know these sticks hold a lot of power. I wish I'd worn a cooler outfit besides jeans, my Nats hat, and a long-sleeved tee. Being a drummer isn't just playing an instrument. It seems to be a complete identity.

I start with a single roll, but I've rolled for barely five seconds when Victoria barks, "Stop!"

Do I already suck?

"You're rolling with your wrists. *Never* roll with your wrists!"

"Uhh?"

"Out of all the bones in my arm, why would I do a roll on one of the weakest links in my body? If you roll with your whole arm, it protects your wrists and will give you more power in the long run. If you ever see a drummer use their wrists, you know they've only got a couple years of playing left. *We're* in it for the long haul. Here—"

She takes the sticks from me and starts up a single roll. It's so smooth and tight, her torso barely moves as her sticks flash past me. I watch as she keeps her wrists locked, bending from the elbow instead.

"Got it?"

"Got it," I croak.

Victoria frowns. "Do you have a sore throat? If you get me sick, I'll be pissed."

Did Mom not tell them about my throat before she bought the gift card? But then again, why would she?

I set this appointment up myself. I scramble to find the right words that will explain why my throat sounds busted without making her pity me.

"That's just how I sound. My throat's damaged."

"Oh," Victoria says, breathing a sigh of relief. "I thought you had something contagious. Okay, now you try."

Victoria being more concerned about her own well-being is weirdly comforting. It's kind of nice to meet someone who can't be bothered.

I try out the roll. It's harder without relying on my wrists, but I can see what she means about power. I can do this for way longer, and I'm not as tired.

"See?" Victoria says. "Practice with your whole arm for our lesson next Sunday. Don't forget to tuck your armpits in close, like they're glued to your sides, so you activate your lats. I want to see doubles and para-diddles, too."

I nod, making a mental note.

"And, Azar?"

"Yeah?"

"Lats are a muscle."

CHOICE BOARDS

MONDAY MORNING + speech therapy = the absolute worst. I stayed up way too late playing drums on my practice pad, and I know the second I speak, Ms. Davolio's going to snitch to Dr. Talbot, who will probably call my mom and have a conversation about bedtimes to make sure my throat is in good shape for surgery. After all, he's the one who wrote my referral to work with Ms. Davolio in the first place. Every speech pathologist has a scope shoved up their nose to know what it feels like, which is how they met. It's a small consolation.

"Choice boards!" Ms. Davolio sings, as if those two words are supposed to make me as ecstatically happy as she seems to be.

Sydney looks at me, like, *Dear god, what now.*

"Choice boards have premade options that you can point to when you can't speak. It's up to the user to create what they want each board to say, but basic words and phrases like *yes, no,* and *Can I go to the bathroom?* are all easy to point to when you can't talk. Which is what's going to happen to you, Azar, after your surgery. You may even use it before then on your vocal rest days."

She holds up a simple choice board with a square for each of the phrases she just mentioned. There's also a section along the side that says *I want to . . .* next to squares that say *play, eat, sleep,* and *sulk.* My eyes narrow at the last one.

"I have some for nonverbal students over at the elementary school, and it works pretty well for them." Great. I'm using stuff that six-year-olds need. What's next? Emotion charts, where I point to how I'm feeling?

"For today's assignment, you're each going to work on your own choice board. Think of all the phrases you use most often and write those down. I've got markers and the laminator machine when you're ready to finalize it."

Sydney balks. "Wait, I have to make one, too?"

Ms. Davolio drops a stack of paper onto Sydney's desk. "Yes, Sydney—you, too."

Sydney sighs, and I feel bad for making her sit through yet another Azar-specific assignment. One of the sample choice boards has a drawing of a girl with the words *I need to* above her. Next to her are a bunch of icons with words like *drink water, do homework,* and *be alone.*

Ms. Davolio leaves the example on my desk. I grab my notebook and tap my pen like it's a drumstick. What are the phrases I use most often?

- *Yeah*
- *No*
- *Um*
- *Can we get takeout?*
- *One, two, three, four!*
- *Which George Clooney movie are we watching tonight?*
- *Shut up, Roya.*
- *Why?*

Ms. Davolio reads over my shoulder and sighs. "Come on, Azar. Let's take this seriously, okay? How about a basic one explaining that you're on vocal rest? Or a simple *Can I go to the bathroom?* for your other classes?"

I put *I want* on my choice board.

"There we go," Ms. Davolio says.

Then I add the words *to die*.

"Azar!" Ms. Davolio pinches the bridge of her nose. "You know what? Never mind. Let's laminate whatever you've got at the end of class. Then you'll be stuck with it forever."

I cross out *to die* and replace it with *to sleep in*.

At least that's one I'll use.

A FORMAL INVITATION

I SEE NADIM, Matty, and Eben at school the next day, and saying hi to them outside of the band room feels strange. I pray this Friday's rehearsal goes better. Everyone's working on learning my song and writing one of their own to share with the band. We'll vote on which other bandmates' song we want to play for the battle.

At least *one* of the songs will be mine.

By the time school ends, I'm so ready to go home and use the choice board for *I want + to sleep forever.* Today was rough, with a pop quiz in math and group work in bio. I am done with socializing for the day.

My phone rings just as I'm walking out the doors. I answer. "Hey, Dad."

"Hey, Azar! Your voice sounds much better."

I step into the freezing February air and switch my phone's audio to my headphones so I can keep my hands in my pockets. "Thanks," I say. At least the antibiotics worked.

"My train gets in Friday night for our February adventure. Want to grab dinner? I'll be staying at a hotel nearby."

Yessss. Dad always takes me out for an amazing meal before whatever parental activity we're doing. I haven't seen him since Christmas. It's been too long.

"That sounds great."

I can hear him smiling through the phone. "Ethiopian food okay? I'll make a reservation."

"Yes, please." Just the thought of the spongy injera bread and stewed meat and vegetables makes my mouth water. Plus, Ethiopian food is soft, which means Mom can't get mad at me for eating something that would be bad for my "throat health."

"All right, I'll see you Friday. I'll tell your mom the plan. Do you want her to come?"

"Sure."

Mom and Dad never married, which is why I suspect they're less angry with each other than my classmates' parents who got divorced. The two of them are more like coworkers than exes. And I don't think Mom's gone out to dinner in months.

"I'll let her know," Dad says. "I love you, bug. See you soon."

"Love you, too."

He hangs up and I head home, ready to practice doing drumrolls with my whole arm.

"Hey, Azar!" Across the parking lot I spy Eben in his full-on lacrosse glory. Lacrosse track pants. Lacrosse sweatshirt. Lacrosse jacket over lacrosse sweatshirt. It's kind of intimidating, to be honest.

"Eben, hey."

He walks alongside me. "So what did you think of Friday's rehearsal? Not bad, right?"

Is he joking? Our first rehearsal was terrible. Why on earth would he think differently? Suddenly I wish I had my choice board so I could just point to the *Whatever you say!* box I should have made.

"Um," I say instead. Eben seems unfazed, though.

"Listen, are you doing anything right now? Practice is canceled, since a bunch of geese tore up the field, and the swim team's got the weight room today. Do you want to come over and work on our report?"

I've never been to a classmate's house before. Eben must see the hesitation on my face, because he adds, "My mom's making homemade mac 'n' cheese. The kind with, like, four cheeses. It's really good."

The thought of going to his house makes me nervous. What if things are awkward and Mom can't get off work to pick me up? But then I look at Eben's glowing face and his warm amber eyes, and I wonder if hanging out with someone new could be fun instead of stressful.

"It's just pasta," Eben explains.

"Okay."

He smiles that huge, open smile that takes up his whole face, and I try not to beam one back at him. If only Sydney could see me now.

THE HOLLINS RESIDENCE

EBEN CHATTERS THE whole way to his house. How is talking so easy for him? I don't mean the *physical* act of talking, which is also hard. I mean he just says whatever pops into his head and doesn't really care how it might sound. It usually takes me a whole paragraph of internal monologuing just to get a sentence out.

"What's your favorite movie? No, wait, favorite TV show!" Eben shouts happily. He's been grilling me this entire walk.

"Umm . . . *Avatar: The Last Airbender,*" I reply nervously. It's a cartoon. I pray that other high schoolers watch cartoons.

"Nice!" Eben says, holding his fist out for a bump. *Phew.*

"Do you watch it?"

He shakes his head. "I have no idea what that is, but it sounds great."

Ah.

We turn onto a block with huge houses, where each home takes up most of the yard and you can definitely stare into your neighbor's window. This must be a new development, the kind of home Holleh Neda says they can build in a couple of months.

"This is me," he says, pointing to a massive house from a row of identical houses. I knew from stalking Eben's socials that his family was wealthy, but this mansion seems even bigger in person.

"Come on," he says, guiding me up a front lawn with little lanterns that light the path. Even in the dead of winter, their yard looks immaculate.

"MOM!" Eben shouts the second he's inside. Their front door, I notice, was unlocked. *How?*

He leads me in, and I almost weep. His house looks like the set of a TV show called *We Have Money!* There's a big staircase in the foyer, the kind they use for prom movies, where the girl walks slowly down as everyone oohs and aahs. Above it is a crystal chandelier, paired with a marble floor.

I start to take off my shoes. My filthy boots are not worthy.

"What are you doing?" Eben laughs. "You can leave your shoes on."

"Oh, I . . . okay." I've never been in a house where

you leave your shoes on. It seems super unsanitary, considering the wintry mix we've been walking through. I gag as they hit the clean floor. Eben leads us into a huge bright-white kitchen.

"Eben!" a woman with bottle-blonde hair calls out from in front of the stove. She wears trendy straight-legged jeans with ripped ankles, a ribbed sweater, and pastel clay earrings.

"Mom, this is my friend Azar," he says, dropping his book bag under the marble countertop before he sits. "She's my partner in English."

"Oh, Azar! What a pretty name. How . . . exotic," she says, her teeth bleached to within an inch of their life. She gives me a big smile and pours us both glasses of milk, even though I didn't ask for one. Who drinks plain milk? She turns back to the macaroni and cheese bubbling on the stove.

I notice she doesn't kiss Eben on the cheek or give him a hug, though I'm pretty sure they haven't seen each other since this morning. Even my exhausted mom will bend over to give me a kiss on the forehead when she comes home late.

Eben chugs his dairy. It must be nice to have a stay-at-home mom ready with drinks and snacks the second you get home. I don't know any other kids who have a hot meal waiting for them after school. Even Roya's mom just unthaws Iranian food from their gigantic freezer for Roya and Ashkan to reheat in the microwave before she leaves for showings.

"Do you like mac 'n' cheese, Azar?" Mrs. Hollins asks loudly. She draws every word out, talking slowly. "Have you had it before?"

Oh no, I see what's happening here. Does she think that because I'm not talking as much that I can't speak English?

"Of course she's had it before, Mom." Eben laughs nervously. And there it is, the second time I've ever seen Eben uncomfortable. It reminds me of how his hands shook before rehearsal on Friday when he was nervous about singing.

"I love mac 'n' cheese."

Mrs. Hollins smiles and spoons a big portion onto my plate. Eben looks ready to pounce on his food.

"Wait, wait!" Mrs. Hollins cries. "Photo time!"

He sighs, holding his fork as Mrs. Hollins whips out her phone and begins taking shots of Eben's plate from every angle. "I'm doing a mac 'n' cheese recipe for my blog," she explains.

"Mom!" Eben whines.

"Oops, sorry, I'm not supposed to talk about my work." She winks at me, like it's our little secret. I turn to Eben, completely bewildered.

"You can eat now," he says quietly.

I take a bite and chew, watching Mrs. Hollins edit the photos.

"This is really good," I croak into the uncomfortable silence. I can see why making macaroni and cheese from scratch is way superior than the organic prepackaged stuff Mom and I eat from the box. "Thank you."

I blink and Eben's already done with his food, his glass of milk completely drained. We haven't had real milk in our house in years. It actually tastes pretty good.

"That was great. Thanks, Mom," Eben says, wiping his mouth. He gets up without clearing his dirty dishes, a criminal offense in my household. I move to put my empty cup and plate into the dishwasher, but Mrs. Hollins gives me a horrified look.

"Oh, no, Azar. I got it. Just leave those with me."

I hand the dishes over and feel even stranger. Since walking into Eben's house, I haven't had to (1) remove my shoes, (2) answer any probing parental questions, or (3) clean up after myself. What strange alternative universe am I in?

"Let's go to my room," Eben says, grabbing his book bag. Are girls allowed in his room? Madness.

I follow him in a daze up the huge staircase to a plush, carpeted second floor. He throws open his door, and I'm assaulted by green flannel. Green flannel bedspread, green flannel sheets, and a tartan kilt framed above his bed seem to be the dominant decor theme. He flops onto his bed, *with his shoes,* and proceeds to open his backpack.

"You can sit there," he says, gesturing to his desk and rolling chair. His desk is practically the size of my bedroom, and it takes up two walls, fitting into a corner. On top of it are all kinds of lacrosse trophies and blue ribbons and even a plaque. I'm starting to get the feeling that Eben is treated like a boy wonder not just at school, but at home, too.

"Okay, so I started outlining my first couple of chapters," he says, opening his binder and showing me his format. He's way further along than I am. And by further along, I mean I still haven't read the book. I begrudgingly admit that he can't be *too* spoiled if he works this hard on his homework.

"Do you want to read what I wrote? If you like it, you can do the same style," he says.

I take the binder from him and scan through his chapter breakdowns, each page packed with notes in those same THEME, CHARACTER, PLOT sections I saw that first day at the library.

"Yeah, this is great." I get my phone out and take a picture.

I hand back the binder, and we sit there in silence for a second. I look down at my hands, not sure what else to say.

"I was actually hoping you could hear the song I've been working on for Friday," Eben begins, his brown hair sticking up all over the place. "Like, for our rehearsal." He looks embarrassed again, and I'm starting to realize that maybe he isn't as confident as I thought.

Maybe this is the real reason he invited me over.

"Sure," I say, perking up. I barely got a chance to hear Eben sing last week.

He gets an electric keyboard out from under his bed. Right as he's about to turn it on, though, I hear someone open the front door. Quick, light footsteps up the stairs follow, and there's a small tap on Eben's door.

"Come in, Adrienne," he calls out.

A five-year-old with blonde hair and the same honey-brown eyes as Eben runs into his arms, clutching him around the neck. "Why didn't you pick me up today?"

"It's Dad's day to pick you up, bean. Look, have you met my friend Azar? She's a really good drummer."

Adrienne gives me a shy smile. "Hi."

"Do you wanna hear me play?" Eben asks, rocking Adrienne back and forth.

She nods. He takes a deep breath and places his hands on the keys.

I've been hoping
That the struggle isn't real.
Been thinking
About the things that we can't feel.

Smiles can't hide everything
When you hate everything, and
They say that it gets better,
But there never is a calendar.

So, smile and wave, take the applause.
Bask in the praise till it rubs you raw.

What's the point of feeling sad
When the gold is glinting?
What's the point of feeling bad
When your team is winning?

He stops suddenly and looks at Adrienne, who's already fallen asleep on his lap. Meanwhile, I feel rooted to the spot, frozen in plaid.

Eben's loud, boisterous voice from the locker rooms is gone, replaced by something fragile and soft. Both Ebens sound amazing, but there's something about this song that I know is rare. There's real feeling and emotion behind it, and it's the kind of song where all he needs is a guitar and a mic. And he definitely doesn't need a drummer like me.

"That's all I got," Eben says apologetically, gently moving Adrienne into a better position on his pillows. She breathes deeply, like she falls asleep in his bed all the time.

My mouth's gone dry. I don't know why Eben decided to show this side of himself to me, but it makes me feel like I've just witnessed something private and precious.

"It was great," I manage to choke out. "Really great."

"Yeah?" He searches my eyes, desperate for approval. But I'm a high school loser with zero social standing. Who cares what I think?

"Yeah." I nod. "You should share it with the rest of the band on Friday."

"Thanks, Azar." He walks over, and instead of giving me a fist bump like he normally does, he gives me a hug. He's so much taller than me that my face goes right into his chest, and I awkwardly pat his back.

"That was terrifying," he admits. I can feel his racing heart through his sweatshirt. I wonder if he can feel mine, too. I'm so close, I can smell his deodorant.

I pull back before I get carried away. "That's what being a songwriter is. Putting yourself out there. Even if it's scary."

"A songwriter, eh? That has a nice ring to it."

"Welcome to the Secret Society of Songwriters."

He laughs, and knowing I made him laugh feels like liquid fire being injected into my veins.

Then I imagine Sydney winking at me, and my face burns bright red. I'm just another girl succumbing to the charms of Ebenezer Hollins, fifth of his name.

CATCHING FEELINGS

FIRST THING IN the morning, I text Roya the words spilling out of me at the breakfast counter.

> **AZAR ROSSI** *7:10 A.M.*: how do you know when you have a crush on someone

Roya instantly responds.

ROYA NAZEMIAN *7:10 A.M.*: I KNEW IT!!!!!!

> **AZAR ROSSI** *7:11 A.M.*: ugh nevermind

ROYA NAZEMIAN *7:11 A.M.*: no no tell me please! Even though I have a pretty good idea who it might be [smirking emoji]

I pull up Eben's social media feed and look at all the pictures of him and his family. I chew my thumb, not sure how to answer.

> **AZAR ROSSI** *7:12 A.M.*: I went over
> to Eben's house yesterday and we
> ~~hugged~~

There's a photo of him celebrating something with his lacrosse friends. How can that be the same guy who sang those amazing lyrics yesterday?

"Azar? You ready? You gotta walk to school, remember?" Mom peers over my shoulder at my phone. "Hey, I know that kid." She points to Eben's face from the photo I pulled up.

"Really?"

"Yeah, that's Samantha Hollins' son. From *The Hollins House* blog. She's famous! I read her all the time when I'd just had you and I didn't know what to do. Eben's six months older than you. She helped me a lot; shame about her divorce."

I google "Hollins House" and click on the first result. Oh my god.

It's an *entire blog* dedicated to Eben and Adrienne.

I click on the first photo, and there, staring back at me, is Eben's toddler face. In a bathtub.

"Yep," Mom sighs. "I bought the same baby bathtub."

The fact that Mrs. Hollins still has naked baby photos of her teen son up on the internet is disturbing. Right next to that post is a new one on the best mac 'n' cheese recipe. The photo looks like the picture she took of Eben's meal yesterday.

I click off the page. For some reason, looking at Eben's photos on the blog feels wrong, even if it is a public website.

"Sorry I can't drive today, Z. But your dad's coming tomorrow. That'll be nice, no?" Mom looks over from the sink, where she's putting in her hoop earrings. I hug her tight.

"What's that for?" she says, kissing my forehead.

"Yeah, Mom, it'll be nice."

"Don't forget your Throat Soothe!" She hands me my curséd thermos, and I step into the frigid air. It's so cold, I have to catch my breath.

"Hey," Nadim says, waiting for me on the freezing landing. He's holding a coffee tumbler in each hand, and he gestures for me to take one.

"My host mom made you gahwe."

"Gahwe?"

"Yes, like espresso, Americano, latte?"

"Oh, coffee!" I'm so grateful, I could cry. "Thank you. I could use a warm drink." *A warm drink that isn't Throat Soothe.*

Nadim beams. "You're very welcome. That's what my name means. 'Person you have a drink with.'"

"Nice." I clink his coffee with mine.

We walk to school, the coffee warming me up with each sip. Even though the tumbler is as tall as the length of my hand, there's maybe only three inches of coffee inside. It's thick and sugary—more mud than liquid. I can feel the caffeine zipping through me. Another icy blast barrels down the wind tunnel that is our morning walk, but the coffee helps me stand tall. Nadim shivers and takes a sip.

"What does Azar mean?" he asks after a while.

"Fire."

"Fire? We call that nar."

"It's a popular name in Iran. Azar is fire. Azarakhsh is lightning. So you get the fire from lightning. There's a famous horse in Persian mythology called Rakhsh, too."

Nadim gives me a long look, his brown eyes almost black in the gray February morning. "It suits you."

"Really?" I almost spit out my coffee. "Never has anyone described me as 'fiery.'"

"The fire's in there," Nadim assures me. "It burns."

Mom named me the American equivalent of Wolf, a name so ferocious, it never fit. I turn away from Nadim's intense stare and quickly change the subject. "You don't have your instrument case with you."

"I keep the electric bass at home to practice and the acoustic bass at school. Too many basses," he explains.

I'm relieved that he's taking our band so seriously. I take another sludgy sip of gahwe. "Have you been working on your song?"

He shrugs. "It's not really a song . . . more like a melody. But I'm excited to show it to you."

We pass Mr. Clarke as we near the front doors. "Azar, say hi to your mom for me!" he calls.

"Ugh."

We push through the front entrance and take a real breath in the warm air. Every year it feels like the winters in the DC metro area get worse, and every summer I forget how bad they are until it gets cold again.

"See you after school? Or maybe we can eat lunch together?"

I freeze. Is Nadim actually asking me to eat lunch with him? I haven't had a friend to eat lunch with since Roya at Stonewall Middle.

"Um . . . sure, lunch sounds good."

"We eat in the back corner." Nadim waves goodbye, and I drain my coffee, wondering what lunch outside of the practice rooms will feel like.

Lunchtime. I scan for Nadim's table in the back corner, feeling awkward as I stand in the middle of the cafeteria. Going straight to the practice rooms means no one can see me be alone, but here I feel exposed.

"Azar!" a voice calls out. A voice that pronounced my name right.

I spy Nadim and make my way over to his full table. He clears a space for me right next to him, and I feel cool and important.

"Hey," I say with an exhale, glad to have found him.

"Azar, these are my friends Nguyen, Ahmad, Winston, and Josefina, and over there is Esther."

I wave at the blur of faces sitting around the table, then quickly look back at my lunch. I can't remember the last time I was introduced to so many people, and I'm pretty sure I've forgotten how to behave.

Nadim gets out a metal tin of stacking containers that reveal fragrant rice, a spicy red stew, and some bread. Nyugen's lunch is just as sumptuous, with rice noodles, marinated chicken, and pickles on top. A quick glance at the rest of everyone else's lunches confirms that I am at the international food table.

"How do you know Nadim?" Nguyen asks, her bright black eyes looking between us. Then she takes a bite of noodles.

I clear my throat. "We live in the same building."

"Cool." She nods.

I take a sip of kombucha, wondering what else I should say. "How about you? How do you all know each other?"

Nguyen gestures to the whole table. "We're all in advanced ESL."

"Oh. I had no idea." I turn to Nadim. There's no way I would have known that Nadim's friends weren't born here.

He shrugs. "It's for the writing. I need to get better if I want to pass my TOEFL."

"What's that?"

"Here we go." Nguyen sighs.

"The TOEFL is the Test of English as a Foreign Language. You need to pass it if you want to go to college in the US or Canada or the UK or Australia. It's really important."

I look around the table, not sure what to do with this information. "Does that mean you won't go to school in Lebanon?"

Nadim's face falls. "Lebanon doesn't have as many opportunities right now. First the port explosion, then the new government, and now low unemployment. My parents saved up a lot of money to send me here."

Ahmad nods to Nadim. "My parents are still in Egypt. I live here with my uncle." He adds something I don't catch in Arabic, and the two laugh. I suddenly feel very stupid for thinking my Battle of the Bands problem was as big as I thought. The stakes for Nadim are much higher than me winning a local music contest.

I get out my hummus and tofu sandwich, praying no one will comment on it, and thankfully nobody says anything.

"Azar and I are in a band," Nadim adds between bites of rice. He pours a bit of yogurt onto it the same way my family does. I do a double take. It's not yogurt; it's lebneh, thicker and tangy-smelling.

"Really?" Winston asks, looking surprised. "Deem, what do you play?"

"Electric bass," he says, looking pleased with himself. I can tell he's enjoying this moment.

"Nadim's really good," I add.

He beams. "Azar's on drums—you should see her." Now it's my turn to blush.

"Oooh, are those kale chips?" Ahmad asks, eyeing my reusable sandwich bag.

"Yeah?" I reply, nervous that he's about to make fun of my hippie meal.

"Can I have one?" he asks.

I laugh, a harsh barking cackle escaping my throat. Nobody seems put off by how rough it sounds, though. I hand him the bag.

"Have them all."

Ahmad's eyes go wide. "Thanks, Azar." He pronounces my name right, too, with the right *a*'s and everything. I could seriously get used to this.

Nadim asks Ahmad something in Arabic, and he gives him a chip. "Yum," Nadim says.

"These are amazing," Ahmad says between bites.

"Glad you like them." I think about that dinky practice room and how this is the first time in forever that I'm not spending lunch there. Now the thought of eating in there feels impossible after sitting at an actual table with his cool friends.

"Here," Nguyen says, passing me a piece of candy. "It's tamarind. I think you'll like it."

"Thanks." I pop it in my mouth, enjoying the sour tamarind flavor softened with sugar crystals.

I hope I get invited back.

TAKE TWO

TODAY, REHEARSAL IS gonna be different. This Friday I've set an actual agenda, and Mom, who's a professional project manager, helped me organize the whole schedule.

"Need help?" Eben stands in the band-room doorway clutching what must be a lacrosse stick, which looks like a yardstick with a tiny, palm-sized net on top.

"Sure," I say casually, while I try to ignore the scent of his deodorant and how it felt to hug him the other day. Or how delicate and raw his song was, and how he played it specially for me.

"Here," he says, reaching over me to grab chairs from the stack in the back. I lower the brim of my Nats hat, hoping he can't see the flush spreading across my face. It's a good thing I wrote down action items today, because the second that Eben's near me, I seem to forget how to function like a real human being.

Once everyone else arrives, I hand out copies of the schedule. It looks like a color-coded, tabulated, sticky-note-covered fever dream. Even Eben looks impressed.

"Are we studying for the PSATs together? Or . . . ?" Matty asks, confused.

I clear my throat. "Since we got off track last time, I figured we could use some structure."

Matty frowns, but he doesn't say anything. Maybe he doesn't understand how footnotes work.

I hit my cymbal with a soft mallet, bringing the rehearsal to order. The gong was too heavy to wheel over.

"Okay, everyone." I stare into Nadim's and Matty's faces, skimming over Eben's so I can have a functioning brain. "Today we're going to finish polishing up the song I wrote and audition contenders for the second song. Sound good?"

Nobody says anything. Perfect. I make a move toward my drum kit.

"Actually—" Matty begins. *Dear goddess, what now?* "I've been working on the guitar part for your song. I was thinking we could do a key change for the chorus? And then Eben could come in with a counter melody on keys. It would sound, like, so raw."

"Umm." I'd already picked the perfect key for this song, since, you know, I'd written it. I feel myself start to get defensive. This is *my* band! Why does Matty keep sticking his nose in?

"Maybe we should just give it a try?" Eben offers. "See if it works?" He gives me an encouraging look, like, *C'mon, Azar—this could be awesome!!!!*

Nadim looks at the floor, saying nothing. I get the sense he doesn't want to be involved.

I grit my teeth. "Fine."

Matty walks me through what he's thinking, and we start the song. Every time Eben sings, my whole body seems to erupt into goose bumps.

We stumble a bit over the changes, but when we finish, all the guys are grinning at each other.

"That was good, right?" Nadim says, his face bright. *Et tu, Nadim?*

"Totally," Matty says. All three of them turn to me.

The truth is, the song *did* sound better with Matty's suggestions. But I thought songwriting was my thing. If I agree to Matty's tweaks, what does that mean about my own talent? Does that mean I'm not as good as I thought?

"Yeah." I sigh, not sure what else to say. "It sounded good."

Matty looks ecstatic, but I feel shabbier than ever. He's already taken the guitar from me, and now he's encroaching on my song, too. I'm used to feeling invisible, but today it stings more than usual.

After we run through the song with the changes a couple times, we go around the room and try out everyone else's songs, my schedule completely forgotten. Matty plays a guitar part he's been fiddling with, Eben sings the lyrics he sang for me at his house, and Nadim reveals his bass line. None of them sound like a finished song that we can vote on, though.

"What if we combined it all into one song?" Nadim suggests. "We go with my bass line, Eben's lyrics, and the guitar melody Matty made." He looks around the room, like he's worried he said the wrong thing.

Being in a band is *hard*. Putting yourself out there when people can reject your ideas is terrifying.

I nod. "That's a good idea, Nadim."

"I love it!" Eben beams.

Nadim exhales, like he's been holding his breath, and we spend the rest of rehearsal figuring out the arrangement for Eben's song lyrics. It actually feels good to sit in a circle and brainstorm together. After writing by myself in my room for years, it's a different feeling to work on a song with someone else.

Nadim is excellent at paying attention to detail, like when the music should crescendo and how we should accent different notes. Matty seems to have a knack for figuring out melodies and brainstorms them out loud on his guitar. And Eben just seems happy to be here, encouraging everyone as they work out the notes. If we had a cheerleader, it would definitely be him.

By the time we finish with our second rehearsal, we've got my song pretty fleshed out, and we have the bones of a second song. Which is good, since March is around the corner.

Nadim and Matty wave goodbye, saying they have plans with their friends, like normal high schoolers on a Friday night. I stay behind to move the chairs, and Eben helps me put the room back in order.

"That was a great rehearsal, right?" he asks.

I think of how defensive I'd gotten over my song and feel a prickle of shame. "Yeah. It was."

We walk out the front doors and into the bitter winter evening.

"It was so cool having other people put music to the words in my head," Eben continues. "Matty's melodies are so good!"

"I guess," I say begrudgingly. Because the truth is, Matty's melodies are *really* good. Better than mine, in fact. And it hurts to have thought I was good at something, only to have someone waltz in and do it better.

"Hey," Eben says, catching the pain in my voice. "Your lyrics are good, too. There's nothing wrong with teamwork making something better. Now your song sounds even more amazing."

I bite my lip. Why does rehearsal always make me feel so exposed? "It's just tough having people pick apart your work, you know?"

"I still can't believe I'm singing out loud in a band," he admits. "It's terrifying."

"I bet."

"I'd better go pick up Adrienne," Eben says, checking his fancy smartwatch.

He gives me a long hug. "See ya, Azar."

He walks away. For the first time in a long time, I liked talking out loud.

I wouldn't mind doing it again.

DINNER WITH DAD

DAD PULLS UP to our apartment in his fancy rental car, and I can see him comb his hair and check his shirt from the upstairs window. Mom has always hinted that Dad has no problem getting dates in New York, but to me he's just Dad. Thick blond hair that sticks up a bit in the back, button-down shirts, and a giant cell phone he always puts on "Do Not Disturb" whenever we hang out.

I'm excited for tonight. Not having a dad who lives close means that whenever we get the chance to spend time together, we make it count. And my dad always makes sure we do something fun.

I shove on a sweater and the gold earrings Maman Bozorg got me for Christmas. Hopefully I look cool enough for a concert.

"Knock, knock," a voice says outside the door. He

always says that, and it always makes me laugh, even though it's stupid.

I open it. "Dad!"

He smiles, the corners of his eyes a little more lined than when I last saw him, probably from late nights at the office. He opens his arms out wide for a hug. As always, he smells like one of those deodorants called Icy Blast! or Extreme Frost! It's comforting.

"Hey, Zazzie." He gives me a kiss on the forehead and hugs me tight. He takes a deep, shaky breath. When he finally lets me go, I walk with him to the living room, where Mom's switching her everyday earrings for something a little fancier. She looks amazing in a black dress and red heels.

"Hey, David. You look nice."

"You too," Dad replies. "Want me to drive?"

Mom gives him an appraising look. "Sure."

My parents aren't *together,* but I love seeing them together. We're almost like the families at Polk. Even classmates whose parents have divorced still get to see their mom or dad whenever they want, since they live close by, while I have to settle for one weekend a month.

Dad leads us to his car, and Mom gets in the front seat.

"How was school today?" Dad asks, finding my eyes in the rearview mirror. "Your mom says you're putting a band together?"

"Yep."

"That's wonderful!" He sounds surprised, but he's the

one who bought me all those instruments. It's inevitable at this point. "You're playing guitar, right? And you're going to compete at a Battle of the Bands contest?"

I clear my throat. "Actually, I'm playing the drums."

"Drums?" Dad looks confused, but he doesn't pry. "Well, that's fantastic, Azar. Really, I'm so proud of you."

"Thanks, Dad."

We pull up to a small strip mall with a dry cleaner's, an appliance store, and an import/export business. At the end is Kerem Ethiopian Restaurant, lit up with Christmas lights. Across the street is a Yemeni place that we go to sometimes, with cinnamon-spiced rice served in huge bowls, and down the block is Eden Center, with the best Vietnamese food on the East Coast. Some of the most delicious food in NOVA is in random strip malls like these.

Dad orders a coffee, Mom gets an herbal tea, and I order a soda. I wait for Mom to correct my soda order and say I can't drink it, but the gods are smiling on me tonight, because she stays quiet, sneaking glances at Dad. Maybe I can even get away with murder, or dessert. Dad puts his arm around my shoulders and squeezes me tight.

"So," he begins. "I have some exciting news."

Mom takes a swig of her tea like she's bracing herself.

"As you know, I've put in a transfer request to our Virginia campus a bunch of times. But this year I was finally approved!" Dad beams, his face breaking into a smile.

"Dad, that's awesome!" I shout, then wince. I chug some more soda.

"I talked to your mom, and that means you and I will get to spend a lot more time together, Zaz." Dad grips my hand across the table, his eyes shining. "I'll get to be there for doctor's appointments, parent-teacher conferences, everything. Big or small."

Happiness surges through me, but even bigger is the wave of relief I feel. *I don't have to say goodbye anymore. I'll never have to wait a whole month again.*

"Congratulations again, David," Mom says, but her smile doesn't reach her eyes. She clinks her cup against his.

Mom's gaze meets mine, and she watches my face carefully. Is she worried I won't be able to spend as much time with her if Dad's here? Doesn't she know I'm a sullen mess without her? I try to say it all in this one look, but I don't know if it works.

"That's so cool, Dad. I can't wait." No matter what co-parenting arrangement we go with, I'm happy he'll be closer. Dad can drive me to my music lessons, and we can eat non-kale dinners at his place. I'll have someone to jam out with as we both mess around on our guitars, being silly. I'll finally have a dad I can see at the drop of a hat instead of after a five-hour drive.

"So, when do you move?" Mom asks, trying to sound casual. But I can hear the tremble in her voice. It makes her sound like me.

"Looks like the middle of April. I'm gonna start looking for a condo tomorrow."

Mom takes a bite of spinach, chewing slowly.

"Does that mean we'll get to see more concerts and stuff?" I ask.

"Concerts, museums, whatever you want. And that means your mom will get some more time to herself, too," he says, looking at her. She gives him a small smile. I can tell something is wrong, but I'm not sure what it is.

For the rest of dinner, I tell Dad about my projects at school, how speech therapy is going, and what kind of music I've been listening to, all of it lubricated by soda. Mom doesn't talk much, only jumping in occasionally to add a detail or two.

Dad looks at his watch. It's fancier than the last one he had. Does Dad's move to Virginia mean he got a promotion, too?

"All right, we should probably head to the concert soon."

Mom nods and stacks her plate onto mine. I take one last bite of injera even though I'm so full, I could burst.

We drop Mom off at home before Dad and I head into DC, and Mom has a sad look on her face. "Be good, okay?" she says, kissing my forehead.

Her earrings tickle my cheeks, and I give her a hug back. I watch as she unlocks our front door and makes her way into the empty apartment. Why is Mom acting so strangely? With Dad here, will Mom be even more stressed out?

"All right," Dad says, rubbing his hands together excitedly. "I've got all of Amy Waters' music on my phone so we can listen to it on the way into town. Sound good?"

"Heck yes."

Dad hits "play," the suburbs of Virginia melting behind us as we take the GW Parkway. To the left I can see the ice-covered Potomac glitter below us, the cliffs on the Maryland side twinkling with houses. The fancy seat in Dad's rental car hugs me close, and I forget about Mom's worried expression over dinner as we take the bridge into DC.

"Look," Dad says. Under the bridge are different letters from local high schools, and I can see the red-and-blue *P* for Polk. The crew team rows on this river and must pass under this bridge every day. "Your mom used to take us here when you were little and I'd visit from Jersey. Those *Exorcist* steps were killer."

"*Exorcist* steps?"

"You know, like from the movie? It was shot here."

I shake my head. "Is this another one of those old-people things? Like Nirvana? And Jimi Hendrix?"

Dad points a finger. "Keep chuckling. One day you'll see how amazing they really are, and you won't find it so funny!"

I giggle. Dad's stern face cracks into a smile, too, and he doesn't look like the intimidating Wall Street suit he is every day at work. He just looks like my dad.

We hit Constitution Avenue, and I press my face against the window. The Washington Monument is lit up like a lighthouse. We pass the Smithsonian and turn just as the Capitol Building comes into sight. I spy tourists taking photos in front of the steps, even in the freezing cold.

Mom and I used to go into DC a lot more before her job got so busy. Every weekend we'd hit up a museum or go to some funky coffee shop in Mount Pleasant or Shaw and stock up on Mumbo sauce wherever we got lunch. Other times she'd take me to Eastern Market and we'd pick fresh produce and pickles from the different stalls.

But we haven't gone in a while. If anything, most weekends Mom and I usually just stay in and zonk out on the couch, exhausted. Going with Dad to a concert feels like an extra-special treat after all the weekends of take-out and TV. We cross onto U Street, where I can already see concertgoers making their way to the venue.

"This area used to look way different," Dad says, pulling into a parking lot next to the 9:30 Club. "Your mom's parents wouldn't even let her go to a concert here unless one of them came with her. It was so embarrassing!"

"Ahem."

Dad looks at me, then back at the venue, offended. "*I* don't count. I'm a hip dad. I'm wearing limited-edition sneakers, see?"

I roll my eyes. A parking attendant leads him to a spot, and we hop out into the chilly night.

"You ready, Zaz?"

I think of Amy's lyrics, how I pray I can be as good as her someday. I nod. "I'm ready."

LIVE MUSIC

WE GET TO the entrance and wait in line in the freezing cold. A scary-looking bouncer with a huge beard wraps my frozen wrist with a neon-orange band and stamps my hand with two Xs. I watch as Dad gets a different stamp, one that probably lets him buy alcohol. I still feel cool, though.

"I can't wait to hear this kid sing," Dad says, taking a photo of the neon 9:30 sign out front for his carefully curated Instagram account, the one that's all pictures of buildings and bridges and skyscrapers.

After listening to her music on the drive in, Dad's become a big, big fan. As in, he might buy a T-shirt from the merch table and put it over his nerdcore button-down shirt and turn into That Guy at the concert.

"Be cool, Dad."

"I saw Nirvana live when I was seven, remember? My cool card knows no bounds."

The second we walk into the 9:30 Club, my heart lifts sky-high. I'm out here in the field, about to see a badass on the guitar, for *research*. Dad has taken me here before, but tonight feels different. Tonight I'm here to study so I can be inspired for our own performance at the battle.

The opening act takes the stage, and I feel like I'm right where I'm supposed to be. *This is where it happens,* I tell myself. *This is the ultimate goal.*

"Do you want anything to drink?" Dad shouts as the indie band from Baltimore starts playing. I've listened to their entire discography, just to be prepared. "Water? Coke?"

Bless my well-meaning father, who has no idea I'm on soda rations, and that I've already had my Sprite for the night. "Coke, please!" I shout. That'll be one of the downsides to him moving closer: he and Mom getting on the same page about my diet.

He flashes a thumbs-up and walks to one of the bars. Alone, I could be a college student or a woman who just goes to concerts every night, all the time, like it's no big deal. *Yeah, nobody would think I was a high schooler.*

I nod along to the music, analyzing the band. They have a keyboardist, a guitarist, a bassist, and a drummer. Just like us. The guitarist and bassist all lean into their mics, all providing backing vocals—should Nadim and Matty back up Eben the same way? Should we make our setup like theirs?

"Here you go," Dad says, handing me a can. He holds out some earplugs. "Is the music too loud for you? I got these from the bar."

I shake my head. "It's fine, Dad."

He shrugs. "I read that ear damage can hurt your Eustachian tube, which . . ."

Can hurt my throat. Sigh. Mom's usually the one who watches out for that kind of stuff. I forgot that Dad being closer also means that I'll have two parents nagging me about my throat.

I take the earplugs.

Soon the opening band finishes, and I feel my heartbeat race: Amy's coming on. I'm about to hear her lyrics *live*.

"Thanks for the tickets, Dad," I remember to say.

"No problem, bug."

Amy takes the stage, and I practically faint: the woman whose lyrics sing me to sleep every night is less than twenty feet away from me. She looks like a proper singer-songwriter, with a cool denim jacket and her hair up in a messy ponytail, an acoustic guitar on her lap. The music begins, and I hear her chilling, haunting words echo throughout the venue.

You were right under my nose,
Standing still all along,
Sending signals to reach me
At a different frequency.

The rest of the night, I feel my soda grow warm in my hands as I focus on the music. Amy's lyrics are just so perfect. How does she encapsulate all the things I want to say? Every stanza has meaning and mood, and it makes me feel a very specific sort of melancholy. How can I ever get my own lyrics to sound like that?

By the time the concert winds down, I feel like I've been in a trance. I've had tunnel vision the whole night, with Amy being the light at the end of it. I don't even notice when Dad gently takes the flat soda out of my hand and goes to throw it out. My hand stays clenched around the air like a claw.

"Azar, you ready to go?"

I blink. A clock in the corner says it's almost midnight, but I feel wired, like my blood has turned into electricity and the only way to expend it is to grab my notebook and fill it with lyrics.

"I can't hear you over the sound of my life-changing experience."

"Come on," Dad says, holding out his hand. "I've got an idea."

He leads us to a different exit, one that takes us past the merch table. And there she is: Amy Waters. She's signing merch and CDs for fans, and Dad quickly grabs an album.

"Go on," he says, handing the CD to me before turning to pay for it. "Shoot your shot."

Is he crazy? Why would Amy want to talk to *me*? My

throat goes dry, and I suddenly wish I had a thermos of Throat Soothe. Too soon, I'm next in line.

When Amy turns to me, I am legitimately starstruck. I float over myself, watching from above as the Azar on Earth is speechless. Dad nudges me.

"Hey," Amy says, smiling, her bleach-blonde hair looking almost purple in the venue's lighting. "Thanks for coming."

"Hnrgh," I reply.

She takes another look at me. "How old are you?"

So much for my college-student ruse. "Umm, fourteen. But my birthday's coming up." *In eight months.*

Amy shakes her head, like she can't believe my answer. "Dang, you're younger than me when I started going to concerts."

"You're worth it," I say quickly, losing all semblance of chill.

"Did you enjoy the show?" She signs the CD and hands it to me.

"You were incredible," I say, my voice husky. Like Cinderella, my throat turns into a pumpkin the closer it is to midnight. Come on, throat! Hold on just a little longer! I think of the soda Dad threw out and wish I'd sipped more. "Your lyrics . . . the songwriting . . . how do you get it to sound so raw?"

Amy laughs. "Well, the most important thing about songwriting is to tell the truth. You can't hide behind anything. You have to put it all out there."

I wish I had a notebook to write all of this down so I could do something instead of nod enthusiastically.

"Are you a musician?" she asks. I know she's being really nice to me, probably because I'm so young.

"Yes," I reply, my voice small. "I mean, I want to be. But my lyrics are nowhere near as good as yours."

"Just tell the truth. I promise, it'll make your lyrics better," Amy says.

I feel another person press behind me, eager to get their merch signed.

"Thanks, Amy. I appreciate it."

"No problem." She flashes me one last smile, and I step out of the line. I'm so shocked I had a full conversation with Amy Waters that I almost black out.

"Dad," I say importantly, "I just met *Amy Waters*."

He grins. "Get used to it, bug. I'll show you *all* the cool stuff." He ruffles my hair and hands me my jacket.

When we step outside, I don't even feel the cold.

FARSI SCHOOL (AGAIN)

ON SUNDAY, MOM insists on driving me to Farsi school, even though Dad offered. Maybe because Dad and I spent all of Saturday in a fog of greasy diner food and apartment hunting without her. He just shrugged and went to another condo listing, but I know the truth: Mom wants to see that dad whose kid is in one of the younger Farsi classes. I'm onto you, Mom. This dad better have a good kabob hookup, or me and Kian will riot.

Today in class we, *surprise,* read more poetry. I think some of the poetry is sinking in, though, because the lesson seems to be a lot like what Amy Waters mentioned at the concert. Poetry is about telling the truth, no matter how uncomfortable it makes you feel. I read the poem we're discussing in class today.

This universe is not outside of you.
Look inside yourself.
Everything that you seek,
You are already that.

"It's about how you have been given all the tools you need," Aghaye Khosroshahi says from the head of the classroom. "Whoever you want to be, there is nothing stopping you." He's bouncing on his toes, excited to share this wisdom with us.

When I walk out of Farsi class later, I'm still thinking about that poem. But then I see Mom in the far corner of the parking lot, talking to that guy and his daughter. The second she sees me, she waves goodbye to them and retreats to her car.

"How was it, Z?" she asks.

"Fine," I say lightly. "And how was your date with Mr. Farsi Dad?"

Mom laughs. "You mean Kevin? A date in a parking lot, how romantic." I notice that she didn't really answer my question.

She pulls out of her spot, and we drive back to the house to meet Dad. He's taking me to lunch before my drum lesson.

"So?" I say, wheedling her. "*Are* you going to go on a date?"

Mom sighs, her eyes focused on the road. "I'm not sure, Azar. He's Polish and Iranian, so he knows what it's like to come from a mixed family, but dating someone is still a lot of work. Especially when you both have kids already."

"Polish and Iranian?"

Mom shrugs. "Apparently they grill kielbasas really well."

I laugh. "Oh my god, Mom, you're such a dork."

She takes a deep breath. "With your dad moving here, I was thinking I could finish my degree. You know, become a full-time student again. David's getting a condo in your school district. You could spend more time with him."

Mom makes another turn and looks over at me, gauging my face for a reaction. But the truth is, I'm happy for her. Mom's job doesn't pay great, and it's been draining her a lot more lately. Getting her degree could be a good thing.

"That's awesome, Mom. If you get your degree, you could get a better job, right?"

"Right," she says. "One I actually enjoy."

"You should do it," I say. "If not now, when?"

Mom pulls over into a random parking lot and turns to me. "Yeah?" she says, her eyes hopeful. "It would be a big change, you know."

"I know," I say. "But you deserve to be happy."

Mom looks out the windshield, lost in thought. "Okay, then. I'll speak to an enrollment counselor and see if my credits can transfer." She gives me a big smile, one that lights up her whole face, even her eyes.

In that moment, I think of my surgery. Of Dad uprooting his life and moving down to be closer to me. Of Mom working up the nerve to take a chance on school again. Finally, I think of the battle, and how it feels to take such a leap of faith.

"We can do hard things, Mom."

She looks away, but not before I see a glassy tear track down her cheek. "That's my girl."

DRUM LESSONS, PART DEUX

WE GET PHO out in Eden Center. Dad drives through the red arches that look a lot like DC's Chinatown's and into a completely packed parking lot, but he still manages to nab us a spot with his New Jersey driving skills.

The restaurant we pick looks more like a cafeteria, with white tiled floors and plain square tables and nearly every seat filled with someone bowing their head over a steamy bowl and slurping. I order beef pho for my throat and hope the soup works its magic. After staying up until 2:00 a.m., scribbling lyrics in my notebook, I can use all the help I can get.

"I checked out three condos in Tysons earlier this morning, and when I drop you off at drums, there are a couple more the broker wants to show me," Dad says.

I nod, adding basil leaves and parsley into my meal. The broth soothes the rough patches in the back of my mouth. Dad always eats his plain, without lime or hot sauce, or even a bean sprout. Mom said she had to explain to him what pho was back in college.

"Did you like any of the apartments?" I ask, sounding like two gravelly stones rubbing against each other, thanks to my late night.

Dad frowns but doesn't say anything. "Yeah, the second one was great, and you'd even have your own bathroom connected to your room. That'd be nice, right?"

I nod, switching from soup to bubble tea. The slimy tapioca in my throat feels even better than soup. Maybe I should just eat Vietnamese food every day.

"It's close to the train, and when you stay with me, we can walk to all the shops and restaurants. Or hop on the silver line into DC and see more shows."

"How often would I stay with you?" It's something I've been wondering, but Mom didn't make it clear when she mentioned going back to college.

"Your mom and I are still figuring that out," he says, scratching at the blue sweater he's wearing today. Even though he's not working, he still looks like he is. On the weekends, Mom wears gaucho pants and tank tops, but Dad seems to relax in business casual. How they ever hooked up is baffling.

My phone buzzes.

ROYA NAZEMIAN *1:16 P.M.*: If you're at Eden Center, can you grab some pickled mango for me

AZAR ROSSI *1:16 P.M.*: already got them. $2.15 plus interest

ROYA NAZEMIAN *1:17 P.M.*: [exclamation point emoji] What percentage interest rate? Is there a penalty for paying it off early via Venmo? Do you even know what APR stands for?

AZAR ROSSI *1:18 P.M.*: i'm eating your mango now

"Zaz, you'd be okay with staying with me, right?" Dad asks, chugging his Vietnamese coffee.

"Duh." I nod. "That's the point of you moving here, right?"

Dad twirls the noodles in his bowl. "Yeah," he says. "Just checking."

He drops me off at the music store, and this time I make my way straight to the back rooms, where Victoria's waiting. I've been practicing drumming by bending at the elbow and not my wrists, and I'm still getting the hang of it.

"Hey," she says, without looking up from her phone. This time she's wearing neon-green eyeshadow and a huge, oversized sweatshirt with the words ATTACK DECAY SUSTAIN RELEASE. There's fuzz on top of her head from where she must not have shaved this week.

"Hey," I say back, the word coming out like a low growl.

"Dang," she says, finally looking up from her phone. "Late night?"

I shrug, trying to be cool. "I was at the Amy Waters concert."

Victoria's eyes go wide. "You got tickets? I'm so jealous! Tell me everything!"

I roll my neck, trying to draw out the moment when I, Azar Rossi, made Victoria Shephard, 19K followers on Instagram, three bands, and a degree from Berklee, jealous. Of course I googled her.

"It was amazing. I even got to talk to her after the show," I gush. "Her lyrics are . . . they're . . ."

"Incredible," Victoria finishes for me.

Her eyes are bright when I look back at her, and I see her face recalculating, like she misjudged me before and she's reassessing me now. *Thanks, Amy.*

"Well, I binged a baking show, so clearly you had a better weekend. Now show me your roll—I wanna see those elbows."

I grab my sticks and warm up for a few beats. Then I demonstrate the single roll I've been working on while Victoria adjusts my form.

"Better," she says. "You're not there yet, but you're not gonna get tendinitis at sixteen like I did, at least."

Mom sometimes wears a wrist guard when work is especially chaotic. It looks like the equivalent of braces with rubber bands, only it's for your wrist. No, thank you.

"How's your band rehearsal going?" she asks, pulling out some sheet music from the cabinet in the corner. "You guys practicing?"

"It's okay," I reply. I know I sound sulky when I say it.

"Just okay?" Despite the shaved head, Victoria's face goes soft in the moment, her full cheeks facing me.

"I thought . . . I thought I'd have more control," I admit.

She nods like I said something she'd expected. "That happens all the time," she begins. "I've been in soooo many stupid punk bands, Azar, it's not even funny. But the best bands I've been in are the ones that don't have a leader, where all of us get a say. Even though you have less control, letting everyone contribute makes the band stronger. Trust me."

I chew over her words. Nadim's voice saying *jam session* echoes in the room's silence.

"But what about my lyrics?" I ask in a tiny voice. "I wanted them to sing my songs, but we're only doing one of mine now. . . ."

Victoria grabs the papers she'd been looking for and places them on my music stand. "Just because a song doesn't have your lyrics doesn't mean it's not yours. You're the drummer, remember? You control the beat, the tempo, the percussion that sets the mood for the song. It's not about whose song is whose, but who can help make it stronger. Don't forget that's your job, too."

Eben's lyrics are going into our second song for the Battle of the Bands, but my drums will be in that song, too. In all my bitterness, I hadn't given any thought to how I'm going to accompany him. Nadim's adding his bass line to it, and Matty has that cool melody. Maybe I can figure out an interesting battery arrangement or use this as an excuse to bust out some cool percussion brushes.

That could work.

Victoria gently pries the drumsticks out of my hands. I didn't realize I was clutching them. "I'm gonna show you a new piece I want you to practice, okay?"

I watch as she drills into the snare, her gaze locked on the music. Instead of regular music notes, drum notes are little Xs on the music staff. She taps out an old military beat, her strokes precise and tight. Her wrists, I notice, barely bend.

"Practice this piece for me. It's got variation in it, so it might give you some good ideas for your band. Remember: working together makes your music stronger. Holding on to your precious idea of control will wreck it."

Her voice is grave, like she's telling me the antidote to a poison. But then again, maybe my attitude *is* a poison. Because I've been letting my salty feelings ruin the fact that *I have a band!*

I take the sheet music from her with reverence. "Okay."

"And the next time you get tickets to an Amy Waters concert, you better invite me," Victoria adds in a warning tone. "Or I'll make you tune all the tympanis in here." Her mouth is a thin line, her eyes flat and hard. "Just kidding. Sort of."

I laugh. I sound like a barking seal, but oh well. Soup and bubble tea can only do so much. "Deal," I promise her.

Dad drives me back to our apartment and slides into

a visitor spot. Mom must have been watching from the window because she hurries down in her bright orange coat. We get out of the car, and I'm relieved the sun's out so it's not completely freezing.

"How was it?" she asks.

Dad's phone beeps. "My offer just went under contract!" he says, his face bright with excitement. "I get the keys in May!"

"Cool!" I shout, giving him a hug.

"That's wonderful, David. Congrats." Mom looks a lot less troubled at the thought of Dad moving here than she did during Friday-night Ethiopian food. If anything, she looks relieved.

"I was thinking maybe Azar could come up for one last weekend in New York?" Dad asks, looking to Mom. "We can discuss it, of course."

That would be stellar. I bet there are already some bands scheduled to perform there that Dad and I could go see.

Mom nods. "Yeah, let's talk about it. That would be nice."

Dad leans in to give her a kiss on the cheek. "Thanks, Niloofar." He turns to me for his goodbye hug,

"I'll see you soon, okay?" His five o'clock shadow tickles my cheek. "I love you so much, Zazzie." He squeezes me tight, and I duck my head into the soft folds of his business coat. Every time Dad comes for a visit, I finally feel like we have a normal family. And every time he goes, it's like a piece of me goes with him.

"Bye, Dad."

"Bye, bug—be good."

Mom and I wave as Dad leaves the parking lot, and the second his rental car's out of sight, I feel myself deflate a little bit. But it won't be forever this time. At least there's that.

NEXT FRIDAY

THE SCHOOL WEEK crawls by, with Friday's rehearsal the only thing to look forward to. I've been practicing the drums after school (and eating lunch with Nadim), but I haven't had a chance to show off the new drum arrangement I made for Eben's song.

When it's finally rehearsal day, I consider just waiting in the band room until 5:00 p.m. Matty has jazz band, Nadim has orchestra, and Eben has lacrosse. Waiting these extra few hours feels like torture. I exit the school, preparing to trudge home alone to wait it out, when Eben hollers at me from the lacrosse field.

"Azar, wait up!" he says, wearing some kind of yoga pant situation with mesh shorts over them. For once it isn't icy cold today, just regular cold, with the sunlight warming me up enough to not have to wear a scarf and gloves. Spring smells like it's just around the corner today.

"Hey," I reply, my voice still choppy from last weekend with Dad. But I guess that doesn't matter. In six weeks, they'll go in there with a laser and zap all my nodules.

"How was your weekend? You saw your dad, right?" Eben asks.

"It was nice. He's moving here."

"That's awesome!" He smiles, shifting his gym bag to his other shoulder. His auburn hair is wet underneath his beanie. "So . . . what are you up to now?"

"I was going to go home and watch Nandi Bushell videos."

"Who? Never mind. Want to get hot chocolate at Café Vert?"

"Don't you have lacrosse?"

Eben shakes his head. "Today's a weight room day, but I ended up doing our workout during gym. Coach doesn't want me to lift again and go too hard."

"Oh. Um . . . Okay." I try hard not to smile through my scarf. Hot chocolate sounds way better than YouTube and my duvet cover.

🎧

Café Vert's about half a mile from school, and a lot of kids from Polk like to pretend they're coffee-drinking adults there. I've never actually gone inside—I've had no one to go with until today. No way would Roya spend money on hot chocolate when she can just make it at home for a fraction of the price.

The second I push through the front door, I feel like I'm in some weird initiation ceremony, like I'm really a high schooler now who gets lattes and cappuccinos and pays five dollars for chocolate powder and hot water.

Eben drops his bag on a small round table and saunters up to the barista behind the long, espresso-colored bar. All around us are people on their laptops and business folks having meetings, plus a couple other kids from Polk who I've seen in the hallways.

I sidle up to Eben, not sure how this all works. Should I pay for his drink? Do we split it? If we were doing this Iranian-style, I'd insist on paying, then Eben would say, *No, no, allow me,* and we'd probably repeat that ritual three times before he lets me pay for us.

If this were Argentinian- or Italian-style, we'd probably already have a tab at this coffee shop and settle up at the end of the month. But this is American-style, with a guy who doesn't take his shoes off before sitting on his own bed and whose parents let him go outside with wet hair. The rules are different now.

Eben turns to me. "What do you want, Azar?"

I clear my throat. "Umm, hot chocolate?"

"But, like, do you want whipped cream? A shot of peppermint? Or butterscotch?"

Eben and the barista stare at me expectantly. I blink.

"Just plain hot chocolate's fine." Thankfully that's a

real thing, and the barista nods and enters it into the cash register.

"I'll have an extra-large peppermint mocha with extra whipped cream, but with oat milk." Eben rattles off his drink order, and before I even know what's happening, he taps his phone onto the credit card reader, the payment zinging through. So much for offering to pay.

"Thanks, Eben. I'll get the next round." I hope that's the right thing to say. Please tell me a line I picked up from watching George Clooney movies from the '90s applies to coffee shops.

He smoothly tucks his phone back into his pocket as he waves at someone he recognizes. "No problem," he says. The super-happy, upbeat Eben I'm familiar with has been replaced by a suave, oat milk–loving gentleman who insists on buying drinks for me. Maybe this golden retriever has got some tricks.

He leads us over to the table where his bag is and pulls a chair out for me, like I'm a lady or something. I inhale the toasty, bitter aroma of the shop, wishing coffee tasted as good as it smelled.

Seeing Eben take a sip from a fancy cup with an upcycled paper sleeve while wearing Lululemon no longer surprises me. But then, just when I think I have him figured out, he drinks with his pinkie up.

The hot cocoa here tastes better than the dairy-free kind Mom makes at home, but I don't say that out loud. I'm no milk traitor.

"How is it?" Eben asks, watching my reaction.

"Good," I say, fishing around in my head for something else to say in return. "Umm . . . how's lacrosse going?"

Eben sighs, leaning back. "It's okay. When I told Coach I'd already done today's workout in gym class, he gave me this big lecture on straining muscles and sports injuries. It's like I'm this secret weapon he's terrified of breaking or something."

I remember what Roya said about how Eben is a lacrosse star. "But you've been playing lacrosse forever, right? You know what you're doing."

He fiddles with the sleeve on his cup. "Coach treats me differently from the other players, benching me for scrimmages and saving me for games. Some of the seniors say it isn't fair. . . ." He trails off.

Sports are so weird. "Gotcha," I say, even though I still don't understand.

"It's been pretty stressful, to be honest," Eben admits, his bright eyes dimming. "If we don't make the playoffs, I'll feel like it's my fault. The other players will think it was a mistake to recruit me."

That's how I feel about the Battle of the Bands. I'm not expecting to win, of course, but what if we completely bomb? I stay quiet. I don't think that's something my bandmate would want to hear.

"Yo, Five!" a Polk student shouts as he walks through the coffee shop doors. He's definitely a junior or a senior, judging from the car keys he's swinging in his hand.

Eben's face morphs from a dejected droop into that

same grin I've seen on his social media feed. "Hey, man!" Eben shouts. "Lacrosse team," he explains to me. "Reed, this is my friend Azar." Reed gives me a nod, probably wondering, *What the hell is* he *doing with* her?

"Yo" is all he says, his huge hands swinging his lacrosse lanyard the way Eben does.

"Hi."

"We're in a band together," Eben adds, leaning back in the wooden café chair. And then he casually puts his arm around my chairback. As if we're . . . As if he and I are . . .

"Oh," Reed says, his eyes wide. "It's like that, huh?"

What is it like, Reed? I don't dare turn around. I feel rooted to the chair now, unable to look at Eben and investigate what this arm-on-my-chair move means.

"Yeah," Eben confirms. "We're doing the Battle of the Bands."

Reed raises his eyebrows. "Better not let Coach know. See ya, Five."

Reed grabs his drink and exits, but Eben's arm is still around my chair. I finally remember to breathe.

"So . . . what's this?" I finally say, gesturing to his extended forearm. I try not to notice how nice and muscular it is. It feels like a pervy thing to note.

"What's what?" Eben asks. Then he looks where I'm looking. "Oh, sorry." He retracts the arm, and I almost wish I hadn't said anything.

"So . . ." I begin.

At the same time, he says, "Yeah . . ."

I look him straight in the eye. "Is this a date? Is that why you got me hot chocolate?"

Eben flushes, and his auburn hair looks even redder, to match his face. "I . . . um . . ." I try hard not to smile as I watch him flail. I've never been on a date before. Heck, I've never even gotten a café drink with a friend. The small space suddenly feels brighter and cozier and more romantic than before. I'm pretty sure I'm on a date with Eben Lloyd Hollins the Fifth.

"My cousin is my best friend. All I do is watch cartoons, George Clooney movies, and YouTube music tutorials. I'm pretty sure your friends think I'm mute. Won't dating me be social suicide for you and your Lax Bro friends?"

Eben looks completely bewildered. "What are you even talking about?"

My bravado loses steam. "Me and you," I croak. "Aren't we, like, complete opposites?"

Eben suddenly yanks on the back of my chair, bringing me even closer. The drumroll of my heart reaches a fever pitch, and I try not to take a huge gulp of his fresh laundry smell. "You're the only person I share lyrics with. And let meet my sister. And makes me feel like I have a lot more to offer than running around on a field hitting people with sticks."

"I did not say that."

"You thought it, though. When you asked me to sing for the band." Eben raises an eyebrow at me.

"Okay, but I didn't say it out loud."

"I think you're really cool, Azar." His amber eyes beam into mine. "Maybe we could get more warm beverages together?"

I smile so big, I can feel cold air on all my teeth, even the ones in the back. "Okay."

Across the coffee shop, I hear that trademark lisp. "See? I knew it!" Sydney cries, pointing accusingly at me. I don't bother turning around.

"Let's get out of here," I say.

Eben grabs my hand, the calluses from my drumsticks rubbing across his rough lacrosse palms, and together, we float out of the coffee shop.

NAILED IT

ROYA NAZEMIAN *5:05 P.M.*: Listen, if he paid for your drink and doesn't expect you to pay him back, he must like you a lot.

        AZAR ROSSI *5:06 P.M.*: now i have to head to rehearsal with him and pretend my face isn't on fire

ROYA NAZEMIAN *5:06 P.M.*: Whenever someone asks me out and I say yes, I just let myself bask in the feeling. You should try it!

        AZAR ROSSI *5:07 P.M.*: what do you mean whenever. How many guys have asked you out

ROYA NAZEMIAN *5:07 P.M.*: Maybe if you weren't such a troll over text I would tell you!

Letting go of Eben's hand when we get to the band room is hard, but pivoting from Date Azar to Bandmate Azar is even harder. All rehearsal, I have to remind myself to not look at Eben when he sings. I can't help it. I watch his Adam's apple bob next to the microphone. It's practically pornographic.

Get it together, Azar.

"We need to take it from the bridge," I croak, pointing a drumstick at Matty. "You're getting off tempo with your solo there."

Matty looks around the room in disbelief. "Me? Nadim's bass line is all over the place!"

"Hey, don't look at me. I am the rock." Nadim huffs.

"I mean, I could have been off, too," Eben says diplomatically.

I snap my gum. "Nope, it's the guitar. You're letting the notes bleed into the next measure."

Matty has never played guitar in a band before. At least Nadim plays bass in orchestra, and Eben has played piano for church in an ensemble. Matty on the guitar, like me, has been a solo act his whole life. But unlike Matty, I'm a drummer, which means I have a metronome buried deep in my heart, where all the warm and fuzzy feelings should be. I couldn't be off tempo now if I tried.

We take it from the top again, but it's no use. Matty's taking up too much time.

"Maybe if we trimmed it a bit . . ." Eben offers.

"Or you could go slower," Matty says to me, like that's a reasonable request.

It's a ballad. How much slower can we go? That's like asking the Sistine Chapel if it could lower its ceiling a teeny bit so you can paint it better: impossible.

I pinch the bridge of my nose. "I think your solo's too complicated. It's too flowery, and you've got a bunch of notes that you don't need. Make it simple."

Matty puts a hand to his chest, scandalized. "I can't just change it now. The song spoke to me. These are the notes it gave me."

I try to summon the feelings of teamwork and collaboration that Victoria spoke of. Instead, I give Matty a scowl. *Do not test me today, Matty.*

"Okay, okay," he says quickly. "Let's give it a shot."

We take it from the top. It's still a disaster.

By the time we make it through our two songs, it's practically 8:00 p.m. They don't sound amazing, and they definitely won't win us any awards, but they didn't fall apart!

Eben plays the last note on his keyboard, sustaining it. Then there's silence. We all look at each other, stunned that we made it this far.

"WE DID IT!" Nadim shouts. "WE ARE A REAL BAND!"

"Being in a band is a state of mind, Nadim. We were *always* a band," Matty says in an annoyingly zen-like voice.

As I look around the band room, I realize it's true: we have a real, actual band. Practicing has paid off. Nadim's holding the bass without looking like he's going to drop it. Matty seems focused for once, instead of having a dreamy look on his face and replying to everything with the word *totally*.

And Eben, well, it's hard to explain Eben. Before, he looked like he didn't fit in the room; like he didn't make sense in the space. But now he looks more at home with a microphone than a lacrosse stick, and that seems like a small miracle.

"Again," I intone.

"Again?" Eben cries. "But we just nailed it!"

"We can do better!"

Something rustles. I spin my head back to Nadim, who is eating potato chips.

"What?" he says. "I'm hungry."

"From the top!" I shout hoarsely. I tap out a *one-two-three-four!* on my sticks, letting my drums do the talking. Nadim shoves the bag of chips into his pocket and starts with the opening bass line.

Just because we got through a song without messing up doesn't mean we're done. Now we have to finesse the music, add in crescendos and accents, make sure every single thing is finely tuned so we nail our gig.

Eben's voice comes in, stronger than our last run-through.

We sound *good*. Better than that, we sound *tight*. After an awkward start, we've got the beat and parts down, everyone giving way to each other. We've hit our groove, and if you'd told me we'd get here a few weeks ago, I would have spurted kombucha in your face.

We're really a band.

We go through our two songs for Battle of the Bands one more time, and I end with a flourish on the cymbals, just like Victoria taught me. Eben grins, and Nadim looks like he isn't calculating what to say in English, he looks so at ease.

Matty smiles at some invisible force I can't see, but then he turns to the group and says, "Now all we need is a name."

Damn it.

He's right.

SATURDAY

WE'RE AT MY grandparents' house again, and even though they've got the heaters on, it's still freezing on their patio. I huddle under a heat lamp next to Roya as I tell her about yesterday's rehearsal.

"Oh my gosh!" she squeals. "Azar, you're a rock star! Your band is going to kill it at the battle!"

I pop a piece of chicken kabob into my mouth. "I know, right?"

"When are you going to let me come see you guys practice?"

I choke. "Why would you want to come?"

"To see you play, of course!" Roya shivers in her baby-blue puffer jacket, holding a cup of tea between her hands. I chew my food slowly.

"You can if you want," I say with a shrug. "But you have better things to do on a Friday afternoon, right?"

Roya looks thoughtful. "Mackenzie Lawler *did* invite me to her birthday party, but this sounds way more fun."

"I get it. You're super popular and well adjusted." I take a sip of tea. "Then you can meet the rest of the band, at least."

"Yeah, and *Eben*," Roya adds. My eyes flick over to Mom, worried she heard what Roya said, but she's in deep discussion with the other adults. They're probably talking about her plan to go back to school and Dad's move to Tysons. I don't feel like telling Mom about my first date and inevitably getting a lecture on birth control.

Roya must see how uncomfortable I am, because she suddenly shouts to our family, "Okay, we're going to go watch a movie inside, bye!"

"Be good!" Mom shouts. "And NO SODA!"

Roya leads me into the basement and pulls something out of her backpack, placing it on the glass coffee table. "Here," she says, "I've been meaning to do this with you."

It's a glossy magazine. "There's a quiz," Roya explains as she picks it up and thumbs through the pages, looking for the right one. "And I think you should take it."

I shrug, grabbing sodas from the fridge. Soda isn't necessarily bad for my throat, but the preservatives in the ingredients list send Mom into a tailspin. I am a terrible daughter. "Fine. But I'm not a big quiz person."

Roya lies on the floor, the magazine pages splayed out in front of her. "Okay, first question: 'Is it easy for you to have a crush on someone?' The answers are 'Yes' or 'Sometimes' or 'I rarely have crushes.'"

I sit down next to her on the thick carpet. "The last one," I shrug. I don't think I've *ever* had a crush on someone until now.

Roya makes a note with her "executive pen," a nice silver one I got her for her birthday a couple years ago. "Right. Okay. Next question: 'Do you find other people sexually appealing?'"

I yelp. "Roya!"

She holds up her perfectly manicured hands, the ones she updates every week with her own at-home gel kit. "Bear with me here, okay? I'm trying to figure something out. And I think you need to figure it out, too. The choices are 'Yes,' 'Sometimes,' or 'Rarely.'"

"Rarely," I say with a sigh, popping in a fresh stick of gum. This kind of stuff reminds me of middle school, where every break during gym or field trips would just devolve into talking about boys, and I'd sit there quietly, not sure what to say.

It's not that I don't *like* guys. I know in some deep, fuzzy place in my mind that I'm straight. Girls who can blabber on about their crushes are completely alien to me, though. How can you have crushes on so many different people?

"Okay, next: 'What is your idea of a good date?' Your choices are 'A one-night stand' or 'Dinner and a movie' or 'Grabbing drinks and talking.'"

I groan, super uncomfortable now. "A one-night stand? Really?"

"Okay, so don't pick that one, then!" she huffs.

"Fine, the drinks-and-talking one."

She flips her hair back around her shoulders and makes a note in the quiz. "Okay, last one: 'What's more important to you?' The answers are 'Being sexually attracted to someone,' 'Connecting both physically and emotionally,' or 'Connecting with them as friends first.'"

I shake my head, beyond uncomfortable now. "Roya, why are you making me answer all these?"

"Azar!" Roya pleads. "Come on!"

"How can you think someone is hot if you don't even know them, though?" I push back. "You can't just see a guy on the street you've never talked to before and be like, *Wow, he's hot! I am sexually attracted to him!*" I cross my arms over my chest, settling the matter.

Roya doesn't say anything. She just stares at me like I grew a second head.

"What?" I reply, my voice getting husky from all this talking. "What'd I say?"

"Umm," Roya responds, like she's searching for the right words. "The truth is, most people *do* just see a guy on the street and think he's hot, Azar."

"Oh." I feel like I just opened the door to a classroom I'm not assigned to.

"Do you know what a demisexual is?" Roya asks, pointing to the magazine.

I shrug. Heterosexual. Pansexual. Demisexual. If it has the word *sexual* in it, chances are it makes me anxious and my eyes skip over the word.

"According to this quiz, it just means you value an

emotional connection with someone over a physical one. Like, you aren't attracted to people the way most of the population is."

I bite my lip. The truth is, I've *never* liked someone before. How can you tell if someone's cute when you barely know them? What if they kick puppies in their spare time, or pronounce *electric bass* like it's a fish? That's worse than Eben's *jalapeño* flaw.

I think about Eben, and how with every conversation we have, my feelings toward him grow more and more intense. Is that what liking someone means?

"Yeah," I say in a small voice. "I think you're right."

I google *demisexual* on my phone, praying it doesn't come up with any gross results. I read out loud: "'Demisexuality is a sexual orientation characterized by only experiencing sexual attraction after making a strong emotional connection with a specific person.'"

"Yep," Roya adds, looking at her magazine. "It means you 'prefer connecting to someone through their personality, rather than physical traits.'"

"Whoa," I say out loud. I feel seen, like my whole body is a tuning fork and it's just been struck. "So, wait." I turn to Roya. "You can just see a picture of someone and decide you like them?"

Roya shrugs. "I mean, they could still be a jerk and we aren't a good match. But yeah, I can be attracted to them. How do you think porn works? They just sit there and talk about their feelings?"

"Roya!" I throw a pillow at her. "Stop!"

She giggles. "Sorry! But aren't you glad you know now? That probably explains why you *never* crushed on anyone. Because you didn't *know* anyone!"

I cover my face with my hands so she can't see how red it is. "Yeah, I guess I am glad that I know. Thanks for the quiz."

Roya pops open her soda. "Cheers," she says, clinking her can against mine.

"How did you know I was demisexual or whatever?" I ask her. The label still feels weird. Maybe I'll drop the "whatever" when I'm ready.

Roya takes a sip of Coke. "One of the guys in my grade is. Everyone in our year took the quiz after that."

"Oh." Roya's entire eighth-grade class feels so much further ahead of me.

"Some people go their whole lives and never learn this about themselves," Roya adds, watching my face carefully. "It's good to know!"

I nod again, not sure what else to say.

"Besides," Roya adds, "now you can tell me all about how you've been *emotionally connecting* with Ebenezer Lloyd Hollins the Fifth."

I throw another pillow at her.

"Tell me I'm wrong!" she says. "First hot chocolate, then true love."

This time she ducks before the pillow can even reach her.

REHEARSAL

FRIDAY. *FINALLY.*

> **ROYA NAZEMIAN** *4:45 P.M.*: Have fun
> with Eben today!! :) :) :) :)
> > > **AZAR ROSSI** *4:55 P.M.*: shut up

I've got the band room arranged the way I need for practice, and I finally found a proper brush set for my drum kit. Not only that, but I dragged over a whiteboard so I can keep a tally of our notes for each run-through.

Matty's the first to show up, with his boyfriend, and Fabián gives him a kiss before saying goodbye.

"Chau, lindo," Fabián calls out.

"Hasta pronto," Matty replies, grinning.

I give Matty an awkward wave hello and go back to

adjusting my drum kit. The truth is, I don't know much about him. I know he's involved in the arts and that he's some kind of South American like me, but that's about it. Him being a grade above means I have limited intel.

I watch from my little corner as he gets out his guitar and makes a call on his phone. The more I get to know Matty, the more it seems like his boyfriend dresses him. Gone are the plain white tees and jeans. Today he's got on one of those fancy sweaters with a toggle at the collar, offset by a pair of ripped skinny jeans and combat boots. His earrings are gold crosses.

"¿Mamá?" he says on the phone. "Sí, tengo que practicar . . . Mmm . . . ¿Milanesas? Bueno, bueno, sí, ya lo hice. Okay, bye."

A cymbal crashes in my brain. He has the *exact* same accent as my abuelo, the same one Mom uses whenever she speaks Spanish. Is Matty Argentinian?

Matty must catch me staring weirdly at him, because he says, "You okay?"

I nod, swallowing down my question. It's not my place to ask.

"Wait," Matty says slowly. "Do you speak Spanish? Did you understand all that?"

"Yeah," I croak. "My grandpa is from Argentina."

"No way!" Matty lights up. "My parents are both from Buenos Aires. That's so cool! You'll have to come over for an asado—you eat asado, right?"

"Of course," I respond, offended. Matty just smiles.

"This is great. Fabián's Mexican, but he says asado is 'too heavy.'"

I laugh. "That's because it is." Having a meal consisting entirely of meat is *not* good for you, but Argentinians love their steak. There's a reason the national drink of Argentina is yerba mate, a leafy juice that helps you poop. It's just about the only green thing Abuelo consumes every day. Matty starts laughing too.

"What are you two chuckling about?" Eben breezes into the band room, this time lugging a keyboard. My heart skips a beat, and I remind myself to breathe when his honey eyes meet mine.

"Our families are both from Argentina. We just had a revelation."

Eben sets his keyboard down. "Wait, I thought you were from Iran?"

"Um, my mom is Argentinian and Iranian. And my dad is Italian." Even though this feels like such a basic part of my identity, I forget that other people probably don't know. I mean, look at my name—Azar Rossi. There's a story in there, for sure. I just don't always tell it.

Nadim walks in. About time. "Hey, sorry I'm late."

Today's the first time we're rehearsing with Eben's keyboard instead of the piano at school, plus we're using Matty's nice amps. Nadim gets out his electric bass, and I note with pride how at ease he now looks with the instrument. I take it as a good omen.

He sits on the chair I placed for him and looks up at me. Eben and Matty take their seats too. It feels strange taking the lead, but I'm starting to realize that I like it. "Today I want to finalize Eben's song and the new arrangements we've been working on." Everyone's nodding as I talk. That's good.

"Eben, you wanna show us your new keyboard line?"

Eben grins, but now I can tell that behind that grin is a sliver of nervousness. *You don't fool me, Ebenezer.*

"Sure."

I sit behind my drum kit while Eben turns on the keyboard and cracks his knuckles. He clears his throat and begins the second song we're performing for the battle, which starts unaccompanied. His strong voice fills the huge band room with just a single breath.

> *I've been hoping*
> *That the struggle isn't real.*
> *Been thinking*
> *About the things that we can't feel.*

It's the same lyrics from before, but when Eben presses into a major chord on his keyboard, the song is suddenly anthemic and larger than life. Matty smiles, nodding in time to the music. Nadim taps his toes, adding a simple bass line of downbeats.

> *Smiles can't hide everything*
> *When you hate everything, and*

They say that it gets better,
But there never is a calendar.

Nadim gives me a look like, *C'mon, Azar!* And before I know it, I'm adding the bass drum. I pump my leg in time to Eben's singing, letting him take the lead. *We're really doing it!* I want to scream. *We're playing to sound good! Not just playing to completion!* Matty joins in, adding a countermelody to Eben's solid chords on the piano. I think of that band from Baltimore that opened for Amy Waters, and how we look like them now.

Eben's voice changes slightly for the bridge, getting stronger and smoother as he finds his groove. I add some snare, like a chef adding spices.

So, smile and wave, take the applause,
Bask in the praise till it rubs you raw.

What's the point of feeling sad
When the gold is glinting?
What's the point of feeling bad
When your team is winning?

Even though this song is what most people would call a ballad, it sounds powerful and inspiring, not sad and gloomy. The last time I heard him sing it, this was where the lyrics had stopped. Eben closes his eyes, ignoring the new lyrics he'd written neatly in the notebook on his music stand, reciting the words from memory.

I've been thinking
About the lives that we can't lead.
Been dreaming about the people we can't be.

I strain to hear his voice over the booming echo my
foot makes every time it touches the bass drum pedal,
so I ease up. Even with the new amps, it's tough to hear
him, and I remind myself to give his voice space. Nadim
and Matty instinctually back off their instruments, too,
letting Eben's voice shine.

With each new day,
I'm stuck in place,
Still in the middle of the race.
Going through motions,
While my heart swims through oceans.
I've been hoping . . .

I stare at Eben as his voice fades out. I had completely
forgotten to accompany him on the drums for the last
stanza, but who could blame me? His voice was so raw,
it felt like it could shatter, and hearing the pain in his
voice toward the end felt like something I didn't want to
mess with.

As his voice tapers off, it's like I can still hear the echo
of the song, the power of the ballad floating in the room,
even though we can't hear it anymore. Victoria calls that
sound the release, when you can still hear the energy in
the silence.

"Wow," Nadim says, dumbstruck.

"That was strong." Matty nods. "You've really got something there, Eben."

Eben's eyes slowly make their way to mine, as if he's most worried about what I'll have to say. I pick my jaw up off the floor.

"That was really, really good."

He smiles at me, his face flushed. It's not the easy grin he turns on for everyone, or the thousand-kilowatt beam I've seen on his social media. This is a tiny, shy smile. The kind that people have when they think no one else is looking. And for a second, it feels like it's just the two of us.

"Nice bass line," Matty adds, turning to Nadim. The spell is broken. Eben looks away, and I take a sip of water, sweaty from playing just one song.

"That countermelody was so good!" Nadim exclaims. "Is that the one you were working on before?"

Matty nods, launching into a spiel about the circle of fifths. I have no idea what they're talking about.

Eben sidles over to me while the other two are distracted. "Nice beat," he says, tilting his head toward my drum kit.

"Thanks."

"What do you think, guys?" he says, interrupting Matty and Nadim's now passionate discussion on music theory. "Wanna try again?"

Nadim nods vigorously. "Yes, please." Matty whoops. Eben looks at me.

"Azar, you ready?"

"Yeah." I smile. "I'm ready."

SUNDAY

THE WEEKEND IS a blur from sleeping over at my grand-parents', Farsi school, and drum lessons. By the time Sunday night rolls around, I need another weekend of doing nothing to feel like I got any rest. Next week is the first week of March, and soon after that is spring break. My surgery looms like a Hans Zimmer score.

"Azar?" Mom says, nudging me on the couch. "You awake?"

"Yeah," I say, taking a sip of kale stew that she made. I search the bowl for a chickpea and chew on it slowly. Mom pauses *O Brother, Where Art Thou?* and turns to me, George Clooney's pencil-thin mustache staring at us.

"So, we haven't really had a chance to talk since your father came to visit."

I nod, putting my bowl down. Mom's clearly gearing up for a Parent Talk.

She clears her throat importantly. "When I was a freshman in college, I dropped out so I could take care of you, which I definitely do not regret." Mom's eyes search mine, like she wants me to be 100 percent sure that I am wanted and loved.

I roll my eyes. "Yeah, Mom, I know."

"Right. But since I'm going to school, I won't be able to pay rent on this apartment, and the lease is up soon. It doesn't make sense to renew it."

"Okay . . ." Where is this going?

"So, I'm going to have to move back in with your grandparents for a while. Save up a bit while I'm still working." Mom sighs, but I'm too stunned to feel bad for her.

"Wait—" I start, hating how whiny I sound. "But what about my room? And my stuff? Their house only has one spare bedroom!"

Mom reaches out to stroke my face, but I recoil.

"Azar, you'll have your own room at your dad's place. Besides, it's only for two years. Your grandparents' house isn't in the Polk school district, anyway."

I blink. What is happening? Is she really saying . . . ? does that mean . . . ?

"You can come over whenever you want, though. Their couch is a pullout, remember?" she says, as if this is supposed to make me feel better.

"But . . . that means . . ." I whisper, my throat choking up too much to speak properly. "That means we won't be living together." I thought Mom was worried that Dad being here meant she'd spend less time with me. But she's making it sound like she doesn't want to spend any time with me *at all.* "That's it, then? You're dropping me off with Dad?"

"Z, come on, it's not like that," Mom says, reading my stormy face. "I just can't afford to renew the lease *and* go to school, since I won't be able to work full-time. Cut me some slack, okay? I'll still be here for you!"

My mom has been the one real constant in my life. No matter what happened, I could always count on her to cue up a George Clooney movie and stroke my hair. Through strep and sinus infections, bad batches of homemade kombucha and SoundCloud sessions, we've been through *everything* together. And now, instead of knocking on her bedroom door, she'll be an entire car ride away.

This can't be real. My life just doesn't work without Mom by my side.

It feels like the second I get Dad closer to me, I lose my mom. It's like we can't ever be a normal family, *ever.*

Don't cry don't cry don't cry.

"Z?" Mom asks. "Did you hear me?"

I get up from the couch and make my way to the front door, grabbing my boots and jacket. I can't breathe in here. The apartment feels too small, too stifling, too in control of our family's destiny. I've never been grounded, never gotten in a screaming match with my mom, never even so much as slammed a door. But now I can feel fourteen years' worth of fights surging out of me.

I spin around to face her. "If you didn't want me around, Mom, you could have just said so."

"Azar, that's not what's happening here! Wait, where are you going? Azar?" Mom's voice sounds anxious in a way it hasn't since Dr. Talbot's office. A small part of me feels bad that I'm making her feel this way, but another part of me enjoys the feeling.

"I'm going to Nadim's," I announce.

And then I slam the door as hard as I can.

🎧

It's almost 8:00 p.m., and I slip and slide my way down the icy stairs to the ground-floor apartments in the dark. When I knock on Nadim's door, a man I've never met before opens it.

"Hi . . . is Nadim home?" I ask. He's got thick-framed glasses and a neat black beard. His copper skin shines like Nadim's, but they don't look related.

"Come in, come in!" the man insists, even though he probably has no clue who I am. Middle Eastern hospitality is hardcore like that.

I step into the warm apartment, the smells of tea and spice surrounding me like a tight hug. In the background I can hear the news in Arabic.

"Azar?" Nadim says, stepping out of the kitchen with a wooden spoon. "Are you okay?"

The person who must be Nadim's host father motions me toward the kitchen, saying, "Please, please," and I slip off my boots before following him to a dining room, where the table's been set.

"Hey, Nadim," I mumble, my face hot from my fight. I've clearly barged in on their dinner.

"Are you all right?" Nadim asks. "You look upset."

My throat feels tight, and my eyes feel puffy as they try to hold back tears. "Do you think I could stay here for a bit?" I ask, my voice breaking.

Nadim's host mom sweeps past him before he can answer. She has a bright pink apron on, and her honey-blonde hair sticks out in wiry strands. "Of course, of course!" she says, fluttering her hands. "My name is Nourie. Have you eaten? Nadim—" she begins, then says something in rapid-fire Arabic that I don't get.

"Yeah, I already ate. But thank you."

Nadim shakes his head. "She's already said she's going to make a plate for you. It's too late now."

"Actually, food sounds great." Kale soup isn't exactly filling.

"Please," Nourie says, gesturing to the dining room.

Nadim follows me to their big wooden table and hands me a glass of water. He looks totally at ease in this space, as if he's lived in this apartment for years.

"I didn't know your host parents also spoke Arabic," I say, watching as Nadim's host mom pours me some tea.

"They're family friends. Their son is in college, so they asked if I wanted to try Polk's exchange program."

"Nice." I nod. Then I fiddle with the cloth napkin on the

table, feeling awkward. I knew I had to leave our apartment before I said something I'd regret to Mom. But now that I'm here at Nadim's, I have no idea what to say at all.

"What happened?" he asks. Nadim's host parents head back to the kitchen to get the food, both of them out of earshot.

"My mom and I had a fight." I take a sip of my water, the grip in my throat easing. I hope Mom isn't worrying about me. For once in my life, I'm being a bad kid. The kind who makes their mother worry all night. I check my phone, and sure enough, there are a zillion texts from Mom, and missed calls, too. It's only been five minutes, but she must be freaking out.

AZAR ROSSI *8:23 P.M.*: mom i'm at
Nadim's in 105 i just need some space

I get an instant reply back.

MOM *8:23 P.M.*: Okay. I understand.
Be home before 10, please.

I put the phone away and turn to Nadim, who still has an open, patient expression on his face. "We're moving," I explain, my voice cracking all over again.

He shifts in his head-to-toe Polk gear, from his blue sweatpants to his red sweatshirt. "I'm sorry, Azar. That really sucks."

"Yeah," I say in a small voice, already thinking of how I won't be living in this building for much longer. "She's going back to school, and she can't afford to keep renting our apartment, so she's moving in with my grandparents on the other side of town while I move in with my dad."

Just then, Nourie sets a heaping plate of food in front of me. There's rice that smells like cardamom, some kind of eggplant dish, and a heaping pile of flatbread. She's also put a couple different kinds of pickles and olives on the outside of the plate, along with a dollop of hummus topped with pine nuts.

"You look too thin, Azar!" She tsks. This serving is enough to feed my mom and me for days.

"Whoa," I balk.

Nadim shrugs. "I told you she'd make you eat. But you're moving? Does this mean I won't see you anymore?"

"My dad's moving into our school district, so I'll still be able to go to Polk. But no walking to school together."

I take a bite of pita, relishing the gluten. Nadim, instead of being sympathetic, like Roya would be, shrugs again. "That sounds like it's a good thing. You don't want to stay in this apartment complex forever. Even my host parents are trying to figure out how to buy their own place and get out of here."

He gestures to the small space and the browning tiles on the ceiling, as if to say, *It's not that great.*

I curl my fingers around the bread, defensive. "I know. I'm just going to really miss living with my mom."

Nadim swipes a piece of bread from my plate, dipping it into some hummus. "Your mom is trying to make sure you can get a better home later. She is giving up a lot. Like my parents did, sending me here."

I chew slowly. "Does it get easier? Living away from your parents?"

Nadim bites his lip. "I miss them so, so much. But I know this will all be worth it in the end. I'm grateful for the opportunity."

I take a deep breath. Nadim's family is thousands of miles away, and here I am, complaining about a short car ride.

He laughs. "Besides, I would love to live in a place with hot water that doesn't run out!"

It's my turn to laugh. The hot water in this building is abysmal. I forgot that moving to Dad's means that I'll be able to shower as long as I want. "Good point," I say. I can feel the anger seeping out of me, being replaced with exhaustion. We're really doing this. In a couple months, my mom and I will no longer live in the same home. My heart aches as it accepts this fact.

I take a bite of eggplant and mix it with the rice on the plate. Nourie bustles in to check on me just then.

"See, Nadim? She eats like a Lebanese!"

"Thank you for dinner," I say. Nourie just tsks again, as if thanking her is an insult. She quickly heads back to the kitchen, where I suspect she's making even more food for us.

"I think she thinks we're dating," Nadim whispers, trying hard not to laugh. I nearly choke on my food.

"If she thinks we're dating, does that mean I can get more pita?"

Nadim grins. "Definitely."

LIBRARY

NADIM DIDN'T MENTION anything about me coming over for dinner to our lunch group, and for that I'm grateful. Even though I've wrapped my head around the move, that didn't stop me from sniffling into my pillow all night. Between my awkward silence with Mom on the car ride she insisted on giving me to school to Nadim giving me an extra-long hug today, I feel like I'm still on edge.

Eben and I meet up in the library after class, and I pull up the chapters I summarized for our English presentation. Spring break is in two weeks, which means we present in three.

He grins. "Nice formatting!" he says, noting how I matched mine to his.

I grimace. "Least I can do, since you'll be the one presenting."

"Oh, yeah." Had he forgotten my surgery already? "Did you like the book?" he says, awkwardly trying to change the subject, as if discussing surgery is taboo.

"It was okay." *The Heart Is a Lonely Hunter* was kind of a bummer.

"I like the girl in the book, Mick Kelly," Eben says. "She pretends to be tough and hard, but she's just a big softie."

My eyes narrow. "Interesting. Do you need anything else from me for the presentation? I can make the Power-Point if you want."

Eben flips his laptop open and smiles. "Already done." It's a flashy grin, the kind that orthodontists show as the "after" picture in their lobby. I remember my conversation with Roya about being demisexual and my stomach swoops. Behind that smile is a really nice person, not just good orthodontia. It makes sense that I'd be into someone who is kind.

"My hero." I beam back at him. I have never smiled as much in my life as I do around Eben.

"So . . ." he begins. I say nothing, waiting for him to finish, when in my head, all I want to scream is *GOD HAVING CRUSHES IS SO AWKWARD WHY DO PEOPLE EVEN HAVE THEM?*

"Are you doing anything fun after rehearsal on Friday night?"

Anything fun? I want to ask. If by "fun" you mean eating the nonorganic ice cream I stashed in the back of our freezer, then yes, I am doing something super fun on Friday. But I know that's not what Eben means.

"Probably just writing lyrics."

Eben nods. "Yeah, cool, no. It's just—um, do you want to do something? Like, we could see a movie? Or grab some food? Or just hang out?"

"Umm," I say, unable to meet his eyes. But my body feels like it's on fire, as if the little prickles I get around Eben have finally caught on to a full flame. Maybe demisexual people don't have a *lot* of crushes, but when we do, we nearly explode.

Eben sits there expectantly, not realizing my body is going through a full combustion cycle. *A date. He wants to take me on a date. That means his outfit probably won't have mesh in it.*

"Yes," I reply, my voice clear and even for once. It's the voice of my dreams, the one that I draft lyrics to. *Thank you, body!* I say in silent gratitude.

"Great," Eben says, beaming.

I nod. I don't trust myself to speak up again, not after the amazing way my throat delivered that *Yes.*

"We can leave after rehearsal," he says, nodding like I'd managed to say something. "And get some food or whatever. Or ice cream. I mean, that's food. If you want." He's nervous again, and I notice his hands shake on the library table. But for once, it's for a good reason. It's because of *me.*

HOME

"AZAR?" MOM CALLS out. "I brought kabob." I can hear the rustle of plastic bags through my bedroom door, a sound that's incredibly rare in this tote-bag-loving household. I sniff the air hopefully, and sure enough, I can smell the real butter on the rice along with sumac sprinkled on top.

Mom and I haven't really talked since our fight. I guess this is her version of a peace offering. I crack open my door.

"Can I just eat in here?" I rasp.

"Nope." Mom shakes her head. "If you want to eat kabob, you gotta eat it out here." She's already setting out place mats on the lip of our kitchen counter, which means I can't bank on the TV to drown out whatever tension there'll be from our shared meal. I sigh and shuffle into the kitchen.

Mom pats the bar stool next to her, and I clamber up. She even got me lamb kabob, the red meat acting like an olive branch. My mouth waters. I reach for my fork, ready to spear a piece, when she slides the place mat out from under me, the food just out of reach.

"So," she begins. "We need to talk about our conversation on Sunday."

Here it goes.

"I know you're upset about moving, but I need you to understand why it's so important to me."

Her eyes are shiny, and I can see her lower lip tremble. A crescendo of guilt rises through me. *I'm* the reason she's trying so hard not to cry.

"When I started college, I thought I was going to join the Peace Corps afterward, or work at the United Nations, or get a job at a nonprofit that's trying to change the world. And even though I *did* eventually get a job at a nonprofit, it's as a project manager. My job is to plan other people's projects. People who went to college. The ideas are not my own. So when your dad said he was moving here, I knew this was my last chance to put my own stamp on the world. Do you understand what I mean?"

I bite my lip, picking apart Mom's words. I never knew she wanted to join the Peace Corps. Or work for the UN. Here I've been dreaming about having my own band and making it as a musician, but I never stopped to think what Mom's dreams were.

"I hate the idea of moving back in with my parents.

It makes me feel nauseous just thinking about being back in that house. But I know it's what's best for us. So by the time you graduate high school and you head off to make your own dreams come true, I'll be doing the same thing. And *both* of us will be on birth control." Mom winks.

I roll my eyes, then reach across her and stab a piece of kabob. I look around our tiny space as I chew. There's the minuscule sink, where our salad bowls can't even fit in the basin, the curled linoleum in the far corner of the kitchen, and the gap between the windowsill and the window that lets in a draft. We have so many memories here, but I'm starting to see that maybe we've outgrown this place.

"I just can't imagine living without you," I say softly, the words harder to get out than if I'd shouted them. "I know this apartment isn't all that great, but it's our home."

"I know, querida. Change is hard. And this is a big one."

"Yeah." I sniff pathetically, for once relishing Mom's pity. Change *is* hard. And uprooting our whole life feels like a big turning point—one I'm not ready to take yet.

"But your dad's place will be amazing, and you can come see me *anytime*. I mean it. Besides . . ." Mom adds, a small smile creeping over her face. "I bet Maman Bozorg will cook like crazy whenever you come over."

"Really?" I ask, eyes wide. "Not just for our barbecues?"

Mom grimaces. "They're going to spoil you rotten. Your arteries don't stand a chance."

I giggle, and it sounds like a choppy stream gurgling over rough stones. Still, it feels good to laugh with my mom. She rests a hand on my shoulder.

"It's gonna be okay, Z." Suddenly, I need a hug very, very badly. I hold my arms out, and Mom squeezes me tight.

"But we're getting rid of the soda fridge in their basement," she whispers.

PRE-OP

BEFORE I KNOW it, it's Friday and we're driving to Dr. Talbot's again for my pre-op appointment. This time next week, instead of sitting in Dr. Talbot's office, I'll be walking to the room at the end of the hall that connects to the rest of the doctors' offices in this building. The one they all use for surgeries. Tracy will close down this office, lock the front door, and assist him in surgery. And then, if everything goes well, I won't be able to talk for a couple days before emerging victorious with my new, fresh voice.

"Azar? Did you hear me?" Dr. Talbot says from across his desk. He's got a coffee cup from the gas station next door (not even one of the good gas stations). He takes a sip and I shudder.

"Yeah, sorry."

"As I was saying, your throat still looks like a good candidate, though it's a little worse than the last time I saw you. That just means our timing is even more important now. You can't eat twelve hours before surgery, since we're putting you under twilight anesthesia, and . . ."

I turn to the window, focusing on watching minivans exit the parking lot instead. I can't help it. I don't know how else to deal with the thought of lasers going *Pew! Pew!* into my esophagus.

Mom scribbles down notes next to me, making up for my mental absence. After surgery, I'll have to be on a liquid diet until Dr. Talbot says I can transition to soft foods. Mom's already started freezing pureed edamame. *Why?*

The thought of going under for surgery makes me nervous. But it's nothing compared to knowing I won't be able to talk, not even the meager amount I already do, for a while.

What if an emergency happens and I need to call Mom? Or what if I need to explain something during band rehearsal but can't? I feel my pulse quicken, and my breathing syncs to its speed. I'd woken up calm and relaxed, but the second I'm back in this doctor's office, I'm sweaty and uncomfortable. Part of me is relieved to finally be fixing my throat, but another part of me is terrified at the prospect of surgery.

"Azar?" Dr. Talbot says again.

"Yep." I nod, pretending to understand whatever he's saying. At the end of the day, it doesn't matter if I know what's happening or not. That laser is coming for me regardless.

"Thanks, Dr. Talbot," Mom says, picking up her purse. I wave goodbye and follow her into the lobby.

Tracy hands me the entire bowl of lollipops.

REHEARSAL

DESPITE OUR AMAZING rehearsal last week, the stakes for today's session feel higher. Maybe it's because of my date with Eben afterward. Or maybe it's because it's the last rehearsal we'll have before my surgery on Monday, which means we really need to do well today. We've got two weeks left until Battle of the Bands now. Our songs need to be absolutely perfect.

Everyone's been tightening up their parts at home, and I'm nervous about hearing our new-and-improved sound together. Especially when it comes to my song, the one with the lyrics I worked so hard on.

Eben clears his throat from the front of the band room, where he's been warming up on his keyboard. "Azar, you ready?" Nadim and Matty come to attention, like soldiers about to salute.

Instead of answering, I click my sticks together. *One, two—one, two, three, four!*

Nadim comes in with the bass line, his notes getting more confident with every week of rehearsal. Before, it sounded like he could barely pluck the huge, ropy strings. Now he's a strong, solid bassist. Matty enters with the melody, his guitar dancing in double time compared to Nadim's slower notes. Then Eben's keyboard fills out the sound. I join in a couple bars later, hitting a simple beat on the snare and the bass, bracing myself for when the lyrics that have been so close to my heart leave my brain and emerge from Eben's mouth.

One, two, three, four,
I don't like this anymore.
Shut it all down,
Hide until they hit the floor.

School's for suckers,
Studying's for losers,
'Cause when we finish,
We're still getting bruises.

The words feel off despite Eben's strong and warm voice, like it's at odds with the song's harsh lyrics. Matty's melody sounds like the wrong arrangement now, the minor chords too gentle for the words I wrote. I can already feel my neck flush red as my deepest thoughts are put out there for everyone to hear without the right arrangement supporting it.

What's the point of smiling when the world is doomed?
Life's stupid when people are consumed
By the screens, the beeps, the blings!

One, two, three, four,
I don't like this anymore.
Shut it all down,
Burn it till it hits the ground.

Caring's for suckers,
And crying's for losers,
'Cause when this is over,
We're just flesh and computers.

We get to the end, and I finish it with a loud cymbal crash, my stick slicing into the golden metal. The room is silent. The notes decay into the linoleum band room's echo, leaving a bitter taste in my mouth.

"That was . . . interesting," Nadim says diplomatically. I can't put my finger on it, but whatever magic we had last week seems to have evaporated today. Our song was . . . okay. Not bad. But not stellar, either. Definitely not enough to win the Battle of the Bands.

"Maybe we can try a new arrangement?" Eben asks, searching our eyes. Nadim looks away.

Matty turns to me. "I think the problem is the lyrics."

The worst part about what Matty's saying is that a small, tiny part of me thinks he might be right. That I'm a terrible songwriter and that this was all a mistake.

He must see the look on my face, because he quickly adds, "Don't get upset, Azar, it's just . . . um . . . these lyrics don't really go deep, you know? It's about angsty stuff, not anything vulnerable. Compared to Eben's song, these lyrics just kind of make fun of everyone else."

Eben's written one song in his life, while I have pages and pages crammed with lyrics and melodies that have been stuck in my head. I can feel my defenses go on edge, itching to fight back and tell Matty he has no idea what he's talking about. I bite my lip instead, not sure how to respond.

"Maybe we could tweak them a *bit* . . ." Nadim adds.

Eben, I notice, is quiet. He doesn't defend the song. It's the last rehearsal where I can still speak out loud, yet we're spending it tearing my work apart. My defensiveness morphs into anger. *Hello?* I learned how to play the drums for this band. I wrote all the arrangements by hand for each instrument's stupid clef. But somehow my lyrics are the one and only problem?

"Azar?" Matty ventures. "What do you think?"

All the thoughts swirling in my head crumble apart. My mouth goes dry, and I'm not sure how to stick up for myself.

"I . . . I . . ." It's one thing to talk a good game in my

head, but it's a completely different one to speak it out loud.

Eben clears his throat. "Maybe we can try it again?" he says. *Finally!*

But Matty shakes his head. "Eben, your lyrics are raw and real. These lyrics just feel sarcastic, like they're afraid of trying too hard. There's a disconnect."

My blood boils.

That. Does. It.

"Who put this band together?" I say, throwing down my drumsticks. It's hard not to take any critiques of my lyrics personally. I'm angry now. "I'm the one who asked you all to be here. I'm the one who put the arrangements together. I'm the one who freaking *switched to drums* so you could play guitar, Matty," I add. "And now you've decided that my lyrics are the problem?"

"Whoa, whoa, whoa," Matty says, holding up his hands. "I'm just trying to give constructive feedback! I mean, we all felt that the song wasn't working, right?"

Nadim and Eben give noncommittal nods, and they feel like knives.

"Well, if that's how you guys feel, then maybe I'm just not a good fit for this band. That I put together."

"Azar!" Eben yelps, shocked. "Nobody's saying you need to leave—Matty's just giving his opinion. Like what we did last week with the arrangement for my lyrics. We changed stuff around for that song, too, remember?"

"Yeah, but this is *my* song," I wail. All I wanted was for someone to sing the lyrics in my notebook out loud. And now they're treating my lyrics like an English paper, crossing things out in bright red ink and giving it a failing grade.

"But this is *our* band, not just yours," Matty retorts. He's right. This isn't my band anymore. It wasn't mine to begin with, if I'm being honest. For some reason I still have this vision of me being THE songwriter, the one with notebooks and ink-stained hands.

I look down at my hands. What am I doing here? How did I get so far away from my original vision?

"You're right," I say, grabbing my sticks. "This was a stupid idea anyway. I don't know what I was thinking, and it's not like I'll be able to defend myself anymore after next week. Tell Principle Saulk he'll have to get road salt on his own."

I push my stool out from the bass drum and stomp to the exit. I take one last look at this space, this place where I thought I could share my real self, then close the door.

"Road salt? Wait, Azar!" I hear Eben protest through the glass door, but I don't turn around.

So much for going on my first real date after rehearsal.

So much for making my dreams come true.

The whole point of having this band was to express myself. What's the point of expressing other people's words when it's already hard enough to express my own?

No thanks.

DRUM LESSONS

"WHY DO YOU look like you swallowed a shot of battery acid?" Victoria asks as I squeeze my elbows into my sides. She insisted I put clementines into each of my armpits. If one of them falls out, then I'm not engaging my lats properly.

Since starting drum lessons, my biceps have gotten beefier. My forearm has this new muscle right where it meets my elbow, and I've learned to keep my shoulders away from my ears. Too bad it's all for nothing.

I don't even know why I came to this stupid lesson, since I left the band. But I was past the window for a twenty-four-hour cancellation, and Mom doesn't know I quit on Friday. This is stupid. Everything's stupid.

"Azar?" Victoria asks, poking me with a drumstick.

I shrug her off. "Why is being in a band so hard? All I wanted was someone to sing my lyrics. That's it! Why did they have to go off and judge me, when I don't comment on their stupid melodies, or how they can't even play their instruments?"

It's the most I've said all day, and I can feel that sandpaper-and-saliva feeling unpleasantly creep up my throat. I should probably moderate my volume better, give my throat a chance to rest and heal so I avoid another painful infection. But with surgery in less than twenty-four hours, who cares? Time to use this bad boy up for all it's worth.

"And how can they be the judge of something as personal as lyrics?" I continue. "None of them take creative writing or anything. Who knows if mine are bad? They're mine—no one should mess with them."

Victoria silently takes a seat on a drum stool in the corner, her eyebrows raised. I'm on a roll now, and I'm not about to stop.

"And another thing—" I point at her with a drumstick. "Why do guys assume everything is up for discussion? At least girls *pretend* they like something before they ask you to change it. But dudes just steamroll all over you!" Even Roya indulges me when I'm clearly wrong. But nobody indulged me at Friday night's rehearsal.

I'm so angry, I've probably squeezed these armpit citruses into orange juice. Victoria pops a huge bubble with her gum.

"You done?" she asks, her two hundred earrings glinting along her earlobes.

"Yeah," I say in a much smaller voice.

"Okay," Victoria says, hopping up from the stool. "So you had a fight with your band."

"I left the band," I interject.

"So you left your band," Victoria says without missing a beat. "We've all been there. I've broken up with every band I've ever been a part of, some of them multiple times. Congrats, kid—you've just hit a musician's rite of passage."

"You've broken up with *every* band you've ever been a part of?" I recoil. "That's . . . a lot of bands."

She nods, her black lipstick twisting into a grimace. "I know. It's not pretty. But think about it—you're a creative group, all of you from different backgrounds, trying to nail something as vague and random as a 'good song.' *Of course* you're going to butt heads. That's the creative process!"

I thought breaking up with a band was this super rare and taboo thing. I didn't know it was this common, everyday occurrence.

"I hate the creative process." I chug some water.

"Take a deep breath. Start from the beginning," Victoria says. I put down my drum sticks and clementines. I have a feeling today's lesson is not going to be about drumming.

"This guy, the guy who plays the guitar, which *I* was supposed to play, said we need to change my lyrics."

"So what'd you say?"

"I basically told him to shove it." I shrug. "And then I left."

Victoria cackles. "God, you remind me so much of myself in high school. I *hated* criticism. It always felt so personal, like they were telling me *I* wasn't good enough."

I nod. "Exactly! Who is he to tell me I suck?"

Victoria gives me a sad smile. "That's the thing, though, Azar. He wasn't telling you that *you* suck. He was telling you he thinks your lyrics need work. And you and your lyrics are two different things. Did anyone else agree with him?"

"Everyone . . ." I mumble.

"Huh?"

"Yes, everyone agreed with him!" I bite back. *Do I have to spell it out?*

Victoria twirls my drumstick across her knuckles like a majorette's baton. I make a mental note to ask her to teach me how to do that. "Okay, so, maybe your lyrics *are* the problem. Which I know you hate to hear. But guess what, Azar? You can fix this! Maybe you should take another look at those words. Figure out if you can make them better. Or rework the arrangements to the song. Maybe it's just in the wrong key. Sometimes when people have a criticism, they don't *actually* know what the right solution is, but they're noticing something is off. Did you think something was wrong with that song?"

"Yeah . . ." I say, drifting off in a tiny, pathetic voice. "But why didn't they fight harder for it? Why did they just all suddenly agree my lyrics were terrible two weeks from the show?"

"Your bandmates want to sound good, and you want

to sound good, too. Try to understand where they're coming from. You only split a band apart when someone is being a dick. And I don't think anyone in your crew has been one just yet." Victoria gives an authoritative snap of her gum, as if to say, *Capisce?*

I sneak a look at my phone screen and see that I have missed calls and voice mails from both Eben and Nadim, along with an essay-length text message from Matty from last night. A small part of me feels happy seeing so many notifications pop up on my phone for once, even if it's for a crappy reason, like quitting the band.

Victoria hands me my drumsticks. "Don't give up on something just because it isn't one hundred percent yours, okay?"

I grab the sticks, my heart sinking. I still don't think I was in the wrong, but with my surgery tomorrow, I'm running out of time to figure this all out.

I hit the snare. Victoria doesn't even flinch.

"Okay," I say.

SUNDAY SCARIES

I FINALLY OPEN my text messages. Not because I feel like I need to say anything to the guys, but because there are messages from Roya I should probably answer, too.

> **ROYA NAZEMIAN** *SATURDAY, 10:31 P.M.*: **Sooo?**
> **How did your date go????? I've been texting**
> **you all weekend! Spill!**

I groan, scrolling away. Which leads me right into Matty's text.

> **MATTY FUMERO** *SATURDAY, 8:00 P.M.*: **Hey Azar,**
> **I know things got a little heated, but I wouldn't**
> **have said we needed to change the lyrics if I didn't**
> **believe you have great lyrics inside you already. I**
> **hope you reconsider leaving the band. <3**

COOLEST PERSON EVER!!! *FRIDAY, 7:34 P.M.*:
Azar, call me back, please.
COOLEST PERSON EVER!!! *SATURDAY, 10:29 A.M.*:
Azar?
COOLEST PERSON EVER!!! *SUNDAY, 9:42 A.M.*:
I just want to make sure you're OK
NADIM HADAD *SATURDAY, 5:45 P.M.*:
I know you're home. Your mom's car is here.
Please answer us.
FABIÁN CASTOR *SATURDAY, 9:13 P.M.*:
why is my boyfriend moping around at my
gymnastics meet and not cheering me on?
did something happen?

I put the phone away and take a deep breath. Time to deal with something even harder.

I grab the piece of paper where my lyrics are written:

One, two, three, four,
I don't like this anymore.
Shut it all down,
Hide until they hit the floor.

School's for suckers,
Studying's for losers,
'Cause when we finish,
We're still getting bruises.

I keep reading, and as I do, I hear a feeble, embarrassed voice in my head. *Matty's right, Azar. These lyrics aren't that great. You can do better.*

Eben's lyrics were honest and bared his soul. What are mine showing? Some cynical, whiny teen?

I take a deep breath and remember Amy Waters' words to me at the 9:30 Club. *Just tell the truth.*

My pencil hits the page, and I pray I am brave enough to bare my soul.

SURGERY

IT'S THE FIRST day of spring break, and instead of sleeping in like everyone else, we're heading down the Beltway toward my doom.

Mom looks even more nervous than usual, her body practically folding over the steering wheel so her face is as close to the windshield as possible. To say she is tense is an understatement.

"You ready, Z?" she asks in a shaky voice.

My whole body feels like it's trembling, and my palms haven't stopped sweating since last night, when Mom cut me off from snacks so I wouldn't have food or water twelve hours before surgery.

"Yeah," I growl. Through the fog of fear, a small part of me notes: *This will be the last time you growl like an old man. The next time you're terrified, you'll get to sound like a fourteen-year-old girl.*

Mom pushes open the door and leads me to Dr. Talbot's office, where Tracy is beaming from behind the receptionist's desk.

"Azar!" Her blonde hair is bouncing. "I got you a tub of ice cream," she whispers loudly, as if we're in on a secret together.

"Thanks," I say in an itchy voice that grinds over my throat. I watch as she locks the front door and presses some buttons on her desk phone, probably forwarding calls somewhere, since she'll be in the operating room with me. She beckons us to the back, and my hand scrabbles for Mom's. She holds it tight, then lets go.

"I can't go in with you this time, Azar." She smiles sadly.

"What?" I demand. It's one thing to go without Mom to that first visit to the gynecologist's office, where they ask you super-embarrassing questions. It's another thing to have to undergo an entire surgery without her.

She must see the panic in my eyes, because she rubs my back encouragingly. "Don't worry, Dr. Talbot knows what he's doing. He's done this procedure hundreds of times. In and out, remember? It'll be done before you know it."

"Five hundred and thirty-two times, to be exact." Tracy smiles. "It's gonna be great!" She gives me a wink, trying to comfort me.

"You can do this, Z. I know you can. I love you." Mom gives me a kiss on the forehead.

"I love you, too."

Tracy leads me down the hallway of patient rooms, softly singing something that sounds suspiciously like *"Operation day! Operation day!"* under her breath.

She then unlocks a door with SHERWOOD DOCTORS' PARK OR on it. Everything inside is white and sterile, and there's a patient's chair that looks like it belongs in a dentist's office, not an operating theater.

Seated at a rolling stool in the corner is Dr. Talbot, thankfully without any of his gross meals. He wears glasses that extend a good couple inches from the bridge of his nose, and when he looks up at me, I see they are two square magnifying glasses, like something a jeweler would wear.

"Azar," he says with a nod. "Good, let's get started. You ready?"

My throat's so dry by this point, I can barely respond. I wish I could have chugged a glass of water, but Dr. Talbot requested I take only a couple sips to brush my teeth when I woke up today. My tongue feels like a dry sponge, and for a second, I consider sprinting out of the room and chugging from the water fountain, voiding my surgery. But I know this is inevitable. I give him a thumbs-up.

"Okay, hop on up," he says, motioning to the chair.

I shimmy myself onto the chair and lie back, crinkling the sanitary paper beneath me. Tracy washes her hands and puts on surgical gloves, and I try hard not to feel queasy at the scent of the latex. A sticker on the ceiling says JUST BREATHE, and for a second, I feel the tiniest bit better.

Dr. Talbot begins his surgery speech. "We're going to do twilight anesthesia. Now, it's not general anesthesia, so you won't be completely under, but you probably won't remember anything, so don't worry."

Tracy gently takes my arm and inserts a needle. I watch as she injects something called "Versed" into me.

"Azar, can you count backward from ten for me?"

"Ten, nine, eight, seven," I begin, my throat aching from the lack of water. Is this the last time I'll ever hear my voice like this? For a second, I almost wish I'd taken the time to say goodbye and record it.

"Azar?" Dr. Talbot says. "You wanna keep counting?"

"Huh?" Why am I counting again? "Two?" My body feels so heavy that it sinks deeper into the chair, melting into the fake leather.

"She's good," I dimly hear Dr. Talbot say to someone. Then everything goes black.

POST-OP

HOW MUCH ICE cream can one fourteen-year-old girl eat? Mom is not a fan of this question, but I am intent on getting to the bottom of it. It's been four days since my surgery, and the only thing that doesn't hurt to swallow is ice cream, yogurt, and, unfortunately, cold Throat Soothe.

"Poke," Roya says, sitting on my bed. I lift up the covers I've been hiding under. Maybe if the world can't see me, it doesn't matter that I haven't spoken in half a week.

Hi, I mouth.

She wrinkles her nose. "Dude, when was the last time you showered?"

I burrow back under my duvet and resume hiding.

"I have some excellent news," Roya says through the blanket. "The odds on your band have improved."

Huh?

"It's no longer fifty to one. It's now twenty to one on you winning, and that's pretty good!"

I text her from under the blanket: **it doesn't matter. i quit the band.**

"WHAT?" Roya throws the duvet off me. "But I bet on you!"

Really? I mouth. *You did?*

"I mean, I was hedging. I bet on some other bands, too." Classic Roya.

"What happened?" she asks, shimmying close. Something crinkles beneath her; an old ice pop wrapper. "Gross." She picks it up with the tiniest corner of her fingers and deposits it into the trash can next to my bed.

I don't wanna talk about it, I mouth back at her.

Roya sighs. "Let me guess. Things got hard and you ran away."

Excuse me? As the older cousin, I do not care to be dragged like that.

She holds up her fingers, ticking them off like a list. "You were too scared to make friends in elementary and middle school, so you only hung out with me. . . ."

Her words feel like arrows, hitting me right in the bullseye. I throw a stuffed animal at her. She ducks.

"You were too scared to put yourself out there, so you put everything into that notebook of yours."

I snatch my journal from my nightstand and clutch it to my chest.

Roya smirks. "And now you're too scared to go through with the battle."

I give Roya my hardest, meanest stare—the one that has quelled Matty and Nadim into submission, the one that makes Colton Tran flinch. But she just smiles back at me like she knows she's won.

And that's when I remember: a birthday invitation from some girl back in fourth grade. I asked my mom if she could make an excuse for me so I wouldn't have to go. Why would I give up a Saturday with Roya for this new, unknown birthday party when I might not have fun?

Then I remember how Colton invited me over for a study group back in middle school. How I didn't even entertain the idea. Or how, according to Eben, everyone at school already knows about my throat and I'm the only one treating it like this big secret. I guess you could chalk it up to me wanting control—of social situations, of my friendships—and making sure I never put myself in situations where I'd feel uncomfortable.

Maybe I'm not as alone as I thought. Maybe I was just scared of letting people in.

I hear the *CLICK* of a phone camera and whip my head up to see Roya taking a photo.

???? says my face.

"Just taking a picture of whatever epiphany is happening in your head there."

I roll my eyes and point my finger to the door. *Out,*

I mouth. We need to leave for the doctor's office soon. I can't have Roya dropping any more truth bombs on my life. Plus, I need to shower.

She saunters out of my bedroom, but not before calling out, "You can't run from this one, cuz. I'd put money on it."

🎧

Mom opens the door to Dr. Talbot's office. He sits at his big glass desk, eating his trademark gas station sushi.

"Azar!" he says. "All right, let's hear it."

I look back at Mom, like, *Huh?* She nudges me forward.

I thought he was going to steam my throat, or at least stick a light in there. For being one of the biggest moments in my life, this sure feels anticlimactic.

I take a deep breath. Here it comes. The smooth voice I was promised. The one that won't make me sound like a chain smoker.

"Azar," I croak, finally correcting him on his pronunciation. "It's pronounced *AW-zár*." But I sound just as scratchy as before. It's less painful to talk, sure, but my voice is still rough. Maybe I need to warm it up first.

"Azar," Dr. Talbot says. "I had no idea I had it wrong. Sorry about that."

"It's okay," I grumble. *Why is my voice still so choppy?*

"Tell me what you ate for breakfast, *Azar*," Dr. Talbot says.

Not gas station California rolls, that's for sure. "A

bowl of yogurt, and more Throat Soothe. Wait, what's happening? I sound exactly the same!"

"Hear that, Azar? There's less friction when you talk. It sounds a bit more even, no?" I see Mom enthusiastically nod from the corner of my eye.

My mouth goes dry. That's what we were aiming for this whole time? Slightly less friction?

"This is the same voice!" I say accusingly. Mom flinches. It's the loudest I've been since the procedure, but it doesn't hurt to raise my volume, though.

Dr. Talbot blinks. "Well, yes, of course. But it's not *as* harsh-sounding. Are you in discomfort when you talk?"

"Well, no . . ."

"Then the surgery was a success! You still have to be on vocal rest for a while, though, to make sure everything heals properly and to prevent infection."

My heart stops. I look at Mom.

"What's wrong?" she asks.

"So just to be clear: This is how my voice is going to sound for the rest of my life?"

Dr. Talbot frowns. "Well, your voice will drop a bit as you mature, and again when you hit menopause, but yes, this is your voice. Did you think it would be completely different?"

I clench my fists. This is as good as it gets. I will always have this rough voice, one with constant vocal fry. I'll never be a singer in a band, never perform my own material. Hell, I won't even be able to sing backup. What was even the point?

This was all for nothing.

Suddenly I can't breathe. I have to get out of here. "I need to go to the bathroom," I say with my stupid scraggly-sounding voice. *Stupid, stupid voice!*

"Azar, you okay?" Mom asks, worried.

I nod and grab my bag. "Gimme a sec."

I head to the bathroom and splash water on my face. *No band. No voice. No date.*

I can't go back into that room. And I can't go back to our apartment and hide out in my bedroom with nothing good to look forward to. I can practically feel the weight of my duvet from here.

I get out my phone. Am I really going to do this? Mom will absolutely murder me.

But I have to get away.

The car from my rideshare app meets me in the office parking lot three minutes later, and I practically sprint to the gray sedan.

"Union Station, right?" the driver asks.

I nod. Then I turn off my phone, and I'm gone.

ESCAPE BY AMTRAK

I SPEED THROUGH what Amtrak calls the Northeastern Corridor, the Acela train making everything a blur. The car's nearly empty, and I press my forehead against the glass and look at what must be Delaware. The last time I went anywhere exciting was to Argentina when I was ten, and since then, I've always taken the bus to visit Dad in New York. I've never gone by train, though. I've blown just about all my birthday and holiday money on this ticket.

The Acela whooshes past Philadelphia and Newark, and soon I can see the outline of Manhattan in the distance. Every time I see it, my heart soars. What if I could live here and be a full-time musician? I couldn't sing, of course, but maybe I could be a recording musician and write lyrics on the side. Then I think about what Matty said, how my lyrics aren't "raw," and I want to chuck this lime-green notebook out the train window.

My phone stares guiltily from the empty seat next to me, as if saying, *Ooooohhh, Azar, you did a bad thing! Don't you want to power me back on and hear how much trouble you're in?* I'm tempted, since all of my music is on there, and I'm starting to get bored of watching the East Coast roll past.

I press the power button, and the screen instantly lights up with messages, most of them from Mom. A *whump* of guilt hits my chest. Mom is probably freaking out. At least she can see my location, now that my phone's on.

> **AZAR ROSSI** *10:32 A.M.:*
> **Mom, I'm okay I just needed some**
> **space. I'm going to visit dad. I'm on**
> **the Acela. I'm sorry**

My phone vibrates with an incoming call from her, but I let it go to voice mail. She must have forgotten I'm not allowed to speak.

> **MOM** *10:32 A.M.:* **I can't BELIEVE you left**
> **without telling me. I nearly had a stroke.**
> **I'm calling your dad now, he'll meet you**
> **at the station. What is wrong with you???**

I chuck the phone back into the seat next to me, facedown. It buzzes some more. At least she's mad at me and not worried. It's an upgrade.

Earlier this year, the only people who texted me were people I shared DNA with. And now I'm here, ignoring *multiple* text messages from a handful of different people.

According to Victoria, butting creative heads is all part of the process. But I still feel angry every time I remember how Matty just dismissed my lyrics like I was the weakest link. And then I feel shame that I'm just running away from my problems again, like Roya said.

Battle of the Bands is next weekend. I pull out my notebook, rereading the song from last Friday's rehearsal, and wince again. Even with my rewrites, it's not any better. I stew in this weird soup of anger, shame, hurt, and insecurity. I want to crawl out of my skin.

Tomorrow, I say to myself. *I'll figure it all out tomorrow.* Today is for enjoying a Friday in NYC with Dad.

🎧

Soon, the conductor's voice crackles over the intercom. "Next stop, Penn Station." Suddenly, the train shoots underground. I watch as people stand up and start throwing away food wrappers and grab their stuff.

It's been a while since I visited Dad in New York. Usually, Mom loads me onto a charter bus that goes directly to Manhattan, but for Christmas I went to New Jersey to see Nonna for a week and we skipped our January visit. My face reflects back at me in the window against the darkness of the tunnel. *Azar Rossi: runaway.*

The car slowly brightens until a packed platform

appears, full of commuters, all of them walking quickly toward escalators and elevators. We slow to a stop, and there, waiting by the newspaper kiosk, is Dad. His eyes scan the train windows and land on mine. He gives me a big frown.

Bleh. So much for Dad being the "cool and fun" parent. He looks just as pissed as I imagine Mom is.

I make my way to the exit, Dad mirroring my moves through the window.

"Azar! What were you thinking?" he says, wrapping me in a hug the second I'm off the train. "How was it? Uneventful, I hope? Your mom is apoplectic."

Great. Dad grabs my bag and leads me to a crowded escalator. "How's your throat feel?"

I get out my phone, its case practically radiating *You're a bad kid!* energy. Then, remembering the choice board in my backpack, I get that out instead. I point to the FINE box.

He squeezes my arm. "I'm glad you did the surgery, though. It'll be for the best. You'll see."

Ha. What does he know? I point to the WHERE box on my choice board, the one I'm supposed to combine with *is the bathroom?* or *is my backpack?* I just leave my finger on it.

"Well, first I'm going to take you to the apartment and make you sit in your room, because you are grounded."

I balk. I don't even *have* a room at Dad's place, just a pullout sofa.

"And then I am taking you to a concert."

My eyes light up. *Who?* I mouth.

He holds up his phone, showing me a picture of a girl with stringy brown hair and a white tank top, clutching a guitar as she stares into the camera. I've never seen her before.

"She's a singer-songwriter, and I think you'll like her. It's a cool venue, too. It'll be good inspiration for your own band performance!"

The smile slides off my face. Dad doesn't know I left the band. I doubt they'll even go to the battle without me now.

I wonder what I'll tell him. Then again, I can't exactly talk. Maybe I won't have to say anything at all.

"And then tomorrow we're seeing your grandma in Jersey," Dad continues. "How does that sound? Weekend with your nonna?"

I give him a thumbs-up.

Dad's phone rings. "Yeah, I've got her. . . . Uh-huh. Are you sure? I mean . . . she can't say anything back. Okay."

Dad holds the phone out to me. "It's your mom," he whispers, even though we're in a crowded station with earsplitting construction going on. Even Dad is scared of Mom right now.

I hold the phone up to my ear. She must hear me breathe, because her tirade begins. "Do you know how worried I was? Dr. Talbot almost called the police. He thought you'd been abducted! To leave without even texting or calling?

I raised you better, Azar! Your father assured me you will not be having a blast in New York City and that this little joyride will have consequences there. And don't even think about—"

I hold the phone away from my ear. Mom's shouting so loudly, I can still hear her with the receiver a foot away.

I deserve it.

CONCERT

DAD "GROUNDING" ME ended up being the two of us eating Chinese takeout in his living room while watching reruns of *Saturday Night Live* music performances. I wouldn't mind being grounded every week if it's as awesome as this.

When the sun starts to set, he changes into black jeans and a T-shirt with a hole in it.

I stare.

His neck looks strange, not strangled by a starched collar. His five o'clock shadow seems like blond down on his face, and his blue eyes look softer without the Wall Street power suit.

"What?" he asks, self-conscious. "Do I not look hip enough?"

I shake my head.

Dad laughs. "You were too young to remember me before I started working. This was how I dressed all the time."

I raise an eyebrow. Dad actually looks like he could be a graphic designer or something, not an investment banker.

"Shut up!" he says.

I didn't say anything! I mouth.

"I know, but I can hear you thinking it."

We hop on the subway to Canal Street and get out near a small alley tucked away in Chinatown. It's freezing, with cold rain coming down in thick drops. This street seems to be where all the restaurants put their huge dumpsters. Great.

"Stop pouting, Azar—you'll like it. I promise."

I pop in a stick of gum to change my facial expression. Why are we even here? It's cold, my boots are soaked through, and all I want to do is curl up on Dad's couch and eat dumplings while watching music biopics.

He gestures to a small door flanked by a bunch of dudes smoking, something that is 100 percent *not* Mom-approved. But he pushes through, and *thump,* a wall of sounds hits me. It's so loud, I lose my breath, and the bass pulses through my chest, my shoes feeling the vibrations with each step.

What I thought was some seedy bar is actually a huge music hall, with a giant, two-story interior with a balcony. It's warm, not from a heater, but from the press of bodies. It smells fuggy and like antiseptic at the same time, the smell of cleaning fluid cutting through the humidity. I instantly unwind my scarf, my numb hands prickling as their feeling returns.

A bouncer puts a bright-orange wristband around my wrist and stamps my hand in cold ink that reads MINOR. People mill around us, holding their jackets in one hand and a drink in the other.

"Come on!" Dad shouts over the roar. "She should be coming on soon!" He yanks me closer to the stage, saying things like "Excuse me, sorry, excuse me" as he shoves us to the front. I try not to make eye contact as we plow through the crowd, and he finally stops in a bubble of space near the front of the stage. He wipes his forehead, the tightness of the crowd making him sweat.

"Can you see okay?" he asks.

"Yeah!" I shout. Then I freeze, remembering I'm supposed to be on vocal rest. Dad doesn't notice, though.

The crowd buzzes with excitement while I hum in my throat, testing for any bumps or scrapes from that one moment of shouting. My esophagus feels smooth, though. Wow.

Even if I'll never be able to sound good onstage, being able to shout without that burning feeling is amazing. I guess Dr. Talbot did a good job. I still close my mouth, though, determined not to get a throat infection after all that surgery.

"Can you put these in? Your mom will kill me if you

get your voice back right in time to lose your hearing." He hands me two neon-orange earplugs. "Sorry we didn't have time to get you a soda," he adds. I put them in.

"LADIES AND GENTLEMEN!" shouts a person I can't see. "Introducing . . . CANDACE HARTNETT!"

The crowd goes quiet, and the music they were piping in between bands fades out. A woman walks onstage. Her curly hair is untamed, and her hands look rough and red. Her jeans and T-shirt make me wonder if she's a staff member setting up the mic for the next act, but then someone hands her a guitar, and I realize that, no, this *is* the main act, the same woman from the photo. Dad won't stop grinning at her like an idiot.

"Hello, New York," she growls into the mic. "My name is Candace Hartnett." Her rough voice fills the room, up to the rafters, and it feels like I've been hit by a wave. I look at Dad, and he gives me a smug smile. Because when Candace Hartnett talks, she doesn't sound like a pop star. She sounds like . . . well, she sounds like *me*. She takes a deep breath, the music starts, and her voice rasps:

Dog-ear the pages of your favorite book—
You'd read me every day.
You left me with notes in my margins.

The rest of the club fades away as I zero in on Candace's voice. She looks so strong and confident, like she knows her voice isn't pretty and she doesn't care. It's clear she has a lot to say and isn't about to let something as pesky as the sound of her own voice stop her.

Only when I taste salt in my mouth do I realize I'm crying.

I wipe my eyes with the back of my hand. It's too much. I never thought I'd see someone like me, someone with the same tools I was given, who uses them to make her dreams come true. What if I already have everything I need? What if I don't need anything else? Instead of anger and frustration, a new feeling blooms in the bitter center of my chest: *hope.*

I look at Candace again, blinking through the tears. Suddenly Dad grips my shoulder, and he isn't smiling anymore.

"Don't let anyone stop you, okay? There are no rules. There never were." He takes a small package from his jacket and hands it to me.

I unwrap it, and it's another notebook, just like the one I've got now. I give Dad a rare smile. Not a pained one or a nervous one. A happy one.

"It's gonna be okay, Azar. I promise." He hugs me, and I let Candace's pebbly voice wash over us both. To everyone else in this venue, she's just another singer-songwriter bringing the house down. They're not thinking about the integrity of her voice or her vocal fry. All they care about is whether the music moves them, and judging from the people swaying and singing around us, it's working.

Dad's words slot into place. I don't *need* to sound like the women on the radio. I don't even need to sound like Candace. I just need to sound like *me*.

It makes me wonder if maybe I don't need to have the perfect voice to get my lyrics out there. Maybe I never needed one in the first place.

I feel the tectonic plates of my soul shift. My jaw unclenches. The space between my eyebrows softens. My throat stops holding all the tension it normally does. I realize how wrong I've been this whole time, and with a new sinking feeling, I realize what I threw away when I quit the band.

TAIL BETWEEN LEGS

THANKS FOR MEETING ME, I write on the whiteboard in the band room the following Monday after school. Nadim, Matty, and Eben are all seated around me in a semicircle, the three of them probably wondering what the hell is going on. Mom let me come to practice after I basically wrote a hundred-page essay on why I was sorry and how I will never run away again. I'm grounded, but at least I can rehearse. Even though Dr. Talbot said my voice sounds better, I'm still on vocal rest until Friday.

Friday. The day of the Battle of the Bands.

Matty raises a hand. I sigh.

"I, for one, would like to reiterate that I am happy Azar is back in whatever form she feels comfortable being in."

We all stare at Matty. Wait, does he think I'm not talking *for fun*?

Eben looks at him, completely bewildered. I can see

dark red flecks in his auburn hair, and I wonder if those parts feel the same as the rest of his hair. I bet if I ran my hands through it, I'd find out.

"Azar?" Eben says expectantly.

Right. Band.

I unhitch my shoulders from my ears, then flip the whiteboard over. On the back are the words I'M SORRY.

The room is silent.

Maybe this was a mistake. I can already feel my face heating up in embarrassment. I forgot that one of the downsides to having friends is that they hold you accountable, and I haven't had to be accountable in a long time.

But now I know that's a small price to pay for friendship.

"We accept your apology." Nadim puffs up his chest, nodding magnanimously down at me. "But you have to promise not to yell at me again."

This time I'm prepared. Not only do I have my choice board, but I labeled my drumsticks last night. I hold up the one with *YES* outlined in thick black marker on the narrow wooden stick.

"Apology accepted, Azar," Eben says very professionally. A little part of me deflates. Whatever spark we had before seems to be gone. "But what are we going to do about the Battle of the Bands? We only have five days left to prepare."

Aha! Excellent question, cinnamon-roll boy of my heart. I riffle through my backpack and hand out the sheets I printed last night.

My hands brush against Eben's, and I still feel that jolt of electricity run through me. I doubt it's reciprocated after I ditched our date, though.

"They're lyrics," Matty says. I hold my breath while everyone reads them. The entire trip back from NYC, I worked hard on creating the rawest, realest song I could. These words have been dredged from the depths of my soul. If these don't cut it, nothing will.

"This is . . ." Matty begins, trailing off.

"Awesome," Eben finishes for him, smiling up at me. "This is really, really great, Azar."

Nadim frowns. "But we have a performance in five days. Is that enough time for a whole new song?"

It is if we get moving ASAP! I almost shout. Instead, I walk over to the drums and slam my YES stick on the snare.

Matty looks at me, and for once we're on the same wavelength. "Let's do this."

Eben stands next to the keyboard.

Nadim grips the bass.

Matty grabs his guitar.

"Yalla!" Nadim cries. "Let's go!"

Eben fiddles with the keys, trying to figure out the right sound for the piece. Matty plucks out some melodies on his guitar. And Nadim works out a sick bass line. We are all finally in the "jam session."

Maybe it's because I can't talk, but I don't feel pressure to control the meeting anymore. I'm happy working on my drumbeats on my own, trusting that my bandmates will figure out their own arrangements. I watch as Matty runs his melody past Eben, and Nadim figures out how to join in. It's nice, collaborating this way. They were right: bands are a team sport.

New lyrics.

New Azar.

Eben starts singing the lyrics softly to himself. I close my eyes, relishing the feeling of having my words sung by him.

Then Eben suddenly stops, with a horrified look on his face.

"Azar." He spins around to face me. "We still don't have a band name!"

Crap.

Matty taps his guitar pick against his teeth. "I mean, do we *need* one?"

I hold up my stick: YES. The regulations specifically say we need one in time for the performance. I just left it blank when I entered us.

Nadim stares out the window, lost in thought. The room goes quiet again.

"How about"—Eben pauses for effect—"Children of Destiny."

Oh my god. I groan silently.

"That one's already taken, habibi," Nadim says diplomatically.

"I think we should be named after something that shows how far we've come," Matty says. "Something that shows we've evolved creatively. Something that shows we are open to collaboration and constructive criticism!" He ends his monologue with a fist in the air. "I give you: Jam Session."

I kind of like it. Eben's nodding to himself, as if he can see the name in his head.

Nadim practically jumps for joy. "Jam Session, yessss! Because that's what we do now! We Jam Session!" One by one, Matty, Eben, and Nadim all turn to me, as if waiting for my permission. Even though this is a democracy, it feels like I'm the guiding light in this moment.

I raise my YES stick in the air.

🎧

Everyone helps me put the room back together after rehearsal for once. But when it's time to walk home, Nadim shoots Eben a look, then quickly says, "I have to go walk home by myself, bye!"

Traitor.

Matty waves and goes to the gym, where Fabián is probably uploading a soon-to-be-viral video or something.

Eben clears his throat.

"Can I walk you home?"

I gulp. I wish I had worn something nicer than a hoodie and my Nats hat for such a loaded walk, but unfortunately, I dress for comfort, not style. I nod.

We push through the front doors and are silent for a

little bit. The sky's gray, but I can sense spring all around me: the black earth, the green buds, and the smell of wet asphalt waking up after a long winter.

"So," Eben begins. I don't know what he thinks is going to happen on this walk, because I'm still on vocal rest. "Was that song about me?"

Gah! I stumble in my boots and shoot him a panicked look. It definitely was about him. I bared my soul, and these are the consequences.

"It's okay, Azar, I won't tell anyone." Eben winks, and I roll my eyes.

Then he grabs my hand and brings it down alongside him. I watch as he threads his fingers through mine, the worn calluses scratching my palm. I remember to breathe.

"This is great," Eben says, staring into my stunned face. "Now you can't talk and list all the reasons that this is a bad idea."

I pinch his hand.

"Ow!"

We walk in silence a bit more, my body buzzing from Eben's touch. *Ebenezer Lloyd Hollins the Fifth is holding hands with me. Like, in a romantic way.* I'm glad it's still brisk out, because my face is beyond molten. I take another breath to steady myself.

"Those lyrics you wrote are amazing. Are you excited about Battle of the Bands?"

I nod.

Eben's quiet a bit more. I can tell he's gearing up to ask something else. "Now that you had the surgery, do you think you'll ever sing? I mean, if you can?"

I take out the new notebook Dad got me and flip to the first page, where he taped a photo. It's of me and Amy Waters, the two of us smiling from across her signing table. I didn't know he'd even taken a photo until now.

I point Eben to the words my dad wrote under the photo.

A portrait of two singer-songwriters.

Eben holds the journal in his hands, then looks up at me. "Yeah, just two singer-songwriters, hanging out."

I get out my phone and type: I thought I needed to sound perfect to be a singer. But I think I just need to believe in what I'm saying and not care what anyone thinks.

We're at my building now. Eben stops on the crumbling sidewalk and gives me a long look. "For what it's worth, I like your voice. I think it's kind of sexy."

I give a hair toss, pretending to primp in front of him. *Damn right, it's sexy!*

"Okay, okay, don't let it go to your head." He gives me a hug. "See you tomorrow."

Bye, I mouth, smiling.

PRE-BATTLE

IT'S THE NIGHT before the show. It's only 9:00 p.m., but I feel wired. So many things have happened in the lead-up to this moment. I've had to swallow my pride a lot, and realize that being on my own was a choice I made for myself, not something that happened to me.

Mom knocks on my door. "Z? I've got the boxes." She gently pushes it open, knowing I can't tell her to enter. In her arms are a handful of broken-down cardboard boxes, all of them pre-labeled with AZAR'S ROOM–DAD'S HOUSE and BASEMENT.

It's really happening. Mom's already enrolled at GMU for her undergraduate degree for the summer term, and Dad's moving down to Tysons Corner next month.

This whole first year of high school has crawled by incredibly slowly, but now things are speeding by too quickly to take a breath. I can't believe that this time tomorrow night, we'll be onstage, and our lyrics will be heard live.

I take a piece of cardboard and fold it into a box that will pack up my life here.

"Did somebody order some boxes?" a familiar voice cries from outside our front door.

"Roya? Is that you?" Mom asks. She opens the door, and there's Roya in a color-coordinated yellow sweater and skirt, carrying a giant box. Behind her is Nadim, Matty, and (gulp) Eben, each of them holding a box as well.

"Come in, come in," Mom says, gesturing for them to step inside and out of the cold.

Huh? I say with my face.

"We have a surprise!" Nadim says excitedly.

"*I* have a surprise," Roya corrects him. She places a box on our kitchen counter and hands me a pair of scissors.

"Anyone want any hot chocolate? I have soy milk and oat milk!" Mom offers.

"Oooh, I'll take an oat milk one," Matty says. He looks approvingly at the crystals collection Mom has on our kitchen windowsill.

"Me too!" Eben calls out. "Thank you!"

Nadim just looks at me, panicked. "You can milk an oat?"

"No thanks!" Roya says quickly. "Come on, Azar, open it!"

I slice open the box. Inside are soft black shirts with JAM SESSION!!!!! in neon-green lettering with an ironic skull on the front. The skull has flames coming out of its eye sockets and everything.

"We've got mugs, dad hats, fanny packs, and, yes, Holleh, even tote bags. Will I need a bigger cut for this rush order? Yes, yes I will."

I put a shirt on even though I'm already wearing a sweater. I don't care. I feel like a million bucks wearing this thing. Like all the blood, sweat, and tears we poured into this band has culminated into this piece of merch. No matter what happens, even if we bomb tomorrow, it was all worth it. I'm smiling so big, I can feel my cheeks dig into my eye sockets.

"Hell yeah!" Eben says, following suit and throwing a shirt on over his Wicking Technology™ henley. Nadim and Matty put theirs on, too, all of us grinning like idiots.

"Stand against that star chart," Roya orders. "We need a band photo before you make it big!"

We press our backs against Mom's wall of horoscope signs. Eben and Matty sling their arms around me, while Nadim makes devil horns with both hands. Roya takes the photo, and I already know I'll want it framed for my new room at Dad's place. Eben keeps his arm around my waist, and I glow almost as brightly as the neon flames on my shirt.

Mom sniffs in a corner, holding a mug of oat milk cocoa in each hand. "My little girl's all grown up and in her own rock-and-roll band."

Mom, I mouth.

"Scorpios grow up fast," Matty says, nodding sagely.

"Careful with that oat milk, Hollins!" Roya barks as Eben takes a sip of his. "I own fifteen—I mean twenty!—percent of all profits from this merch, including that shirt you haven't paid for yet!"

"I'm never taking this shirt off. I'm going to buy twenty just so it can be my new uniform," Eben informs her.

"That'll be four hundred dollars," Roya instantly calculates.

Mom, I notice, is staring at the spot where Eben's hand touches my hip. She arches an eyebrow. *Birth control,* she mouths.

"Jam Session!" Nadim fist pumps out of nowhere.

I look around our packed apartment. This will probably be the last time we have any guests over. I'm going to miss this place. But now, being surrounded by my friends and family, I know I can re-create this feeling anywhere.

All I have to do is let them in.

BATTLE OF THE BANDS

WE MADE IT. After all the rehearsals and fights and cracked hands and drumstick blisters, we've finally arrived at the Battle of the Bands. Did I get any sleep last night? No. Did anyone else in the band? From the look of Eben's shaky hands, Nadim's nervous laughter, and Matty nodding and smiling so much he looks like a dashboard ornament, I don't think so.

We zip through sound check in five minutes, the whole event a well-oiled machine. The greenroom is packed with other bands, many comprised of high school seniors with intimidating smiles. Backstage, however, is complete pandemonium, with people running all over the place and shouting things like "Where's my pick?" and "I lost my pedal!"

I find a quiet spot near the fire exit and hyperventilate at the thought of performing in front of an audience.

Mom, Roya, and my grandparents are here, along with some classmates and Anthony Staples himself. What if I mess up in front of them? What if my hands turn into spaghetti and I suddenly can't clutch my drumsticks? I listen to the other bands like I'm underwater, their music barely reaching me. It all feels so surreal.

Eben taps me on the shoulder, making me flinch a mile high. "You okay?" he asks.

I nod through my clenched jaw. Even though Dr. Talbot said I was okay to speak today, I still haven't done it yet. I've been too nervous to say anything coherent, anyway.

"Jam Session, you're up next!" shouts a man with a headset and a clipboard.

Oh my god. What are we doing?

Nadim and Matty make their way over. Nadim looks just as green as I do. I can't help noticing how different he seems. He's in jeans and a T-shirt, his curly hair longer and shaggier than when we first started talking. He looks way more comfortable in his skin, even if he looks like he's going to spew.

"All right, you're up!" the man with the clipboard says, and before I know it, I can hear our band name being announced over the roar of applause. We step in front of the black curtain and onto the stage, and I'm blinded by lights that seem hot enough to fry an egg. Eben leads me by the small of my back toward my kit, which is good, because I feel like I'm going to black out and stick my foot into my bass drum.

"Hello, everyone! We are Jam Session—thank you

so much!" Eben yells into the mic, copying what past bands did onstage. I sit on my drum stool and fiddle with the height, adjusting the cymbals, snare, and toms to my level. There isn't much time to talk to the audience, though. "Get in, get out," the stage manager had told us.

This is really happening. We're really here. I'm not fantasizing anymore. If I pinched myself, nothing would change. It's unreal being in a setting you've imagined in your head so many times. I take a deep breath. *It's time.*

Eben turns around to look at me, as if to ask, *Are you ready?*

Was the first wave ready to attack on D-Day? Was that monkey ready to be shot into space? Was I ready for Mom to switch me to a pescatarian diet? No! But I bite my lip and nod. Here goes nothing.

CLICK, CLICK, CLICK, CLICK! My drumsticks count out the beat in 4/4 time, and before I know it, we're off! The intro to our first song is simple, and I hit the snare and bass drum leisurely as I keep tempo with Nadim's bass. Matty's guitar comes in, followed by Eben on the keys. And then his voice.

> *I've been hoping*
> *That the struggle isn't real.*
> *Been thinking*
> *About the things that we can't feel.*

I'm in the zone. I'm so laser-focused on maintaining tempo that I almost forget we're really performing. We've rehearsed Eben's song so many times, my muscle memory has taken over, and I try not to think too hard about what I'm doing. Because if I do, I'll realize I'm playing in front of a live audience on a real stage at a proper concert, and my hands will slip and this whole song will come crashing down.

We're on cruise control, our ensemble sounding tight as we all hit our marks with precision. And we should—this is the song that we've worked on the longest.

I take a peek past the lip of the stage and see the outlines of people, their heads nodding along, and I falter a bit on my snare beat. *Holy crap. Real humans are enjoying our music.*

When my sticks hit the hi-hat, something warm and light floods through me. *Happiness. This is what happiness feels like.* Maybe we have a shot at this. Maybe we can actually win this thing!

I slam my stick into the cymbal for the last note, letting the crash fade out on its own. The audience cheers, and I'm pretty sure I hear someone who sounds like my dad give a loud *Whoop!* from the audience, even though that can't be right. He isn't moving here yet.

The echo of the song dies out, and the four of us lock eyes with each other. Nadim looks like he can't believe he pulled it off, but Eben and Matty seem confident and pleased. Did they know we were going to do well?

"LELELELELELE!" someone ululates from the crowd. "Yalla, habibi!" Nadim smiles into the audience. He turns back to our gang with a new burst of confidence on his face.

Eben approaches the mic.

"Ladies and gentlemen, for our next song, we're going to have a slight change in vocals," he announces.

Wait, what? I almost drop a drumstick.

Matty gestures to the stage manager, and before I know what's happening, someone with a headset is placing another microphone in front of my face. Were the cymbals not coming through the sound system? Who can't hear a *cymbal*?

Eben hurries over. "This was always your song, Azar. You got this."

I stare at him blankly. "Huh?" I say out loud. It's the first thing I've said all day. It doesn't sound rough, per se, but it doesn't sound as smooth as Eben's voice, either.

"Your lyrics! It's time you sang them!"

My soul practically leaves my body. "You want *me* to sing?" I gasp, covering the new mic with my hand. "Are you insane? We actually have a shot at winning this thing!" In the back of my head, I notice that it doesn't hurt to talk. It feels easier, as if my voice doesn't need a running start. I haven't sounded this even since elementary school.

"Your voice is perfect for this song, Azar. It always has been, even without the surgery. And I don't want to win if it means hiding you behind a drum kit." Eben squeezes my shoulder and walks back to his place by the keyboard before I can argue with him.

I frantically search for Nadim's eyes, silently begging him to call this whole thing off. But instead, he gives me a thumbs-up. *Curse you, Nadim!*

I turn to Matty. Matty, who has a way better voice than me. Matty, who should probably be the lead of his own band one day. He pulls something out of his pocket and waves it at me: it's a bundle of sage. And that's when I know I've been outnumbered.

I gulp. After seeing Candace Hartnett perform, I know I have what it takes to sing out loud. But is it enough for a packed audience? For a real, honest-to-God performance?

"Z?" Eben asks into the mic, looking back at me. I can feel the audience getting restless. Our precious ten minutes are quickly running out. Here it is. The moment I've been waiting for. This is my chance to show the world what I can do.

I twirl my drumsticks. I've gotten pretty good at it, thanks to Victoria's help. "Okay."

Eben's face cracks wide open, his eyes crinkling with happiness. "Awww, yeah!" he shouts into the microphone. The audience starts clapping again.

I clear my throat, quickly humming to warm it up. My hands clutch the sticks, fingers trembling. *CLICK, CLICK, CLICK, CLICK!*—a foot that doesn't feel connected to my body pumps the bass drum pedal. It's now or never.

I stare down the barrel of the microphone and close my eyes, my lyrics ingrained into my memory from staring at them all week. And then I let everything pour out of me.

I don't want to catch another spark—
Dreams always die better in the dark.
If I take one more chance, it'll kill me.
Who cares about happy?

There's nothing in life that you can lose
If you stay safe with all your rules.
It's Friday night and I'm not lonely.
Netflix consoles me.

But when your eyes meet mine
And you set my world on fire,
Whatever hurt you're gonna be
Is worth it just to feel something—

'Cause . . .

I'm scared, I'm freaking terrified at the thought
    of you and I.

I try to wrap my head around more than just my
Little life.
Whatever happens, there's no going back.

I'd say let's just stay friends,
But I'm a terrible liar and this is a heart attack.

Since this song is anthemic, I don't have to sound beautiful, I just have to say it with feeling. My voice is gravelly and unconventional, but it's even, and I can hold and sustain each note like I've got a humidifier right next to me.

It doesn't sound pretty; it sounds *true*.

Halfway through, I open my eyes, and I notice that the lights have dimmed and there's a spotlight centered right on me. Eben, Nadim, and Matty are in the dark, and I can sense the heat of everyone's gaze as they try to see me through the cymbals. My hands move on their own, my voice struggling to keep up.

Adrenaline floods my system, and as I let out each note, I feel in control. *I can do this*, a steady beat says deep inside me. *I can do this. I can do this.*

We reach the bridge, and I finally look out into the crowd. There's Mom, Abuelo, Maman Bozorg, and Dad, too! I see Roya, and even Victoria, who actually looks like she's smiling. Everyone who's rooting for me is here. And for the first time in a long time, I'm rooting for me, too.

Life is easier if your default's No
Choosing to stop and not pass Go
And did I forget to mention?
My mom's my best friend?

Planet Earth is already screwed.
Who cares if this song's killing the mood.
What's the point if we're doomed to die
By the year two thousand fifty-five?

But when your eyes meet mine,
And you set my world on fire,
Whatever hurt you're gonna be
Is worth it just to feel something—

'Cause . . .

I'm scared, I'm freaking terrified at the thought
    of you and I.
I try to wrap my head around more than just my
Little life.
'Cause whatever happens, there's no going back,
I'd say let's just stay friends,
But I'm a terrible liar and this is a heart attack.

We built in a drum solo before I knew I was going to be the one singing. A small part of me wonders if I should just skip it and play it like the normal space between verses.

But then I lock in my shoulders like Victoria taught me and hit the toms for all they're worth, slamming between the snare and the cymbal as my right foot pumps the bass and my left foot drills the hi-hat pedal. I feel like an octopus, my limbs twirling around.

Sweat's pouring down my face, but I don't care—this is it, this is my moment to shine. I come up to the end of the solo and do a run across the entire kit, using my whole arm in a way that I hope makes Victoria proud. Then Matty's guitar comes in, right in time for his solo, and I let the snare hits grow soft. I hear a few claps in the audience, and I finally catch my breath before I close out the song.

How dare you reanimate my heart,
How dare you light up this dark.
Who gave you permission to breathe in life
And open me up with your blunt knife?

'Cause . . .

I'm scared, I'm freaking terrified at the thought
*   of you and I.*
I try to wrap my head around more than just my
Little life.
'Cause whatever happens, there's no going back.
I'd say let's just stay friends,
But I'm a terrible liar aaaaaand . . .

I let the note draw out, ratcheting it up with a double snare roll.

I said yes, I gave in,
Now I'm waiting for my world to cave in.

There never was so much to lose,
Until you made me see you.

For the first time, I want more—
I can't ignore how I want an encore.
It's your fault, I have you to blame
For setting my world aflame.

There's Matty with the final power chord, and—

I'm
So
Scared.

My voice cracks on the last word despite the surgery, but I don't mind. I end the song with one bass thump as Eben holds the keys for a fade-out. I finally look up, only to realize that the whole band is staring at me. Eben's grinning from ear to ear, Matty is giving me the wise nod of a sensei who always knew I had it in me, and Nadim looks so excited, I worry he might wet his pants.

"Thank you, Jam Session!" the emcee shouts.

I gulp oxygen and someone hands me a towel. When I wipe my face, it comes away sopping wet. Now I know why drummers are always shirtless or in muscle tees.

Eben motions for me to stand up, and I take a bow with the rest of the band, holding my YES and NO drumsticks. Even if my voice is back, I think I'm going to hang on to these for a while.

The applause washes over us, and I smile into the crowd.

"¡DALE, AZAR!" Abuelo hollers.

"Well done, Miss Rossi!" shouts a voice that sounds suspiciously like Principal Saulk.

"Let's give it up for Jam Session!" says the emcee.

I make my way out from behind my drum kit, my legs still shaking.

I did it. No matter what happens, even though we probably won't win, I'll always be proud of this moment.

I clutch my drumsticks in my fist as I punch the air.

"YEAH!" I shout, for the first time in forever.

AFTER

IT'S FINALLY QUIET. The roar in my ears is gone, and I think my face is back to a normal color. The high of the concert has worn off, but something new has filled its place. I feel myself stand taller, and I relax my jaw. I take the deepest breath I've taken all year.

I did it. I sang in public.

Nobody laughed. Nobody taunted me. We didn't win, not that we expected to, but that's okay. I got something even better. *Confidence.* I feel at peace. Angry thoughts aren't swirling around in my head, and neither is my desperate desire for control. I feel like a new person now, one who's competent and capable. Plus, I don't owe James K. Polk High School a thousand dollars anymore.

It feels pretty great.

I've already helped Mom pack up most of our apartment this morning. All that's left is to unpack our stuff at my grandparents' house and my dad's condo. Tomorrow, we're going to IKEA so I can pick out new bedroom furniture.

But this Saturday afternoon is time just for me. I sit in the empty band room, gathering my thoughts and replaying everything that happened last night, from me almost dying onstage to us getting ice cream afterward.

This is the space where I've grown the most in these past months, and where I've taken the most hits, too.

Now when I look at my drum kit in the corner, instead of feeling anxious, I just feel happy. Maybe I'll stick with the drums after all.

A door opens. I slowly turn around.

"Hey," Eben says quietly, like he can tell he's interrupting something. "Roya said you'd be here. After she invoiced me."

I smile. "Hey."

"There's something I want to show you," he says. For the first time ever, Eben's just wearing jeans and a T-shirt. I don't think I've ever seen him in civilian clothing before. Even last night, he wore a moisture-resistant shirt "for all the sweat."

"Okay." I move to collect my things, but Eben stops me.

"No, in here."

He walks to the upright piano in the corner, the one we used before he brought in his keyboards. He clears his throat, looking seriously uncomfortable. "I wrote you something."

"You wrote me a song?" After all these years of writing songs for myself, I never imagined that someone else would write one for me.

Eben plays a chord, and my breath stills. He closes his eyes, and then he sings. He sings and sings, and I soak the words up. They tell me all I need to know.

The last note fades away, and I'm rooted to the spot. Something bright and wonderful soars through my chest.

His eyes meet mine, and instead of being in some band room that smells of spit valves and cork grease, we're in our own little bubble.

And then Eben stands up and puts one of his hands over the other, his palms touching, his fingers interlocking in a way that looks familiar.

SNAP! His hands click together, the sound echoing throughout the space.

SNAP!

I can't believe it! It's the complicated two-handed snap of Iran, the one that made George Clooney an Iranian American obsession. Eben's mastered it.

"How do you know how to do that?" I cry. "*I* can't even do that!"

He gives me a shy smile. "Your cousin Roya showed me after the show last night. She said it's important."

I walk over to him on shaky legs. "That. Was. Amazing," I say in my low, husky voice. I like the way it sounds now. I'd never swap it for anything else.

I reach for his hand. "Come on, Ebenezer Lloyd Hollins the Fifth."

He grins and wraps his arm around me. "I like the way you say my name," he says. "It sounds like a grizzled old detective, tired of working the beat."

"Get used to it," I growl again.

He leans over and kisses me, and for once in my entire life, there is no beat, no rhythm, no tapping in the back of my brain.

Everything goes blissfully quiet, and I give in to the silence.

MAY

ON THE LAST day of speech therapy, the room is decorated with stylish streamers and balloons. There's even a cake.

"What's going on?" I ask, picking at a pink polka-dot streamer that hangs from the ceiling.

Ms. Davolio beams. "You've both graduated from speech therapy!" she says. "This is your last class. Y'all have made me proud."

"Wait, really?" I spin around to look at Sydney. She looks just as shocked as I am.

Ms. Davolio nods. "Yep. Dr. Talbot says you've made progress with regulating your volume after surgery, and Sydney, your *s*'s are sssssomething elsssse!"

"Seriously?" Sydney says without a lisp. "That means I have a free elective next year!"

That's right. I almost forgot.

"That means I can take band next year. That means I can play percussion!" I say out loud. I'm doing that more. Saying things out loud. "Thanks, Ms. Davolio."

"Yeah, thanks," Sydney says, nodding enthusiastically. "This is going to be so amazing."

"I got this cake from a real bakery, not some off-market shop that Dr. Talbot goes to," Ms. Davolio says, winking at me as she cuts into it. She hands me a piece.

I laugh. It's a harsh, barking sound. But that's okay. I take a bite.

"Yum," I say. It doesn't taste as forbidden now that I live at Dad's and he allows gluten in the house, though.

Ms. Davolio hands a piece to Sydney.

"Are you going to Emerson's birthday this weekend?" Sydney asks, taking a bite.

"Yeah, Eben and I are going," I say. "I'll see you there?"

"Ooooh," says Sydney, waggling her eyebrows. "See you there."

Ms. Davolio hands me a plate with a few slices of cake wrapped in plastic. "For your band," she explains.

"Thanks, Ms. Davolio. Thank you for everything."

"You're welcome, Azar. Now, don't forget to visit me, okay? And invite me to your next concert!"

"I will."

After the battle, we decided to keep Jam Session going. Nadim is going to stay another year to finish studying for his TOEFL, and Matty's going to stay with us while he also works on his own pieces as a solo artist.

Besides, there's always next year's battle. And we may have a shot at that one.

I exit speech therapy for the last time, and there's Eben, twirling his lacrosse lanyard and wearing a vintage Misfits tee.

"Hey, Z," he says, hooking an arm behind my back.

"What up, E."

He smiles, kissing my forehead. "I've got some new lyrics. You ready for practice today?"

I hold up one of the drumsticks I always keep in my back pocket.

Yes.

**TURN THE PAGE FOR
MORE FROM**

Olivia Abtahi

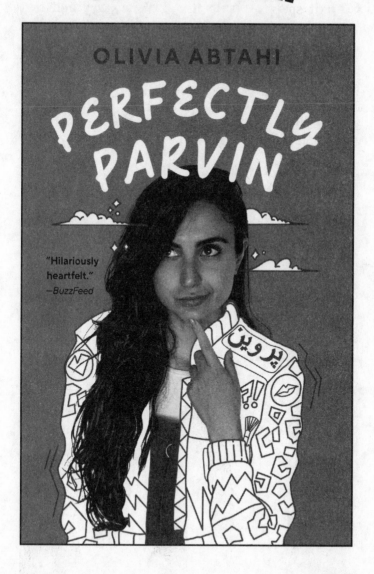

AUGUST

· · ·

THINGS I HAVE GOING FOR ME:

- My BFFs, Ruth and Fabián
- Summer vacation at the beach
- Parents who let me order pizza last night
- An awesome aunt who teaches me how to do my makeup over video chat
- ~~Good grades~~ Decent grades

BUT MOST IMPORTANT:

- A boy who I like . . . and who I think might like me back

Tuesday

THE BEACH
1:00 P.M.

"Wesley!" I ran toward the dunes. The beach was packed with families and rogue sun umbrellas that threatened to hit someone in the wind. Seagulls circled overhead, waiting for someone to drop a stray French fry from their lunch onto the sand. Was it the most romantic spot? Not exactly. But who cared? I'd made friends with a cute boy, and he was waving back at me. "Come on, Wesley—they found it!"

He smiled that shy smile that made his braces sparkle, and I swooned.

"Let's go," he said from across the beach. Wesley was tall and gangly, and he wore cool board shorts with elephants on them. Obviously, I had a massive, massive crush on him.

I ran toward him in my pink bikini. Mom had helped me wax just about every part of my body to be able to wear this thing, and I was abnormally proud of it. If only Wesley knew how much I'd done to look like the rest of the girls here at the beach—the ones who definitely didn't need to worry about shaving their toes. All Iranians came with their own carpets, and half Iranians like me were no exception.

I caught up with him, and we hurried over to one of those guys with a metal detector, the kind they waved around the beach looking for lost wedding rings. He was digging frantically toward something, and more people gathered to see what it was. He kept saying things like "It's a big one!" or "Definitely from a shipwreck!" and swatting away kids who tried to help, saying it was "his discovery."

Too bad he was digging for the fake treasure Wesley had helped me plant last night. The metal he was searching for would barely buy him a soda if he scrapped it for parts, and it was hard to not laugh and potentially spoil the whole thing. Wesley clenched my arm, willing me to be quiet, but I could tell he was struggling to be silent, too. My skin prickled where he touched it.

"I see it," the man cried. "There's gold in there, for sure!" He had on a bucket hat and a big stripe of zinc oxide on his nose. He looked like a demented camp counselor.

Wesley grabbed my hand, his whole body vibrating with quiet chuckles. I'd never held a boy's hand before. It felt nice, though a bit sweaty. Maybe all boys' hands were sweaty?

We watched as the gold digger unearthed a metal box and threw it back up onto the sand. He clambered out of the hole he'd dug. A hush fell over the whole beach, waiting to see what was inside.

The lid creaked open.

"AHHHH!" he screamed. He slammed the lid shut and turned to the huge audience now waiting around the hole. Only, his face was completely blue.

"It sprayed me!" he spluttered. "It's booby-trapped!"

"BA-HA-HA-HA-HA!" I cackled along with the rest of the crowd. I'd rigged the box to squirt ink the second it opened and filled it with rusty tools to set off the metal detector. Wesley and I'd both agreed that since this was our last week at the beach, we had to leave with a spectacular prank. But this was better than anything I could have imagined.

"I can't . . . breathe . . . ," Wesley wheezed next to me, tears streaming down his pale face. His eyelashes were so blond I could barely see them.

The metal detector man tried to wipe the ink away with a beach towel and got sand in his eyes instead. "Whatever's inside must be even more valuable to be protected!" He blinked rapidly as he addressed the group. "We'll need to get the authorities involved!"

I couldn't take it anymore. "THAR SHE BLOWS!" I screamed in a bad pirate accent, bursting into laughter. The man with the metal detector flinched and stumbled, almost tripping over his "treasure." A mother next to us gasped, yanking her child away from me. Clearly, we looked deranged.

I turned to Wesley. "Let's go." We'd be long gone before "the authorities" got here. "Race you!"

We ran toward the ocean, shouting "Yarrr!" and "Avast, mateys!" Wesley held my hand the whole time.

Wednesday

THE BOARDWALK
8:00 P.M.

The next night I led us to the shops by the beach. "Do you want to get some ice cream?"

Wesley nodded. It was our last day together, and I was weirdly quiet, even though I'd spent the whole summer talking his ear off. Wesley was a good listener like that.

We'd met that summer on the beach. I'd spied Wesley

watching me play backgammon a few weeks ago, when Dad had gotten all the other Middle Eastern people vacationing here in on his game. I'd noticed how Wesley's parents were the kind of people who were absurdly proud of their fancy cooler, and how his dad wore a gold college ring on his finger. All their beach towels were monogrammed.

I finally asked Wesley if he wanted to play, and when he said yes, his mom and dad looked terrified and moved their umbrella farther away. Who doesn't like backgammon? Still, he hung out with us anyway.

Wesley was cute and skinny with sandy hair bleached blond by the sun, and his lips seemed permanently chapped from the salt. He didn't talk much, but he was always interested in what I had to say. Whatever I suggested, from ice cream to boogie boarding, he usually said yes. For once, I had a friend at the beach while my BFFs, Ruth and Fabián, were stuck in the DC suburbs.

Though I was secretly hoping Wesley and I could be more than friends.

We got our ice cream cones, walked to the water, and sat down on the cool sand. I shivered in my dress. Wesley wore a nice sweater that brought out the blue in his eyes, and I wondered if he thought my brown eyes were just as beautiful.

"Are you cold?" he asked.

"A little." I took a bite of my freezing cold ice cream.

"Here," he said, putting his arm around me. Whoa. He didn't even pretend to yawn or anything! Friends didn't just sling their arms over each other, did they? Oh, wait. I did that with Ruth and Fabián all the time. Either way, I hoped Wesley would break out of his shy shell and make a move.

After all, starting high school with a boyfriend would be

amazing. Everyone in middle school had already coupled up by the end of spring, and Ruth and Fabián had even turned people down. It was time for me to get a boyfriend of my own, even though nobody from middle school had been interested.

Wesley didn't even have to be my soul mate or anything, just someone who would laugh at my jokes and hold my hand. Knowing someone thought I was cute would probably be the best feeling in the world. But I had no idea. It hadn't happened to me before.

"Are you nervous about school?" I asked, inhaling his sweater's salty, soapy smell. Wesley was from my part of town back near DC and was starting at the same high school as me. He didn't know anyone going to James K. Polk High, since everyone else from his private school would be going on to Sacred Heart High. He said his parents were switching him because it made more "economic sense," but I think that just meant that James K. Polk was cheaper, as in, free. I would have been freaking out about the change, but Wesley didn't talk about it much.

"I'm a little nervous," he admitted. I could feel his arm shaking as he rested it on my shoulder. He leaned into me.

"Yeah?" I breathed. We were really close together now. *C'mon, Wesley!* I signaled with my eyes. *Make a move!*

He gulped. "Yeah."

Just then, my phone buzzed in my pocket. Mom and Dad were probably texting me to come home soon since we had an early drive back to Northern Virginia in the morning. Not now, parents! Couldn't they tell Something was about to happen? I had no idea what that Something was, of course, but it felt important.

"Listen, Parvin," Wesley said suddenly. He pronounced

my name the way it was spelled, even though the proper pronunciation in Farsi was PAR-veen. I'd never bothered correcting him.

"Mm?" I replied. Was he going to ask me to be his girlfriend? Or even better, his date to the fancy Homecoming that Polk High threw every year? Or what if he was just going to tell me his arm had fallen asleep, and yank it back?

But instead of saying anything, he leaned toward me. I realized what was happening just in time and shut my eyes.

His face crashed into mine, the imprint of his braces digging in. I'd never been kissed on the lips before. It felt like eating a melted Popsicle, only with more teeth.

It's happening! my brain kept shouting. *THIS IS REALLY HAPPENING!* Thank god I had gotten my braces off before coming to the beach, otherwise they would have tangled with Wesley's. This was a dream come true.

He pulled away. I wiped my lips. Kissing was messier than I thought.

"I think you're really cool, Parvin," he said.

Finally! A boy liked me! I didn't want to leave the beach and drive home tomorrow. I wanted to stay in this moment forever.

"Thanks, Wesley," I said, not sure what else to say. My bright orange lip gloss was all over his face, and somehow by his right ear. "Er, you're pretty cool, too."

He wrapped a thin arm around me again.

"Will you be my girlfriend?" he asked, his face super serious. Which was hard, considering all the lip glitter shimmering on it.

YES! I fist-pumped in my mind. This night was going

better than I could have imagined. *YOU'RE GONNA START HIGH SCHOOL WITH A BOYFRIEND! HA-HA-HA-HAAA!*

"Sure," I said casually, as if my head wasn't filled with exploding fireworks. "That would be cool."

Wesley grinned. "So, is this our first date?" he asked, inching so close I could see the freckles on his face. I felt like I was seeing a different side of Wesley—someone who was more confident than the boy I'd dragged around the beach all summer.

I laughed. "Is this a normal first date? Is this what people usually do?"

But Wesley just smiled even wider. "Normal is overrated, Parvin." And then he kissed me again, lip gloss and all.

Friday

JAMES K. POLK HIGH ORIENTATION
5:00 P.M.

To say I had anxiety about starting high school was an understatement, but freshman orientation night was supposed to help with that. Right when it felt like we'd gotten the hang of middle school, we were punted off to a building five times its size and made to start all over again.

At least Fabián and Ruth were starting with me, and I'd get to see Wesley after being apart for a couple of days. Just the thought of starting high school with a boyfriend made me giddy. I was a girl with a boy who liked her. That fact alone was enough to get me through tonight.

My phone buzzed with a WhatsApp message from my

aunt in Iran, followed by a picture of flowers. Why did Iranians always message each other bouquets of flowers?

My whole body vibrated with happiness. *Everything was coming up Parvin.*

"So, where's this boyfriend of yours?" Fabián asked, grabbing a seat next to mine in the auditorium. I scanned the crowded theater for Wesley but didn't see him yet. I'd worn my favorite floral T-shirt, and Ameh Sara had helped me with a special silver eyeshadow tutorial earlier today. My outfit was perfect for my Wesley reunion.

"He'll be here."

I'd told Fabián and Ruth everything the second I came home that night from the beach, my lips still tingling. Fabián had kissed plenty of boys and was not impressed. Ruth, however, was in shock that I had somehow landed a kiss at all.

Fabián just chuckled, his brown skin more tanned since the last time I'd seen him. "Remember when you told everyone you had a boyfriend in fifth grade? And it turned out he was a cartoon?"

"He was very lifelike!" I elbowed him, mussing up his perfectly styled outfit. Fabián put a lot of effort into looking sophisticated but also liked to pretend he didn't care.

"Go easy, Fabián," Ruth piped up, her straight black hair in two high buns for her "special occasion" hairdo. Thank you, Ruth. At least someone was a true friend around here. "Let her be delusional if she wants to be."

"Yeah!" I said, sticking my chin out defensively. "Wait . . ."

"Parvin, can you blame us for thinking this guy sounds too good to be true? You do tend to exaggerate." Fabián patted my arm kindly.

"I never exaggerate!" I cried.

Just then, the lights in the auditorium dimmed, and the whole theater fell silent.

"Welcome, freshman class!" a voice called out. Electronic music blasted from the speakers and lights flashed. We watched as a bunch of teachers entered from stage left and began to dance very, *very* badly.

"I think I'm gonna have a seizure." Fabián shuddered as our eyes were massacred by the faculty's terrible (but enthusiastic) dance moves. Then he began streaming it on his phone, for posterity. Teachers waved their arms, inviting us to dance with them as Ruth sank lower into her chair. Nobody joined them.

"WHOOOO!" I shouted, just because I felt a little bad for the grown-ups who were dancing so hard up there. One of them gave a pained smile, like she knew how embarrassing this whole thing was.

"GET IT!" Fabián shouted, still filming from his phone.

The music suddenly stopped, and microphone feedback echoed throughout the auditorium.

"Generation Z? Meet Generation WE!" a man shouted. He wore a brown suit that looked two sizes too small, and had the kind of expression that can only be described as "desperate." He stepped into the spotlight, clutching his chest as he tried to catch his breath, his round baby face so red it looked like a cherry.

"Let's give it up for our amazing teachers!" He gestured toward the staff who'd been awkwardly swaying around him. A teacher took a puff of his inhaler.

"My name's Principal Saulk, and welcome to James K. Polk High School freshman orientation!" he shouted, spittle flying from the patchy beard he was trying to grow. "And here are your student ambassadors who came to share their high school experiences!"

Principal Saulk gestured to a group of students standing on the side of the stage, and one of them quickly grabbed the mic. She wore head-to-toe black and had pale skin and dark purple hair. She looked cool, in a terrifying way.

"High school," she whispered into the microphone, "is a prison."

"Becca!" Principal Saulk shouted. "You're not supposed to be here!" He chased Becca offstage, but not before she bowed to the rest of us.

"That was amazing," Fabián said into his phone. He had shared the performance with his followers, and I could see comments like "BECCA4EVA" and "We love you Fabián!!111" fill his livestream feed as he pointed the camera at the stage. Being a dancing sensation on Instagram meant Fabián had thousands of fans. But I could barely get him to be a fan of believing I had a real, flesh-and-blood boyfriend.

"High school's not *actually* a prison, though, right?" Ruth twitched, looking upset despite her sunny-yellow K-pop T-shirt. "Making high school a prison would be *illegal*, right?"

I shrugged. Middle school hadn't been a prison, per se, but it hadn't been a walk in the park, either. Who knew what high school would be like? My dad had gone to James

K. Polk High decades ago, back when he was fresh off the boat from Iran. His advice was zero percent helpful.

My heart sank as every student ambassador following Becca gushed about high school, almost as if to make up for Becca's warning. I got the feeling Principal Saulk had chosen a very select social group to speak at orientation, full of good-looking seniors who were thriving. He had completely stacked the deck.

Where was the student ambassador who talked about how it was okay to be nervous and sweat too much and accidentally walk into the boys' bathroom like I had before assembly? Because that was the ambassador for me.

Ruth was so excited for orientation she'd drafted a list of questions and kept squirming in her seat, waiting for some kind of Q&A. She'd even brought her own name tag, with custom gold foil that glinted in the auditorium lights, while everyone else used the stickers provided by the school. Meanwhile, Fabián ignored all the speakers and answered questions from his zillion social media fans. I don't think he looked up from his phone once.

"Being a high school freshman can be intimidating, for sure," a guy on the football team was now saying. "But it's, like, so much more chill than middle school, you know?"

No! I wanted to scream. *I don't know! So tell me what I don't know!*

"It's, like, way harder, but also, more relaxed?" he went on. Oh my god. Of all the students they could have chosen for orientation, they went with the vaguest person ever. When were we going to go over the important stuff? Like, when did we have to take the PSATs (and were they optional)? Was showering/being naked in front of my classmates after gym class mandatory? And did the vending machines have Hot Cheetos (and where were the vending machines)?

But most important, where was Wesley? We needed to start plotting our next prank, like swapping all the ketchup dispensers in the cafeteria with hot sauce or something equally romantic. I glanced around at the auditorium full of five hundred kids, hoping to find him.

James K. Polk was so big I wished it showed up on Google Maps. Ruth, Fabián, and I got lost just trying to find the auditorium. I honestly wished my parents were here for once so they could ask embarrassing questions that were secretly helpful. All of Ruth's questions in her binder were about the arts and crafts closet and whether you could use the industrial-size paper shredder in the front office. Her obsession with crafting was out of control, and I hoped she'd keep it together so everyone could assume we were just as popular and cool as the ambassadors onstage. If only for a couple hours, at least.

"And, like, there's a new squat rack in the gym? So. There's that."

"Thank you, Kyle!" Principal Saulk started clapping enthusiastically. I didn't think Kyle was actually done speaking, but then again, Kyle was clearly useless.

Fabián unglued himself from his phone. "Do you think he's why our football team is so bad?"

"All right, everyone, we're going to go ahead and break out into tour groups. Outside the auditorium are student ambassadors in blue and red shirts—please line up next to one. No more than ten people per group, please!" Principal Saulk shouted before shimmying offstage.

"Finally," I groaned.

Ruth whined, clutching her binder. "I didn't get to ask any of my questions!"

"Come on, Parvin," Fabián said, holding out a hand adorned with rings in the shape of snakes and skulls.

And then, out of the corner of my eye, I saw Wesley. His sandy-colored hair had been chopped off in favor of a buzz cut, but he still looked cute, despite his white polo and khakis. That was strange, since he usually wore a T-shirt and jeans. But at least I could finally introduce him to my friends.

"Wesley!" I waved. "Hey!"

Wesley turned around, and I almost swooned then and there. His braces were off (gasp!), and he looked like a completely new person. He gave me a small wave from where he was sitting next to some students I'd never seen before, and I dragged Ruth and Fabián over.

"Hey, Parvin," he stuttered, getting up quickly. He herded me away from the people he'd been hanging with, clearly wanting to have me all to himself.

Gosh, it had only been a couple days since we'd last seen each other, but I'd missed the shy, nervous way Wesley talked. I couldn't stop staring at his braces-free teeth. Just smelling his brand of soap again made my lips tingle from that night at the beach.

"Wesley, these are my friends," I exclaimed proudly. Hah! Now I had proof that Wesley wasn't made up! "Meet *the* Fabián Castor," I began.

"Charmed," Fabián purred, sticking his hand out, palm down, like he was a duke or something. Fabián had high standards for boys, and he didn't hold his hand out to be kissed by just anyone. I could tell he thought Wesley was handsome, too.

Instead of taking Fabián's hand, though, Wesley just stared at the black nail polish and rings Fabián wore. I watched as his eyes tracked up Fabián's frame, noting the motorcycle boots, the frayed black jeans, and the smoky eyeliner. I thought Fabián looked amazing today, but from the way Wesley cringed, maybe I'd been wrong.

"Hi," Wesley squeaked, keeping his hands in his pockets.

"And I'm Ruth Song." She gave a quick wave, trying to gloss over that awkward moment, but Wesley took a step back. Ruth dropped her hand, self-conscious.

What was going on? Why was Wesley acting so weird?

"Wes? Are you feeling okay?"

"These are your friends?" he asked. Then he glanced back to the group he'd been sitting with. They all wore the same kind of Polite Youths outfit Wesley had on and were just as pale as his white polo. I followed his gaze and was met with a wall of frosty looks.

"Do you know her?" one of them called, gesturing to me. He wore a button-down shirt and something my dad called "slacks." He looked like he was preparing to run for senate—or at least student-body president—both of which could be possible here in Northern Virginia. His name tag said **HUDSON**.

"A little bit," Wesley replied. *A little bit?* Hello! You just asked me to be your girlfriend! For some reason this Hudson guy thought Wesley's response was hilarious, because he started laughing coldly at me as he walked over.

"What kind of name is Parvin, anyway?" Hudson read my name tag, pronouncing it Par-vin, and not PAR-veen, like Ruth and Fabián did. What was going on? Why wasn't Wesley sticking up for me? I felt my friends bristle beside me, ready to step in.

Too late. "Don't you have some used cars to sell?" Fabián sneered, gesturing to Hudson's outfit.

"Yeah!" Ruth added, a bit unhelpfully.

But in that moment, I could have kissed them both. Fabián and Ruth were my ride-or-die BFFs. They weren't going to let just anyone make fun of me. After all, making fun of me was *their* job.

Wesley stared uneasily at the floor. Why was he friends with this jerk? And why wasn't he saying anything? I was starting to get annoyed now.

"Let's go over here," he said finally, leading me alone to an empty hallway away from Hudson and his crew. Gone was the happy twinkle in Wesley's eye from whenever he saw me. Now he looked as nervous about high school as I felt, and he kept running his tongue over his braces-free teeth.

"How do you know those guys?" I asked. *And why won't you look at me?* It felt like the second I'd introduced my friends, Wesley had clammed up. Was he intimidated by how awesome they were? Being BFFs with an influencer could be nerve-racking, sure, but Fabián had been on his best behavior just now.

"They go to my church, actually. I didn't know they'd be here until yesterday."

I nodded. I was glad he was starting school with some friends, even if they seemed dumb.

He still wouldn't meet my eye.

"Wes?" I took a step closer, reaching for his hand. But he shoved them both into his pockets.

Fabián and Ruth gave me a sympathetic look from where they waited over by Wesley's church friends. They were probably wondering where the hysterical boyfriend I'd bragged so much about had gone. I'd told them how funny Wesley was, but he was completely different from the boy in front of me.

For someone who had asked me to be his girlfriend a couple days ago, Wesley sure wasn't acting like my boyfriend.

"Listen, Parvin," Wesley started, finally making eye contact. "I've thought about it a lot, and I think it's better if we just stay friends. You're just . . . a little . . ."

My heart stopped. I held my breath, waiting for Wesley to explain the punch line. This had to be a joke, right? Who dumped someone two days after asking them to be their girlfriend?

"Loud," he said finally. He gestured to all of me, as if I could read his mind and understand what that meant.

I gasped. *Loud? Moi?* This had to be another one of Wesley's jokes, like the time we covered the lifeguard chair in body glitter.

"Shiver me timbers, Wes," I snorted, remembering how much he liked my pirate-speak earlier this week. "Good one, Captain!"

But Wesley just shook his head. "It was fine at the beach and all. But things are different now. You're just really . . . um . . ."

He looked at the ceiling tiles, as if he'd find the right word up there. "Too much."

This couldn't be happening. This had to be a prank.

"What does that even mean?" I chuckled, but it was a strained, shaky sound.

He remained silent. I reached for his hand again, but he kept it in his pocket. "We're still on for hanging out after orientation, right?" I pressed. I had already scoped out the school's parking lot, and if I moved each assigned parking space over by one, Principal Saulk wouldn't have a spot to slide his Prius into tomorrow. It was the perfect trick, and I needed Wesley's help since Fabián and Ruth refused to help with my little schemes anymore.

"Ummm," he said uncomfortably.

The laugh I'd been holding back for when he yelled "Just kidding!" died in my throat. Was this really happening? Wesley had never mentioned before that I was "too loud" or "too much" all summer. He had seemed happy enough listening to me explain why mint chocolate chip was the best ice cream flavor, or why I still wore bronzer even though my skin was already pretty bronze.

Wesley just shook his head. "Sorry, Parvin. I don't think you should be my girlfriend anymore."

He walked away, back to his church friends.

And then I died.

— ACKNOWLEDGMENTS —

THIS BOOK WOULD not have been possible without Nina LaCour's Slow Novel Lab. Thank you to Nina and Fer de Avila for holding my hand throughout my dreaded Second Book anxiety. I am so grateful, and I don't think I could have done this without the course.

Thank you to my agent, Jim McCarthy, for being my absolute rock. The whole team at Dystel, Goderich & Bourret are such big champions of my work, and I am so appreciative of all you do. Thank you to Mary Pender-Coplan and UTA for being the wonderful stewards of my stories for the screen.

Thank you to Stacey Barney, my editor, for always pushing me to be a better writer. Two books in and I feel like we are just getting started! And thank you, Caitlin Tutterow, for making the process as smooth as possible.

To Kate Heidinger, my first reader, my dear friend: Thank you for reading all of the random things I send you. It means so much to me. Ditto to Romy Natalia Goldberg, who is the best critique partner a girl can ask for. I'm so excited for you and your own publishing journey. A million thank-you's to Crystal Maldonado, Axie Oh, and Aminah Mae Safi for your incredibly kind blurbs for this book.

Huge thank-you to the team at Penguin Random House, Nancy Paulsen Books, for shepherding this book through. Nancy Paulsen, Debra DeFord-Minerva, Jacqueline Hornberger, Ariela Rudy Zaltzman, Suki Boynton, Cindy Howle, Lathea Mondesir, Felicity Vallence, Shannon Spann, Kara Brammer, James Akinaka, I am so grateful for all that you do. Thank you, thank you, thank you.

This beautiful book was designed by Kristie Radwilowicz, with cover art by Kervin Brisseaux. Thank you for the most gorgeous, fierce cover ever. But more than anything, thank you to PRH for always making sure the girl on the cover matches the girls in my books.

Khayley mamnoon to Shahram Shiva of Rumi Network for the beautiful translations. And thank you to Caeli Duerson for lending me your speech pathology knowledge—how I wish you'd been my therapist when I was younger!

Massive thank-you to booksellers, librarians, and educators who have shoved my books into readers' hands. Especially the librarians at the Denver Public Library and Arapahoe Libraries for being so supportive and helpful.

It takes a village to raise a family, and I am so grateful for the help of Gavyn Madison and Charlene Marshall. My family and I appreciate you both so much.

To my parents: Thank you for encouraging my love of music and reading. Thank you for driving me to those ENT appointments and talking to all the specialists. Thank you for driving me twenty minutes away to the school with Spanish immersion and speech therapy. You said that one day I'd stop complaining and be grateful you spent over an hour to take us to that special school, and you were right. Mil gracias. Los quiero mucho.

To AG, fourth of your name, thank you for supporting me through all the ups and downs, through thick and thin, through both good news and rejection. You prioritize my writing and career in ways I sometimes forget to. Thank you for being my biggest cheerleader; I absolutely could not do this without you.

Lastly, to my child, second of your name. I drafted this book when you were just a few weeks old. I would place you on my desk as you slept and wrap you around my body as I stared at a blank screen. Like Azar, you're a quarter Iranian and Argentinian. What will that mean for you? You get to decide. And if you ever wonder why Mommy made you drink Throat Coat every day, now you know. I love you so much, my darling, perfect kid. Never be afraid of finding your voice.